———————— ★ ————————

A key turned in the lock. The door swung open, and the hall light came on. Will pressed his cheek against the side of the desk.

The figure was slight and wore a watch cap pulled down over his ears. Will didn't get a good look at his face because he moved fast, but he guessed that the clothes he had found in the duffel bag would be a perfect fit. The figure slung a climbing rope over his shoulder. He turned the hall light off and shut the door.

Will listened to the stranger's footsteps disappear off the porch. The car started, the lights sprayed across the mantelpiece and vanished.

———————— ★ ————————

"Offering realistic characters, striking autumn scenery, a fast pace, and a clear, strong plot, this first novel is fresh and accomplished."

—*Booklist*

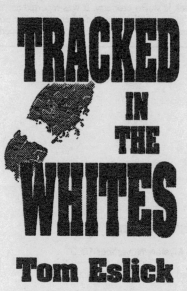

TRACKED IN THE WHITES

Tom Eslick

WORLDWIDE.

TORONTO • NEW YORK • LONDON
AMSTERDAM • PARIS • SYDNEY • HAMBURG
STOCKHOLM • ATHENS • TOKYO • MILAN
MADRID • WARSAW • BUDAPEST • AUCKLAND

TRACKED IN THE WHITES

A Worldwide Mystery/November 1999

First published by Write Way Publishing, Inc.

ISBN 0-373-26327-9

Visit us at www.worldwidemystery.com

Printed in U.S.A.

TRACKED IN THE WHITES

ONE

OUTSIDE Will Buchanan's window, lightning cracked and jarred him awake. Thunder rumbled, followed by driving rain that pelted against the down spout. He got up to close the window. The birches outside whooshed above his head as a gust picked up an aluminum lawn chair, sent it tumbling across the yard, and pinned it against a hedge.

Laurie's voice came out of the darkness. "Are you all right?"

"Yeah." He slammed the window shut. It suddenly felt too quiet in the room.

"You were moaning," she said.

He lay on the bed and ran his hand down his stomach. It was moist from sweat. "Must have been dreaming," he said. Lightning flashed in the room, and he counted seconds until he heard the thunder again. He figured the storm center was four miles to the east.

"Who's Jeanne?" Laurie said.

"What?"

"You called out her name."

He reached for Laurie but she stiffened at his touch. What had he said in his sleep? He wanted their last night in this room to be special. Tomorrow the dormitory annexed to his apartment would be filled with freshman boys. "What's the matter?" he asked.

"Is Jeanne someone real?"

"She was." The rain drove heavier now. It drummed against the window. "God. Listen to that," he said.

"You mean she's dead?"

"Yes."

"Are you going to tell me about her?"

"Why is this so important?"

"Oh, Will. Just tell me, please."

He waited a moment and let his hand rest on her arm. He tried to piece together the dream. He had been rock climbing, leading Jeanne up White Horse Ledge. As he tied in and called down to her, he could see the rope slip slowly from her harness like a snake uncoiling. "Jeanne was Jonathan Tyler's wife," he said quickly, trying to jolt himself back to this bedroom, this storm.

Laurie sat up. "The singer? You know Jonathan Tyler?"

"Yes." In his mind's eye he could still see Jeanne falling, her mouth open in a grotesque silent scream.

"Does he know you moan over his dead wife?"

Will swallowed hard. "I can't help what I dream."

Laurie rolled away from him.

He stared at the dark outline of the ceiling fixture. He could feel Laurie slipping away from him, and he knew he had to tell her something. But where to begin? He couldn't explain to himself why he hadn't been able to forget about Jeanne. "Two months ago she fell from a balcony."

Laurie stirred, suddenly animated, and turned back to face Will. "I remember reading about it."

"I guess she was on my mind because their daughter is coming with the new students tomorrow."

"God. The kid just lost her mother and Jonathan's sending her away?"

"She's been having trouble adjusting."

"I can imagine."

"Jonathan wrote me a letter and thought a year at the school might be good for her. He talked about how she needed structure in her life..." Will closed his eyes and envisioned Jonathan's crimped handwriting, the terse phrases he used to describe his daughter's problems.

"And that's all you have to tell me?"

"I'm trying to give you a reason why I dreamt about Jeanne. Isn't that what you want?" He reached for her hand but she pulled it away. "You don't want me to touch you?" he said.

"I want to hear the story."

"This isn't the easiest thing to talk about, you know."

Laurie sighed. "Never mind then."

It had been a lot of years since he shared anything with anyone. He was still getting used to having someone in bed with him on a regular basis. His hand felt empty lying open, palmup. All right. He would tell her...something. "The night Jeanne died, Chicago had a bad thunderstorm. I guess my brain was making connections."

"Were you there when it happened?"

"I was in town, yes."

"They thought she jumped, right?"

"That's what they said."

"But you don't believe it?"

Will hesitated. "It was a tragic fall, plain and simple. An accident."

"And they ruled out homicide?"

"God, Laurie. Why do you always suspect the worse?"

"Because I'm a cop. Was there a suicide note?"

He sat up. "If you want to grill me, why don't you switch on the lamp and shine it in my eyes?"

"Just tell me if there was a note."

"No. There wasn't a note."

They grew quiet together. The thunder grumbled distantly, like an old man clearing his throat. The storm had rolled over them.

"Will..."

"What is it now?"

"Did you hear that? It sounded like it came from the bathroom."

"I didn't hear anything." He lay back on the bed and listened for night sounds. "Probably the rain," he said.

"No. I definitely heard something."

He went to the bathroom and switched on the light. His eye caught the open window. The floor was wet. He checked the cat bed and Butch was missing. He had closed that window himself before turning in, and Butch had been tucked away, puffed up like a dustball in his bed.

When he came back to the bedroom, he found the light on. Laurie was dressing. "What are you doing?"

"What does it look like?"

He watched her look for her clothes, not knowing what to say to her. "Butch is gone," he managed, finally. "The window's open."

"Maybe he got tired of living here."

"It's the middle of the night, Laurie."

"I'm following Butch's lead."

"But it's still raining."

"I won't melt."

He approached her and she backed away. "You're upset because I had that dream." It was a statement, not a question.

She pulled on her jeans and struggled with the buttons. "Will, how long have we been seeing each other?"

He thought a moment. "Six months?"

She shook her head. "God. You don't even know how long we've been sleeping together."

"Seven? Eight? I don't know. I haven't been counting."

"It's been long enough for you to at least drop the guy's name. I mean, Jonathan Tyler, for crying out loud."

"Maybe I didn't think it was important. What's he got to do with us, anyway?" She reached for her bra. He grabbed it from her. "This isn't fair," he said.

"The point is I don't know you." She snatched her bra back. "It's been eight months, seventeen days, by the way." She glanced at the digital clock. "And eleven hours. But who's counting?"

"Come on. Let's go back to bed."

"That's not going to solve our problem." She reached for her holster, but Will got there first.

He pulled out the pistol, a stainless steel Smith & Wesson 659. "Why do you always carry this thing, anyway? Worried about drug runners in Saxton Mills?" He was sorry he said it as soon as the words came out.

"Give me the pistol, Will." She waited.

He put the piece back into the holster. He handed it to her and watched as she hooked it on her belt. "Don't you think you're over-reacting a bit?"

She tucked in her shirt. "I don't think so." She slipped on her Bïrkenstocks and walked into the hallway.

Will darted in front of her and blocked her exit out the door. "I don't want you to leave."

"Get out of my way, Will."

"I'll tell you anything you want to know."

Laurie folded her arms in front of her. "Are you going to let me go?"

"I used to be in a band with Jonathan."

Laurie let her arms fall to her side. "What?"

"You wanted to know everything."

"You don't mean 'Waggoner's Lad'?"

"I played bass."

She shook her head. "You played bass with Jonathan? I didn't even know you were a musician."

"I'm not. I mean, I'm not any more."

A trace of a smile played on Laurie's mouth. "Wait a minute. You are kidding."

He raised three fingers. "Scout's honor."

"It was a trio, right?"

"Jonathan and I and a girl named Grace Diccico. We had one hit."

"A Childe Ballad." Laurie said. "It began, 'Hard is the fortune of all womankind...'"

"How do you know that?"

She paused. "I think I still have the album."

"Then check it out. You won't recognize me, though. I'm the skinny guy with the Abe Lincoln beard smiling maniacally on the back cover. My protest days."

She made a rolling motion with her arms. "Keep going," she said. "What does this have to do with Jeanne?"

"Can't we at least sit down?" He led her to the sofa in the

living room. He felt a chill, suddenly aware of his nakedness. "You sure we can't go back to bed?" he said.

She didn't say anything.

He thought about putting some clothes on, but didn't want to chance her leaving while he was in the bedroom. He grabbed an afghan off the sofa and wrapped it around himself. He sat down on the sofa, she in the chair opposite. "Jeanne and I were lovers," he said. "It was a long time ago." He waited for a reaction but there was none. He leaned forward and continued. "I had been going out with Jeanne for a few months when the record hit big. This was the summer of 'sixty-five."

"'Sixty-five? I was ten years old."

"Great. I needed to hear that."

"Sorry. I won't interrupt anymore."

"We were flying high. It's funny. That song launched Jonathan's career, but—as you probably recall—it was Grace who sang it. Even though Jonathan was the leader, she was the driving force behind the band. He thought the song was too depressing, that no one would like it."

"And Jeanne?"

"Like I said. We had been going out. One night I introduced her to Jonathan." Will got up from the sofa and began to pace. "We were at this bar. I can remember the look on his face when he saw her." He started to say something more, but the memory stirred his anger even though a lot of years had passed. "You can guess the rest."

"She ditched you for Jonathan?"

"I wanted to kill him. She had been the best thing for me."

"So what did you do?"

"I quit."

"And that's when the group broke up?"

"One album, one hit. Jonathan went on his own then, and you know the rest of his story." Will stopped his pacing. He looked at Laurie. "That's how I know Jonathan."

"What happened to Grace?"

"I don't know. Rumor had it she'd become born again—joined some fanatic religious order."

Laurie got up from her chair. "You still love Jeanne, don't you?"

Will hesitated. "I had gotten over her. It took a long time. Then, last year Jonathan called me out of the blue. We got together. When I saw her again I wasn't prepared for the hurt to return. It's stupid, I know. Then, while I was in town she died. She fell..."

Laurie reached out to him. He shook her hand and held it awkwardly, like it was something that might break. "I want to be with you," he said. "I don't talk about things much. I don't try to hurt you on purpose."

"I know," she said, and squeezed his hand. She got up to leave.

"Where are you going?"

"My shift starts at eight a.m."

"I've told you everything."

She walked toward the door.

He threw off the afghan, grabbed an umbrella and raincoat from the closet, and followed her. He held the umbrella over her head as she got in the car. She slammed the door. He knocked on her window, and she opened it a crack. "What do you want me to say?" he asked, hearing desperation in his voice.

She smiled up at him. "I think it's time we had a little break, Will. Things are happening too fast for me."

"I thought we were getting along okay."

"You keep things too much inside. You won't let me in."

"I'm trying, Laurie."

"Don't call me for a while, okay?" She cranked the window closed. He rapped on it again. "Will, come on. Let me go."

"This *is* about Jeanne, isn't it?"

She just looked at him. "That's what I like about you, Will. You have such command of the obvious."

"But she's dead."

"Not to you she isn't." Laurie turned the ignition, gunned the engine and drove off.

He stood in the rain and watched the tail lights of her Bronco disappear. Laurie's words came back to him. It was true, he held things inside, but he couldn't help dreaming, damn it! He lifted his head and the rain patted his face. No wonder he lived alone. He had better luck talking to his cat.

On his way back to the apartment he heard something behind him. "Here, Butch," he called. "Come on, you stupid cat."

A light went on in the house across the street—Miss Cora Roberts, who lived alone. He ducked behind a tree. All he needed was Ray Carson, Laurie's deputy, to show up. Ray loved to scatter-gun raccoons off garbage can lids. He snugged closer to the tree and listened to the water drubbing his feet. He waited ten minutes before the light went out.

Back inside his apartment, he heard a meowing coming from the bathroom. He opened the bathroom door and Butch raced out. The cat was riled about something; he never moved that fast.

Will caught up to him in the living room. "Butch. Come here!"

Butch hunched in the corner by the sliding glass door.

Will switched on the overhead light. Butch was wearing something around his body that glittered. A closer look revealed some sort of cat raincoat with Velcro tabs holding the thing together. "Where did you get this?" he said.

Butch meowed.

Will stooped and stroked his head. "Here, let's get it off."

Butch wasn't in any mood to be touched and Will had to struggle with him. He finally got the coat off Butch and examined it. The coat was shiny red, rigged with sequins and metal buttons. In white spangled letters across the back were the words: "Jesus Saves."

"Been out making a fashion statement, Butch?" He tried to smooth the cat's fur, check to see if he was hurt, but Butch would have none of it.

In the kitchen, still in his raincoat, Will poured himself a shot of Laphroig—neat—and sipped it, savoring the musty bite of single malt on his tongue. He sat on a stool and arranged the cat coat on the kitchen counter as Butch hopped up on it. His tail flicked at Will's arm, and he got his motor going. Will got another shot glass from the cupboard and poured a small amount of the Scotch into it. He set it out for Butch and refilled his own. "Who put this froofie thing on you, Butch?"

Butch busied himself with tongue laps.

"You're just supposed to sip the stuff." Will moved closer to him until his face was opposite the cat's. "Come on, Butch. Who's playing tricks on us?"

The cat coat was the latest of some practical jokes. Last week Will had found two pink flamingoes on his lawn; two days ago, his garden hose had been split down the middle and uncoiled all over the front lawn.

There had to be only one explanation: someone had been in the house while he and Laurie were in bed. Someone opened the bathroom window, took Butch out and returned him, dandified, while he was seeing Laurie to her car.

TWO

SOMEONE WAS KNOCKING on the sliding glass door, which came into focus as Will slowly opened his eyes. Then he looked down at his lap: He still had his raincoat on, but it had opened in the night since he'd been sleeping sitting upright—spread-eagle. He pulled the raincoat around himself, went to the door, grabbed the handle, and slid it along the track. He stared silently at a man who was dancing from toe to toe on the back porch, rubbing his hands together.

"You Will?" the man said.

"Yes." Will felt the Laphroig as a heavy cloud at the base of his skull.

"I guess you're the one I'm supposed to see. Mind if I come in?"

Will thought about Butch and the cat coat. "Just who are you?"

"The headmaster sent me. You're the head woods nerd, right?"

Will measured him. "I'm in charge of Orientation, if that's what you mean."

"Yeah. Yeah. That's it. Listen. Can I come in? It's colder than penguin shit out here."

Will hesitated, but the man already had one foot in the house.

"Name's Franco Delacorte," he said. He extended his hand. "I tried the front door. No one answered."

Will noticed the mat of dark hair on the back of Franco's hand as he shook it. He felt stupid standing there in a raincoat and was about to concoct some explanation for it when Franco interrupted his thought.

"If this is a bad time, I can come back," he said. Franco's

eyes—cow brown—seemed oddly set, wedged in between a prominent nose slightly off center.

"No. Not at all. Let me put on some coffee."

Will led Franco to the kitchen and suggested he sit at the counter. Will scooped coffee into the filter, poured water into the coffee-maker, and turned it on. All the while, he felt Franco's eyes watching him. There was something immediately irksome about the man, like the proverbial bastard at a family reunion. He cautioned himself not to make quick judgments. He turned to face him. "Listen. I'm going to get some clothes on. Just make yourself at home."

He checked the bathroom on his way to the bedroom. Butch was curled up, narcotized. In the bedroom, Will peeled off the raincoat and stared in the mirror. It wasn't long before he was aware of a presence in the doorway.

"God. What happened to you?" It was Franco's voice. Will turned. "You look poached. You spend the night in a lagoon?"

"Do you mind? I'm getting dressed."

"Sorry. Just looking for the WC."

"You passed it. It's on the right."

"Gotcha." Franco left.

Will toweled off with the bedspread, getting angrier the more he thought about the intrusion. Franco had to have seen where the bathroom was on his trip down the hall, which meant that he'd deliberately come into his room. Will listened at the door and could hear the toilet flush, faintly, from down the hall. He composed himself. Just answer the man's questions and get rid of him. He threw on jeans and a clean T-shirt, and went back to the kitchen.

He found Franco in the living room. "So, you're the new guy," he said.

"I'm the new language teacher, if that's what you mean."

"I didn't know if you were going to show. We were taking bets—"

"We?"

"Other faculty members. When you weren't there for the meetings, we were guessing—"

"Often a bad thing to do, don't you think?" Franco was facing the wall, talking to it. "I wanted to be there, but I had a personal problem." He turned. "Would you like to hear about it?"

"No. Listen. I didn't mean anything—"

Delacorte picked up a magazine from the coffee table. *"Backpacker,"* he said, the lines around his eyes smiling. "Pretty racy stuff."

"Want some coffee?" Will asked.

"No thanks. Never touch the stuff."

Will paused, carafe in hand. "I thought you said you wanted some."

"Never said anything of the kind. I believe you said, 'Let me put on some coffee.' The word 'coffee' never crossed my lips."

"How about tea?"

"Gives me the farts. Postum. Got any Postum?"

"No."

"It's okay. I don't much mind."

Will went to the kitchen for coffee and Franco followed. While he was at the counter, he stoppered the Laphroig and put it quickly in the cupboard.

"You know you've got a dead cat in the bathroom?" Franco said.

"What?"

"I poked him a little. He didn't move."

"Oh, he's okay. Had a bad night, that's all. Listen. Did Knox explain about SMOOT?"

"Just that I'm supposed to traipse through the woods with you and a bunch of girls."

"Done much hiking?"

Franco made an noise that sounded like his face sprang a leak. "The closest I've been to the woods is the Arboretum in Washington."

Will stared at Franco and studied his body shape. Franco had a paunch, but there was a muscularity about him that suggested he had once been an athlete.

"What the hell does SMOOT mean?" Franco asked.

"Saxton Mills Outdoor Orientation Trip."

Franco smiled. "Clever. Your invention?"

"Nope. A student dubbed it a few years back. I guess it stuck."

Franco picked up a piece of driftwood on the counter. "What's this crap, anyway? The place is stacked with it."

"Just things I like to collect. It's found art. You've heard about that, haven't you?"

Franco looked at the curved piece of driftwood. "What's artsy-fartsy about this?"

"If you hold it to the side it looks like an otter."

Franco twisted the piece and studied it. He shrugged his shoulders. "If you say so."

"Don't you see it?"

"No."

"You're kidding."

"Looks like a hunk of wood to me."

Will took the piece from him. "Here. I'll show you."

Franco took hold of his arm. "Look, I could give a shit. I really came over to see if you could get me out of this SMOOT thing."

Will looked down at Franco's hand on his arm. "I don't think so. This is the way we begin each school year."

"Why?"

"It's a great way for new students to get to know each other. Cuts down on homesickness."

Franco removed his hand. "Knox said you were the man to go out with."

"You'll have a good time."

"Made you out to be some latter-day Davy Crockett."

"I like being in the woods."

"Yeah? Well, I don't. I imagine I could make life pretty miserable for you out there. Be a real burden."

Will looked at him. "You serious?"

"Think about it. Maybe there's something else I could do. Some support role, maybe."

"That's between you and the headmaster."

"But you could pull some strings, right?"

"Nuh-uh. I don't have that kind of influence."

"Suit yourself."

"Do you have equipment?"

"Converse High Tops. That's about it. See what I mean?"

Will looked at Franco's feet, then back to his face. He wore a grin like an attitude Will wanted to crush. This man *was* going on SMOOT if he had anything to do with it. "We can fix you up, no problem," Will said.

"What if I get hurt?"

"You won't."

"Suppose I get blisters and can't walk?"

"You'll persevere, I'm sure."

"How do you take a dump?"

"Just like a bear."

"Are there bears?"

"If we're lucky, we might see one."

"Lucky?"

"Saw a moose last year."

Franco shook his head. "Well, I guess I don't have much choice."

"Not if you want to teach at Saxton Mills."

"So, what should I do?"

"Meet me at the picnic for new students and their parents."

"Picnic? What do you people have against buildings, anyway?"

THREE

IT WAS almost noon and Will still had one kid who hadn't checked in—Berkeley Hutter, a ninth grader. He'd give him another fifteen minutes.

He located the list of names for his SMOOT group and walked outside to wait. He stared at the list—five girls—one of the names was Dee Tyler. He usually led a boys' group, but he figured the trip would offer a good opportunity to get to know Jonathan's daughter.

He soon spotted a kid hauling a suitcase up the hill. He walked over to give him a hand. "Hey, how you doing?"

"I can't find my dorm." His glasses were fogged from crying.

"Are you Berkeley?"

"Yes."

"You're in luck; I'm your dorm parent." He held out his hand. "I'm Mr. Buchanan." Berkeley's hand felt small and limp. He was barely five feet tall.

Berkeley sat on his suitcase. "I've been dragging this thing all over campus."

"You by yourself?"

He nodded. "My parents left me at the front gate."

Will smiled at him, all the while thinking that some parents should be either shot or sterilized, whichever was most painful. It always amused and saddened him to think that he—charter member of the socially challenged who kept things inside—sometimes was more of a parent than those who saw biology as a license to practice abandonment and mental anguish. He clapped his hand on Berkeley's shoulder. "Well, you made it," he said. He glanced at his watch. "Come on. Let's get you settled in."

BY THE TIME Will arrived at the picnic, Headmaster Perry Knox was in the middle of his welcoming speech.

"...and so I challenge each of you to take advantage of your Saxton Mills education, beginning here and now with SMOOT. If you're like the many who have graduated, you will be telling war stories about SMOOT for a long time. We've been running this program for almost twenty years now"—Will sighed as he listened for the punch line; he had heard it all before—"and as far as we know every one has come back."

Laughter rippled through the crowd.

He searched the throng of students and parents, seeing if he could spot Dee. He had never met her and had to rely on his recall of the picture in the application folder. His eyes settled on a young girl with dark brown hair leaning against a maple tree. She had Jonathan's nose. Dee Tyler, it had to be. He thought of working his way through the crowd, but something about her was off-putting. She was by herself, arms folded hard across her chest and Jonathan Tyler was nowhere to be seen.

A burst of applause meant the headmaster was finished. Catherine Tripp, Director of Admissions, began calling out names of the SMOOT leaders.

Will heard his and Franco's names. He walked toward Catherine, and his group began to assemble, parents in tow, as, in turn, their names were called. Will waited a moment for Franco, but he didn't show, then led the group to a grassy area beneath an ancient maple, the leaves edged with a hint of scarlet subtly announcing the approach of fall.

"If you would just take a seat, here," he said squatting in front of the tree. "Why don't we begin by everyone introducing themselves?" He looked straight at the girl to his left. Her blond ponytail stuck out the back of her baseball cap and she was fingering a small crucifix attached to a gold chain around her neck.

"Me?" Her face reddened.

"Yes, just tell everybody your name and something about yourself."

"Well, I'm Patty. I'm from Ohio; it's, uh, flat. And this is my dad," she said gesturing to her left. Her father identified himself as Frank, began to say something more, then stopped. He deferred to the girl sitting next to him.

"I am Michiko from Japan," she said. "I have just landed here."

"We are very tired," her mother added, smiling.

"Japan is a long way from New Hampshire," Will said. The statement fell flat, and he heard his words echo in his head. A silence sat on the group. He always hated this time, this getting-to-know-you stuff. What was that first girl's name? Patty? He checked the list. He always had trouble with names and tried to think of a mnemonic. He wrote down Ponytail Patty. He couldn't think of anything immediately for Michiko, and then was suddenly aware of time passing. When he looked up, the Japanese woman was still smiling at him. He was about to say something when a tiny, fragile voice barely disturbed the surface of the silence.

"Dee. My name is Dee."

Heads turned toward her. She was hiding behind her hair.

"And can you tell us something about yourself?" Will asked.

Dee jerked her head, and her hair flew to one side. "The only reason I'm here is because my father made me come. I hate it already." It was still the same, small voice.

Will cleared his throat. "Well, we'll try to change that."

Dee didn't look convinced. "Where are we going, anyway?" she asked.

"I'll explain in a minute."

"Do we have to hike far?"

"It's not bad at all."

"How far?"

"Dee, please. I'd like to hear from the others, first."

There was a slight upward movement to her shoulders. She picked at the grass.

"Well, I'm Anita from Charleston, South Carolina." Anita's

strident, Southern inflection cut the air like the twang of a mouth harp. She turned to Dee. "Is your daddy really Jonathan Tyler?"

"Yes," Dee said.

"It must be great to be his daughter."

"Yes," she said. "It's great."

"Where is he now? Is he here?" This came from the girl sitting next to Anita. She was painfully thin, and Will wondered how she was going to carry a pack.

"Excuse me," Will said. "Can we find out first who everybody is?"

"Oh, I'm sorry," the skinny girl said. "I was just curious, that's all." Her face glowed as she flicked at the thick red curls on her forehead. "My name is Elsa, and this is my grandmother, Mrs. Petrie. My mother like couldn't come because my stepfather had his like appendix out, although he's really my second stepfather and I don't really like know him. You see my father died when—"

The grandmother patted Elsa's knee. "That's enough, now."

"But he wants to know something about us, Gram."

"Not that much." The grandmother turned to Will. "I think you're going to have your hands full on this trip, Mr. Buchanan."

This sent a chuckle through the group. God bless the grandmother, Will thought. "I'm sure we'll be fine," he said.

"My father is rehearsing his band in San Francisco," Dee said, without looking up. "That's why he isn't here."

"I just love his new album," Elsa said.

"Especially 'Two From Nothing,'" Anita added. "It's such an awesome song."

"Well, it doesn't look like we'll be at a loss for words on the trail," Will said. "I'm Will Buchanan, and I teach science courses and also manage the woodlands at Saxton Mills."

"So, we can assume you know something about the woods," Mrs. Petrie said.

"I should. I'll put it that way."

"You see, Elsa," the grandmother said, "there's nothing to worry about."

"Now," Will said. "I'm sure you heard Headmaster Knox's speech about why we begin each school year with a backpacking trip, so I won't belabor the point."

"Are you leading this trip by yourself?" Patty's father asked.

"No. I have a co-leader. He, ah...was called away unexpectedly. He should be here soon, though." Where the hell was Franco?

Will handed out copies of the topo map of the Sandwich Range in the White Mountains. "I thought I would trace the route for you, so you would have an idea of where we're going. As you can see, we begin at the Greeley Ponds Trail and spend our first night camped somewhere below the Tripyramids." As Will ran his finger along the route on the map, out of the corner of his eye, he saw Franco slip into the circle. "Then on the last day we'll walk out the Oliverian Brook Trail."

"Wow, that's quite a walk," Franco said.

Will's head snapped up. "I'm glad you could make it, Franco. While I fold the map, why don't you say a few words about yourself."

"I'm the new guy," he said more to Will than the group. "I've been hired to teach French and Spanish. I know next to nothing about the woods, but we're in good hands with my friend Will, here. He puts Natty Bumpo to shame."

Will felt his face color. "And so, tonight," he said, trying to brush over Franco's remarks, "we'll meet in the hockey rink to sort out the food and get our packs together."

"Packs!" Franco said. "No one told me I had to carry a pack."

FOUR

WILL FOUND Perry at his office. "The man's a complete jerk," he said.

Perry got up from his desk and closed the door behind him. "Who?"

"Franco Delacorte, that's who."

"Oh."

"Do you know what he did?"

"I have a feeling you're going to tell me."

Will was going to tell him, oh yes, he was going to tell him, all right, but what were the words to describe Franco? "First, you set him loose on my apartment."

"I did what?"

"Then he embarrassed himself and me in front of the whole SMOOT group. He's got one parent wondering if her child should go because she thinks Franco isn't fit to lead."

"Oh, great. Who is it?"

"Anita Feldman's mother."

"I'll have to find her before she leaves."

"Perry! The fool didn't even know he had to carry a pack, he shows up with no equipment, and to top it all off, he tells everybody in the group he thinks SMOOT is silly."

Perry sat down on the couch opposite Will's chair. "Where is he now?"

"Wreaking havoc somewhere."

"I can't remember you ever being this upset about anything."

"Did you tell him about SMOOT?"

"Of course. I laid it out for him."

"Then why would he..."

"I don't know."

Perry got up from the couch and walked to the window.

Will stared at his hands. "Why would you hire such a—"

"Complete jerk, as you put it?"

"Sorry. I guess I'm out of line."

"You know how weak our language department is, Will," Perry looked out the window. "He comes highly recommended."

"I don't want to go out with him, Perry."

"Who would you put him with?"

"I wouldn't let him go with anyone. I'll just do it myself; I've done it before."

Perry turned to him. "How many years have we been doing this, Will?"

"You said it this morning—almost twenty years."

"And SMOOT was your idea to begin with, remember?" Perry laughed.

"This is funny?"

"I'm sorry, Will. It's just that I can't believe somebody could get your goat so easily."

"Then you don't know Franco Delacorte."

"Are you sure there's nothing else bothering you?"

"Of course I am." But Perry's question gave him pause. Was he mad at Franco or mad at himself? His mind flashed on an image of the tail lights of Laurie's Bronco.

"Look, Will, I know Franco hasn't had much experience, that's why I put him with you."

He stared at Perry. "The guy doesn't even have a pack."

"Fine. We'll get him one. I'm sure we have enough rental gear."

"Why don't you take him out with you?"

Perry smiled at him. "And deny you two the chance to become pals?"

Will shook his head. He always marveled at Perry's ease with people, and he was more a friend than boss. Will had joined Perry in the early 'seventies when the school was struggling to make it, and now, over twenty years later, the Saxton Mills' School was at full enrollment while competitors were scrambling to fill beds. "How do you do it, Perry?"

"What?"

"Work your way around me?"

"It's part of my job," he said. "That's why I'm the head-master."

"And why I'm not."

"I didn't mean it that way."

"I did."

"I'll have a talk with Franco," Perry said. "I'm sure this is just a misunderstanding."

"I still can't believe he doesn't have a pack."

"Will you stop with the pack? Look, I'll take care of his equipment and make sure he's at the hockey rink at seven."

"I bet he'll be late."

"If he is, I'll fire him." Will knew Perry would do just that. "Now, all I ask is you take him out and introduce him to the beauties of the wild."

Will sighed. "Some people belong on the subway, Perry."

BUTCH CAME OUT into the hallway, meowing for his supper.

Will picked him up. "How's the head?" The cat squirmed, clawed at his arm. "Little hung over?"

Will let him down and went to the cupboard for cat food. He opened the tin, scooped it out into a plastic bowl, and placed it on the floor. "Got you some new stuff; it's called 'On Sale.'"

Butch nosed the dish and backed away. He sat and flicked his tail.

"Oh, come on, it can't be that bad." He picked up the bowl, opened a drawer, and pulled out a fork. He sniffed. "Umm." He jabbed with the fork, lifted a morsel to his mouth, and took a bite. "Hey. This is heaven."

Butch jumped on the counter. Will loaded the fork and extended it. Butch circled, stalked. He inched forward, sniffed again. He twitched his head like there was something stuck on the tip of his nose. He rubbed his nose with his paw, hopped off the counter, and ran into the bathroom.

"How come you're so spoiled?" He wagged the fork in the

direction of the bathroom. "What are you going to do when I'm gone, starve to death?"

Will took another bite. It really wasn't that bad. He had a whole case of it. A little mayo, two pieces of white bread, and he would have lunch for a month.

He chewed, remembering Laurie had agreed to feed Butch while he was out on SMOOT. He would go to the police station after he got everybody packed up—make sure she knew to give Butch the gourmet stuff. He felt better knowing he had an excuse to see her.

Suddenly, a rancid after-taste of glutinous fish eyes and crab innards hit Will's palate. He tried hard to swallow, wiped his mouth with the back of his hand, and figured he'd better brush his teeth if he didn't want Laurie to keel over, or have every cat in the neighborhood follow him into town.

With the faucet running, Will couldn't hear the knocking coming from the front door. When he paused in his brushing, the sound was barely audible. Damn! Probably Franco looking to scrounge a pack—the man was impossible. He wiped his mouth on a towel, stormed to the front door and ripped it open.

"Mr. Buchanan?" It was Dee Tyler.

"Oh, I'm sorry. I startled you."

"It's okay. I forgot to give you this." She handed him a piece of paper. "It's from my father."

"Oh, sure. Well, great." Will opened the note. It was just a few telegraphic words: *Hi, Will. Had a schedule conflict. See you Parents' Weekend.* Will looked up from the note to Dee. "So your father told you something about me?"

"Just that you were friends a long time ago."

"That's right." They exchanged glances. "Why don't you come in?"

"Okay. I'm not doing anything, anyway," she said.

Will showed her to the living room and motioned for her to sit in the overstuffed chair. He cleared off CDs from a ladder-back chair he found near the stereo and sat opposite. "Are you settled in?"

"Yes."

"Have any trouble finding your dorm?"

"No. Our chauffeur knew exactly where to go."

"Chauffeur. I see." Will thought of something else to ask her, but it flew away. She was hiding behind her hair again. "All set to go in the woods?"

"No."

"We're going to have a great time." He clapped his hands. Dee jumped. A silence followed. He wished he could whistle, or yodel—anything to make it easier between them. Maybe she could smell the cat food on his breath.

"I'm really scared of the woods," she said.

"No reason to be."

"Are there any wild animals?"

"None big enough to carry you away." Dee gave him a quizzical look. "Listen, Dee. Did you mean what you said at the picnic? About not wanting to be here?"

"Yes."

"Don't you think it's a little early to be making judgments?"

"Oh, I like the place. I mean it's okay for a hick town. It's just that Walt's not here."

Will hesitated. "Your boyfriend?"

She nodded. "And I told my father it wouldn't do any good shipping me out to some dumb school because I'd just run away."

Will paused. "You're not planning to do that, are you?"

She parted her hair and looked at him. It was the first close-up look she had allowed him, and he was startled at how pretty she was. "I'm in love with Walt," she said. "That's all that matters."

FRANCO WAS ON TIME. "Listen," he said. "I didn't mean to cause trouble."

"Right," Will said. "I guess you talked to Perry."

"Yes sir, I did. And I want to apologize for my behavior."

"You do?"

"It was regrettable. I should have known better." Will raised his eyebrows. "I know, I know," Franco said. "It's hard to believe from the way I carried on, but I truly am sorry. Will you accept my apology?"

Will tried to read his eyes. Was he for real? "I guess so," he said.

"Good." Delacorte rubbed his hands together. "Now what can I do to help out?"

"We have to get the food organized, divvy it up."

Elsa and Anita entered the rink, humped over from the weight of their packs. Their voices were lively and could be heard over the sounds of those assembling. Fast friends, Will thought. Seeing Elsa again sent red flags waving: She was painfully thin, with training-bra breasts; he wondered if she had an eating problem. He made a mental note to watch her at meal time. Elsa the Eel.

Franco looked at the array of bagged pasta, soup mixes, cheese. "How are we supposed to carry it all?" he asked.

"In our packs."

"But mine is full; I don't think I can stuff another thing in it."

"I guess you'll just have to make room." Will waited for a retort.

Franco only smiled. "Here I go again," he said. He put his heels together, bowed his head. "I defer to your expertise in packing."

Dee arrived, with Patty right behind her.

"Anyone seen Michiko?" Will asked.

"She couldn't find some of her stuff," Anita said. "She might be a little late."

"I suppose we can get started. Why don't you just dump your packs out." The girls hesitated. "Well?" he said.

"But we just packed them," Anita said.

"I need to check to make sure you've brought the right gear. We have to get the food in anyway, so you might just as well dump them."

"Mine, too?" Franco asked.

Will nodded. He noticed Anita watching the exchange. He could tell she was still nervous about going in the woods with Franco. Her mother had done a good job encouraging her doubts, a dynamic Will didn't need, but would the new Franco dispel them? He wondered what Perry had said to him.

Michiko straggled in. "I'm so sorry to be late," she said.

Will smiled. He looked at her pack, something resembling a boy scout soft pack. It would have to be replaced. It suddenly occurred to Will how out of place Michiko must feel. If it wasn't enough just to go away to school in a foreign country, she was also fighting jet lag, and on top of that, she would soon be plunked down in the middle of some woods in North America. He would have to be sensitive to this, especially at the start of trip. A passing thought disturbed him—this was usually the only way he *could* be sensitive—if he made a note of it and planned it. He was pleased with himself that he had the girls' names down pat. Anita was easy to remember because of her southern twang and mother angst, Elsa because of her bony arms and legs, Patty with her ponytail, Michiko from Miles Away, and Dee—well, because she was Dee.

Most of the other girls' equipment was in good shape. All had pack straps, suitable sleeping bags, and enough layers to keep warm. He looked at Franco's gear. Perry had done a good job outfitting him.

"As soon as I've checked you out, you can help Mr. Delacorte with the food," Will said to the girls. "I have to see about the other groups." Will walked away before Franco could say anything.

Being overseer of operations was part of Will's job, but the real reason he wanted to leave the group was to test Franco and his new-found desire to help. Over the years Will had developed efficient logistics, and he was pleased, as he roamed the hockey rink, that the process of getting the groups organized was going especially well. He watched Delacorte out of the corner of his eye as he made his rounds of the groups. The girls pretty much kept away from him.

He looked at his watch. Dee's unexpected visit to his apartment had prevented his leaving for the police station, but maybe there would still be time to see Laurie after the packing up. He returned to the group and found the pile of food gone.

Elsa was helping Michiko adjust her pack and Anita and Patty giggled over whose was heavier. Dee sat on hers, looking dejected. "I don't think I can carry this very far," she said.

"You won't have to," Will said. "Tomorrow's an easy day. Mostly flat."

"I hope so," she said.

Will looked at the portion of food piled next to his pack. He turned to Franco. "Am I pulling my weight?"

"Well, I've got a little extra in my pack. I thought since you had the stoves—"

"No. Give me an equal share."

"It's no problem, really."

Will studied Franco Delacorte's face again, trying to read behind the eyes. They really were like a cow's: deep, brown, and impenetrable.

"I HAD TO TALK TO YOU. I'm leaving first thing in the morning."

"I thought we weren't going to see each other for a while." Laurie turned to go back to her desk.

"Wait," Will said. "This will only take a minute."

She folded her arms. "I've got a lot of paper work."

"A minute?"

She looked at her watch. "You've got one minute."

He reached into his pocket. He pulled out a tin of *Gourmet Gato* and placed it on the counter.

Laurie looked at it. "A token of your affection?" she said.

"Butch is a spoiled brat." He picked up the tin and handed it to her. "He won't touch the other stuff."

Laurie didn't move. "You came down here just to tell me that?"

"You remember you were going to feed him, right?"

"Get Ray to do it," she said.

"Butch doesn't like Ray."

"Then find somebody else."

She went back to her desk and sat. She opened a folder.

Will stared at the tin on the counter. "Butch really likes having you around," he said.

Laurie moved to the file cabinet, folder in hand. She opened the drawer, hesitated, then returned to the counter. She picked up the tin of *Gourmet Gato* and walked back to her desk.

FIVE

"THE TAUT-LINE HITCH works best," Will said. To demonstrate to the girls, he fastened a piece of parachute cord through the middle grommet of the tarp, and with the free end went around the trunk of a beech tree. He crossed the cord, went under and up, and pulled—then tied two half hitches. "Got it?"

Patty stepped closer. "Do it again."

"Who cares?" Dee asked. "Why not just tie a granny knot?"

"Because you can adjust the tension by just pulling on it." Will showed them how to do it.

"That's neat," Elsa said. "One more time."

Will showed her again. "Now, why don't all of you split up and string some tarps? We need one group of three and one of two."

The girls took no time dividing up. Dee and Michiko seemed more than happy to be together, away from the chatty threesome of Patty, Elsa, and Anita. All day, they had motored down the trail while Dee and Michiko had struggled to keep up.

"Interesting," Franco said.

"What?"

"Human behavior. How personalities gravitate toward each other."

Will grabbed the other end of the tarp. "You learn a lot about people out here," he said. He cut another length of cord, tied a girth hitch through the grommet and pulled. The tarp rose off the ground. "You'll have a pretty good read on them by the time this is over." He finished tying off on another tree. "Okay. Your turn."

"You serious?"

"Of course. You didn't think I was going to do it all, did you?"

"Well, I thought since it was the first day..."

"Sorry. I'll take care of supper, though. You finish up; I'll get the stoves going."

"What do I do?"

"Just pull the sides out and fasten them."

"What was that knot again?"

Will wagged a finger. "You weren't paying attention, were you?"

Franco grinned. "I guess you caught me."

"You want to tie as low to the ground as possible." Will took one of the ends and strung it out. "Sometimes you can use a root."

"Okay. I think I've got it," Franco said.

Will left him on his own. He pulled out the stove bag from his pack, scouted around and found a flat spot for the kitchen, retrieved the two billy cans—#10 tins with wire handles—from Michiko and Patty and walked to the stream. He hopped across rocks until he reached the middle and paused, listening to the water swirling around the rock where he stood. He hunched over, dipped in one billy can, then the other, then stepped from rock to rock back to shore.

At the kitchen he called to the girls. "Whoever's carrying the cheese, I'm going to need it. And the pasta." The main course would be macaroni and cheese.

He pulled a stove from the bag, pumped it, and set it down. He turned the red lever to the light position, struck a match, and watched as the flame rose. He pumped fifty times. The yellow flame turned blue, and he heard the familiar chu chu chu as the fuel began to vaporize. He set the red lever to run and put the billy can full of water on the stove. He repeated the procedure with the other stove.

He sat on his haunches and watched the construction of the tarps. From a distance, they at least had an A shape. He could see Franco working furiously on the tarp and wondered if he had been wrong about the guy. All day long and no complaints.

As usual, his first hunches about the girls were wrong: Elsa wasn't the one he had to worry about; she was wiry but strong.

Anita tended to screw around a lot but she was clearly a leader in the group. And Patty? Too early to tell. She seemed to be getting along well with everyone, though. Dee was another story. She wasn't well-placed with Michiko because they both tended to drag the other down. He was appalled at the depths of Dee's negativism. He'd had to talk to her twice about swearing. What the hell kind of a father was Jonathan Tyler?

"The secret's in the sauce," Will said, stirring the cut-up cheese into a mixture of powdered milk, freeze-dried onions, and potato buds.

"The pasta's done, I think," Elsa said, poking at it.

"Franco," Will said, "you want to help her drain it?"

"Me? I don't know anything about cooking."

Patty stepped forward. "I'll do it."

"Far away from the water source, please." Will said.

After they returned, Will poured the cheesy sauce over the drained pasta, stirred it. "So, we had a pretty good first day," he said. "Any complaints?"

"I think it's neat out here," Elsa said.

Anita gave Elsa a playful poke in the arm. "I'd like to complain about Elsa: She keeps falling down."

Elsa giggled. "That's because Anita keeps stepping on my heels."

"I do not." Anita shoved Elsa and she fell, missing the billy can full of boiled water by inches.

"Okay, okay," Will said. "Cut it out before somebody gets hurt. I want you to have a good time out here, but you've got to calm down a little and keep the noise down."

"Why?" Dee said. "Who's going to hear us out here?"

"SON OF A BITCH."

Will looked over at Franco, curled in his sleeping bag, a wool hat pulled down over his ears, his nose sticking out. He was careful to aim his headlamp away from Franco's eyes. "What's the matter?"

"I guess I didn't tie the tarp right."

Will took off his shirt, climbed into his sleeping bag. "You did a good job. I was just doing some fine-tuning."

"Fine-tuning, my ass. You re-tied every knot. I watched you."

"Sorry. I like to stay dry." Will switched off his headlamp and settled in.

"How can you sleep without a shirt on?" Franco said. "I'm wearing a wool jacket and my teeth are clacking."

"Warm-blooded, I guess."

"What the hell do I look like, a lizard?"

Will paused. "Sometimes."

"What?"

"Just kidding."

Will could hear Franco shifting in his bag. "I know today was an easy one," Franco said, "flat as Broadway. It's tomorrow I'm worried about. Are we really going off the trail?"

"It's just a short bushwhack over the ridge in front of us."

"You said something about a slide?"

"The South Slide of Mount Tripyramid."

"What kind of slide?"

"A rock slide."

"Doesn't sound inviting."

"It'll be fun."

"You like this shit, don't you?"

"I guess I do."

"And you really know where we are?"

"Yes, Franco. I know where we are and I like this shit."

One of the girls screamed.

Will sat up.

"Oh, my God!" Anita yelled.

Will could hear them scrambling toward his tarp. "What's going on?" he shouted.

"Now what?" Franco said.

Will turned his headlamp on. Elsa, Anita, and Patty knelt at the front of the tarp and Anita stuck her head inside it. "Someone's out there!"

"Calm down," Will said.

"I was going to the bathroom and he was staring at me," she said.

"How could you see?"

"I had my flashlight."

"Did you shine it on him?"

"No."

"Then how can you be sure?"

Dee and Michiko joined the group. Dee dropped to her knees beside Anita. "What's wrong?"

"Nothing," Will said. "Nothing at all. It's dark and we're in the woods; sometimes you *think* you see things."

Anita turned to Dee. "I *know* somebody's out there."

Will adjusted his wool cap. "I'm sure it was shadows playing against your flashlight."

Franco sat up, flicked on his flashlight, and held it under his chin. "Maybe it was a ghost."

"A ghost!" Elsa shrieked.

"Oh, great." Will said. "He was only kidding, Elsa. Now, why doesn't everybody just go back to their tarps? Nothing is going to happen. Franco and I are right here."

Anita stood up. "If I see him again, can I come back?"

"Me, too," Elsa said. A chorus of "me, toos" followed.

Franco rolled over on his side. "Oh, that'll be fun."

"You'll be fine." Will said to them all. "Go back and get some sleep."

IT TOOK A GOOD HALF HOUR for the girls to settle down.

"Thanks for mentioning ghosts," Will said. "It really helped."

"I was being serious."

"You believe in ghosts?"

"'The woods are lovely, dark, and deep.'"

"What the hell is that supposed to mean?"

"Means what it says."

Will listened for night sounds. He thought of Butch and the cat coat. Could someone have followed them?

"Was the tarp really that bad?" Franco said.

"What?"

"I spent a lot of time on it. Then you go and rip it apart."

"You tied a nice spinnaker." Will waited for a response, but nothing came. He rolled on his back and stared into blackness. Anita couldn't have seen anything. Her eyes were playing tricks on her, that was all.

WILL LOOKED UP AHEAD at the girls strung out on the rock slide. Dee and Michiko were at least twenty-five yards up, and Patty and Elsa were so far ahead, he could barely distinguish them. He had no idea where Anita was. "Hold it up," he shouted and turned to Franco.

Franco's face was red, his chest heaving. "I can't go any farther," he said. He looked like a myocardial infarction waiting to happen.

"We're more than halfway."

"My feet keep slipping and my shoulders are killing me."

Will checked the sky. A heavy dark cloud encircled the ridge. "Go back down then."

"No. I can't even *look* down."

Will fought the urge to put his hands around Franco's throat. He chose his words carefully. "We're exposed out here. Weather's coming."

"You got me into this mess."

Will didn't hesitate. "These girls are my first responsibility," he said. He climbed away from Franco until he reached Dee and Michiko.

"What's wrong with Mr. Delacorte?" Dee asked.

"Nothing. Just a little slow today." Will looked up. Patty and Elsa sat on an outcropping of rock, waiting. He shouted, "Is Anita with you?"

"Up there." Patty pointed where the cloud had spilled over the ridge. "She really took off."

Will brought his attention back to Dee and Michiko. "Listen, you two wait for Mr. Delacorte." He looked down. He could see the top of Franco's hat bobbing toward them. He was still a good two hundred feet away. "When he gets here, make your way up to Patty and Elsa and stay there." He took off.

He tried to spot Patty and Elsa, but the trail had taken a long switchback away from the rock outcropping, and they were hidden from view. He worked his way up, hoping they had stayed put. He found them huddled together. "Get another layer on, and put on your wool hat, too."

"How come it got so cold?" Patty asked.

Will dropped his pack. "It's important for you to keep warm. I'm going after Anita." He stooped, looked straight at them. "When the others get here, I'm counting on you two to make sure they don't get cold. Understand? And stay together—no matter what, stay together."

Will left them. He scrambled up the slide, feeling a great deal lighter without his pack.

The mist grew heavier and the visibility dropped to a few yards. When he finally reached the trail junction below the summit, it felt as if he had been hiking for hours. He checked his watch; about twenty minutes had passed since he'd left Patty and Elsa.

Connecting with the Sleeper Trail, their route off the Tripyramids, called for traversing the slide, then heading down and across to where the trail entered the woods. It was tricky going even in good weather. He studied the rocks and picked up Anita's wet footprints. As he suspected, she had missed the junction and was headed toward the summit. He called her name, but she didn't answer.

The mist clung to Will's wind shirt. Her trail began to disappear in the fog. He stopped and called her name again. Listened. Took a step. "Anita!" he yelled.

Then faintly: "Here. I'm up here."

His heart leapt at the sound of her voice, but he could tell that she was pretty far away. The rocks angled more sharply upwards and he lost his footing a few times as he walked deeper into the cloud. He finally found Anita near a large rock with scrub growth poking out of a crack. She wore just the T-shirt and shorts she'd begun the day with.

"Where is everyone?" she asked.

"Just below us." He grabbed her pack, dug deep, and pulled out her polypro jacket. "Put this on."

"I'm not cold."

"Do it." He watched as she struggled with a sleeve. Her movements were slow, uninspired. "Where's your wool hat?"

"I don't know. I can't remember."

Will put on her pack. "Let's go. Just follow where I walk." He led her back down to the trail junction where he dropped her pack, took hold of her shoulders and looked her in the eyes. "I've got a job for you, Anita," he said. "You have to find your hat. I'm going back and get the others. You stay here."

He left her rummaging in her pack for her hat and began his descent.

The switchbacks disappeared in the dense fog. He stumbled and caught himself. He slowed down his pace and had to guess where to place his feet, feeling his way down the slide. He felt like he was walking in a dream, and time began to play tricks again, but he kept working his way down. Then below, shrouded in mist, the group appeared. He retrieved his own pack and put it on. "Everybody okay?"

"I'm freezing," Dee said. "Are you sure you know where we're going?"

"Maybe we should wait here until it clears," Franco said.

Will didn't acknowledge them. This was no time to chat; he had to get them moving. He started climbing again.

The girls caught on and followed without hesitation. Franco reluctantly brought up the rear. At the trail junction, they found Anita sitting on her pack, hugging herself, her head down.

"I couldn't find my hat." She was crying. "Please don't be mad at me."

Franco placed his hands on his hips. "This looks like a good place to camp."

Absurd. The man's totally absurd. To camp in the middle of a slide on a severe angle was absolutely ridiculous. "All right. Listen up," Will said. "We have to traverse this slide—watch your footing. We can rest when we get off this thing."

Franco said something. Michiko jerked her head up and looked back at Franco. At first, Will thought it was the thickness of the air that prevented his hearing, then he realized he hadn't understood because Franco had spoken in Japanese.

THE RAIN DRUMMED on the tarp.

"This isn't going to leak, is it?" Franco said. He switched on his flashlight and ran the beam along the fabric overhead.

Will refused to look at him. "It's seam-sealed," he said.

"What does that mean?"

"It won't leak."

"How do you know all this stuff?"

"How do you know Japanese?"

"I don't. Just some phrases."

"Didn't sound that way."

"If you say so. You're the boss."

"Just drop the goody-goody shit. I know you don't mean it."

Franco laughed. "Still pissed at me, I guess."

"You could have gotten us killed."

Franco lay back, exhaled loudly. "A bit melodramatic, don't you think?"

"Melodramatic!"

"Yeah. What's the big deal? We didn't hike together, so what?"

"You think these girls know where they're going?"

Franco thought a moment. "Well, I suppose they could have gotten lost." What? Franco sees the light? "Maybe lost, but not killed. No. Definitely too melodramatic."

Will rolled away from him. Just two more nights and he'd be rid of the man. He tried to concentrate on the rain.

Franco turned off his flashlight, shifted in his sleeping bag. "I think I felt a drop," he said. Will didn't answer him. "Did you hear me?"

"It's probably condensation. Go to sleep."

"Condensation? That's another word for water, isn't it?"

"Oh, Christ."

"What did I say this time?"

"Go to sleep, will you!" Will burrowed deep in his sleeping bag so his head was covered. He began to count backwards from one hundred.

"How come you don't like me?" Franco said.

Will came up for air. "Are you deliberately trying to piss me off?"

"I just think you're unfair. I still don't know what I did to warrant such abuse."

"Abuse!"

"All I did was take a little longer than the rest."

"You caused the group to split up."

"Well, so what?"

"We've been through this, Franco. You already agreed the girls could have gotten lost. It was raining, remember? It was cold."

"What difference does that make?"

"Haven't you ever heard of hypothermia?" Will waited for a response. He could feel the heat rising from his bag.

"Actually," Franco said. "No."

"I don't doubt it."

"What is it, anyway? It sounds positively gruesome."

"Never mind."

"How am I suppose to learn anything if you won't tell me?"

Will sat up. "Because, Franco, I think you could care less about hypothermia. No, cancel that—I think you know what hypothermia is and you're just trying to bait me."

"Well, that's a hell of a thing to say."

"And that's why I don't like you. I don't trust you. You are a lizard."

"Are you finished?"

"You wanted to know."

"What about Michiko? I cheered her up, don't you think?"

"Not bad for knowing only a few phrases."

"What can I say? Languages are my business."

"Where did you learn Japanese?"

"I am far from fluent."

"And you wonder why I don't trust you."

"We can't all be Boy Scouts."

If Will were standing he would have punched him. Instead, he rolled over. He gave his air mattress a wicked left cross.

"Wait," Franco said. "What was that?"

"I didn't hear anything."

"Quiet."

Will listened. "It's just the rain coming to get you, Franco."

"Very funny."

Both men were silent.

"It's nothing," Will said.

"At least I know how you feel about me," Franco said.

"The veil has been lifted."

"I have a good ear for languages, you know that?"

"Who gives a shit."

"I am a cunning linguist." Franco laughed. "It's an oral activity."

"You're a sick man, Franco."

This time Will heard the noise, a clanging of metal on metal.

"There. That's it," Franco said.

Will climbed out of his bag, pulled his boots on.

"You're going out there?" Franco said.

"I won't melt." He felt a strange echo to his words, then he remembered: Laurie had said the same thing when she was walking out on him. He stood outside listening, the raindrops falling off the hood of his poncho, beating a tattoo on his feet. Faintly, a low metallic ring, like a distant church bell tolling, sent a shiver through him. The wind shifted, blew rain against his face, and the low sounds mixed with cacophonous chiming.

He walked in the direction of the sounds, relying on his night vision. He hoped the pelting rain would cover any noise made by his footfalls. He took measured steps, stopping every now and then to listen. The gurgling of Downes Brook told him he was headed east. The wind dropped. He waited. A sudden gust sent a single low tone, like a death knell.

He was close now. If someone were there, Will would have the upper hand. The sounds began to pick up again. He parted branches, stepped over a rivulet. He was almost in the brook. He backtracked, took a more northerly route. Then he ran into the thing. It was all over him, bonging around his ears. He flailed his arms, fell backwards. He fumbled for his flashlight and aimed the beam upwards illuminating an enormous wind chime, suspended from the branch of a large oak. Will got to his feet, sprayed light on the contraption. It was made from spent shell casings of various sizes. He reached up with his knife, cut it down and stashed it in the brush.

SIX

THE SUN BROKE THROUGH just as the group made it to Camp Rich below the summit of Mt. Pasaconaway. All day they had hiked in a clinging fog, and all day the wind chimes bonged in Will's mind. Whenever they stopped to rest, Franco pulled him aside and questioned him about what he had found, and the more he harped on it, Will began to feel that somehow, some way, Franco knew exactly what he had found and that he was playing games with his head. The problem was, Will didn't know the rules, so he played dumb. Maybe as Franco talked, he would slip up and reveal something that would give him away.

Will walked ahead and checked the shelter. It was occupied.

"Can't we just kick them out? There's only three of them," Dee said when he returned.

"Plenty of spaces to camp."

"But you promised us."

"I'm sorry, Dee. This hotel doesn't take reservations. Time to scout out tarp spaces."

After the girls left, Will turned to Franco. "I'd appreciate it if you'd oversee them," he said.

"I thought you didn't like my knots."

"Just help out, will you?"

"And what are you going to do while I'm working?"

"I might watch from a distance."

"Bullshit!" Franco took a step closer, lowered his voice. "How come you won't tell me what you found last night?"

"Nothing to tell."

"All that bonging. Then it stopped. Kaput!"

"It's a mystery."

"You know what I think?"

"Not even half the time."

"I think you're a lizard." Franco turned on his heel and walked away.

Will shook his head. There was something primitive in Franco's movements, as if his arms were stretched too long from tree swinging or toting a huge club.

ONE OF THE HIKERS at the shelter had started a fire in the stone fireplace. When Will approached, he was smacking at the smoke that blew back on him.

"I guess that wood's pretty wet," Will said.

The man coughed. "Lucky I got it going at all." He stepped out of the smoke and pushed his hand out. "Name's Arthur Wallace." His grip was strong. He wore a black checked jacket and an uneven beard. "This is my wife Bette and Arthur, Junior." He gestured toward the shelter. Bette smiled at Will. Their son, early teens, gave a half-hearted nod. "I'm real sorry about taking up all this space," Arthur said.

"No problem. We couldn't all fit in there anyway."

"I knew I should have brought that tent." Arthur looked at his wife.

"You were worried about the extra weight, remember?" she said.

Arthur patted his belly. "Guess I've got enough to carry as it is."

"Have you seen anyone else on the trail today?" Will asked.

"Some day hikers near the roadhead this morning."

"Did you come up the Cutoff?"

"Yes."

Will took a step closer. "Did you pass anybody on their way down?"

"No. You're the first ones we've run into."

"I see."

Arthur thought a moment. "Oh. There is someone else here, though," he said.

"In the shelter, you mean?"

"A ranger. He's got a tent back there." He gestured toward

the rear of the shelter. "He's been out cutting deadfall. When he comes back you could ask him about your friend."

"Who?"

"The one you're looking for."

Will hesitated. "Oh yeah," he said. "Thanks."

"You bet."

"Well, I guess I better check on my kids," Will said. "Light's fading fast."

On the way back to the tarp site, he met the ranger coming up. He was slight and wore shorts underneath his rain gear and carried a bow saw in one hand and an ax in the other. "You with them?" the ranger asked, pointing the ax in the direction of the group.

"I'm in charge, yes." Will relayed the information about the school. "I've got the permits if you want to see them," he said.

"Won't be necessary. You people do a good job."

"Appreciate it." Will looked at the ax in the ranger's hand, then back to his face. His wispy blond mustache gave him a boyish look. If there was one person who might have seen someone suspicious, it would be this man.

The ranger let the ax fall and put out his hand. "Name's Nick."

Will introduced himself, then asked: "Have you been cutting near the Sleeper Trail?"

"No, why?"

"I thought you might have seen someone."

"Who you looking for?"

Will paused, wondering how his concern was going to sound to the ranger. "I think we're being followed." The ranger was clearly waiting to hear more. "Oh well, it's probably nothing," Will said.

WILL STOLE OUT of the tarp when he was sure Franco was asleep. The moon was three-quarters full, the night crisp. The front had pushed through; the wind was picking up from the north and lowed through the trees. He headed in the direction of the shelter along the perimeter of the clearing. The ranger's tent was about fifty yards away; the glow from his lamp cast him in silhouette.

Hiking with the group had made it impossible to tell if they had been followed, but he didn't doubt it for a minute. The wind chimes signaled something larger than a practical joke, perhaps a bold stroke, meant to alarm him, rather than just annoy him; it really only made him angry. Tonight he would stay up, move about, see what he could come up with.

The ranger turned his light off.

Clouds skirted the moon. Will moved with the wind to hide his footfalls when he headed back to the group, retracing his route.

He sat on a rock with a clear view of the tarps. When the wind dropped, he could hear Franco snoring. There was a rustling to his left, so he approached in the direction of the noise and frightened a pair of chipmunks investigating packs. They scurried away.

He continued on and circled the camp, locating the trail that led to the summit. He walked up a few yards to a water source, stooped, and cupped his hands to drink.

The summit of Pasaconaway was less than a half mile. As many times as he had been to Camp Rich, he had never missed an opportunity to go to the summit. He had planned to have the girls make the short ascent in the morning, but now had second thoughts because of all that had happened. Better to get them out as soon as possible and camp close to the road.

He was sure the girls were safe here, though, that if anyone was still following them, they would not take a chance of being discovered with all these other people around. He was too wired to sleep and decided to go up and free himself from the canopy of trees and all things Franco. Toward the top, foot placement was difficult, but he managed with care and trail memory.

Unlike bald faces on Bondcliff or Liberty, Pasaconaway is spruce-covered, except for outcroppings of rock. He headed on the trail that led through the trees to an overlook. The sky opened up and he could see the dark outline of Whiteface off to the southeast. It was too cold to stay long. He sought the shelter of a spruce grove, a place he had once spent the night. The wind spanked his jacket; he pulled his wool hat closer to his ears, sat on the soft needle-covered floor, leaned his back against a rock and dozed.

He woke to the sun on his face. He had not planned to stay the night and felt his shoulders ache from being curled against the rock. As soon as he stepped out on to the overlook again, he could tell the weather had changed—the wind was coming from the south and it was warmer, even at this early hour. Overhead, a hawk rode the wind. He studied it.

He wanted to stay, but a growing sense of urgency that he couldn't identify, like an itch he couldn't reach, told him he had better return to camp and get busy on breakfast. He walked on the trail that traversed the summit, thinking of Franco, hoping he was still asleep. The sleeping dog should lie.

He dropped down onto the switchbacks. As if his thoughts could conjure, Franco's shadowy form appeared, huffing up the trail, hands on knees.

Will stopped.

Franco looked up. "Buchanan!"

Will took a step, waited. "Hello, Franco," he said.

"Where the fuck have you been?" Franco leaned against a tree. His breath came hard.

"What is it?"

"Dee!" Franco took another breath. "She's gone."

"Gone! What do you mean she's gone?"

"Disappeared. Jesus, Buchanan. We've been looking all over for you."

SEVEN

AT THE CAMPSITE, Will found the ranger talking with Michiko, who was crying. As he came near he heard her say: "Dee went to the bathroom. She didn't come back."

Will joined them. "When did this happen?"

The ranger looked relieved that Will had arrived. "Early this morning, apparently," he said.

Will asked Michiko, "Did Dee say anything to you before she left the tarp?"

"No. I don't think so. I was asleep and..." She began to cry again.

Elsa came over and put her arm around Michiko. She sent Will a look of betrayal—the captain who had abandoned the ship.

Will was vaguely aware of a squirrel making chucking noises in a tree overhead. Anita and Patty hugged each other. They seemed to be waiting for him to say something, but before he could open his mouth Franco straggled in, out of breath.

"She show yet?"

Will ignored him. He put his hand on the ranger's elbow and steered him away from the group. "Have you looked for her at all?"

"No. I just barely got here myself." The ranger's voice was flat and unaffected, which had a calming effect on Will. Here was a man he could work with.

Arthur Wallace and his family soon arrived. "Can we be of assistance?" Arthur asked.

Will thanked him. What a blessing to have other adults besides Franco. "Perhaps you can. We're discussing what to do now." He addressed the ranger. "Are you carrying a radio?"

"Yes, in my tent. I'll go call in." He turned to go.

Will stopped him. "Let's not panic," he said, more to himself than the ranger. He imagined search and rescue teams, dogs, helicopters—the whole enchilada. "She probably just wandered off. Let's give ourselves two hours—if we don't find her by then we'll organize a full search."

Franco walked up to them. "Will somebody tell me what the hell's going on?"

"Look, Franco," Will said. "I want you to get the girls to the roadhead. We'll call in for a pickup. Just wait for the van to meet you."

"You want me to lead them out of here?"

"I'll show you the trail on the map. It's easy to follow." Will reached for the inside pocket of his jacket and pulled out the map.

Franco shook his head. "I can't read that thing. Too many squiggly lines."

"Look for trail signs. You can't get lost."

Franco squinted at him. "Wanna bet?"

He should have known better than to ask for Franco's help. It was a brief instant, but Franco's cow brown eyes flashed impish pleasure, like he had been waiting through the whole trip for this moment. "Forget it," Will said. He shoved the map back in his pocket. "Stay with Michiko. Maybe you can find out something more from her. Speak to her in Japanese; it might help."

Franco snorted. "That'll be a short conversation."

"This is important. I want you to find out everything you can."

"About what?"

"About what she remembers: the last time she saw Dee, whatever. And interview the others, too." Will turned back to the ranger. "Just you, Arthur, and I. We'll fan out. I don't think Dee's above us because I just came from there."

The ranger nodded and checked his watch with Will's. "I'll start over by my tent," he said. "Arthur can stay on the trails, and you can keep to the east. We'll meet back here in two hours."

Will looked at Mrs. Wallace. "And if you could help with the girls, that would be great."

She smiled and placed her hand on his arm as she walked by. "It's going to be okay," she said. "I'll take care of them."

After they left, Franco said, "Well, I guess I know my place."

Will moved closer, stood toe to toe with the man. He felt a rush of heat on the back of his neck and said, "Don't start with this," under his breath.

"Sure. I'll just hang with the womenfolk."

"It's important that someone take notes. If we can't find Dee, the police will want details."

"Now I'm the secretary."

Will's nose was almost touching Franco's. There was a faint, stale smell of peanut butter on Franco's breath. When had he had time for breakfast? "What are you trying to do? Make me punch out your lights?"

"That wouldn't be good form, Will. Grace under pressure." Will wheeled away from him. "Wait a minute," Franco said. Will stopped but refused to look back. "It's just a little detail. I mean, I need some guidance here."

Will spun around. "What is it?"

Franco held his arms up in the air, then he let them fall to his sides in mock exasperation. "What do I write down about why you deserted us?"

WILL PICKED UP footprints leading away from the tarp, but they disappeared at the edge of the clearing. He combed through dense brush, looking for broken branches, turned-up soil, anything that would suggest a struggle. There was nothing. At times he called out Dee's name, but there was no response.

At the end of two hours they reassembled.

"You guys have any luck?" Will said.

Arthur gestured with his hands. "It's like she just vanished."

The ranger looked at Will. "You think she ran away?"

"Maybe. Better call in now. Make sure the school sends a van to the Oliverian Brook roadhead. I'll get the kids out and meet you back here." He gathered the group together. The girls formed a tight circle around him.

Franco didn't join in. He sat on his pack, his hat over his eyes.

"I know this is hard on all of you," Will said to them. "We haven't found Dee, but I'm sure she's okay."

"My mother was right," Anita said. "It's not safe out here."

Michiko started crying again.

Will put his hand on her shoulder. "You've got to be strong," he said. He turned back to the group. "We have to help each other as we walk out. Let's get going."

BY THE TIME they reached the Pasaconaway Cutoff it was almost noon and they were all hungry, but Will pushed on since it was all downhill. He was antsy and wanted to get back up on elevation to scout for Dee. With each step he resented Franco even more, especially now that he seemed to be going out of his way to hinder their progress by walking by himself in the rear, a good fifty yards away from the last girl.

In another two hours they came to the junction of the Oliverian Brook Trail. Will dropped his pack. "Let's have lunch here," he said.

He pulled out the map. The trail leading out was easy, and it wouldn't take much in the way of map-reading to walk it. Will figured it would save him another three hours if he could head back up to Pasaconaway from the junction. He would give Franco one last chance to help out. He motioned for him to come over.

Franco let the pack slip off his back. He walked with his back hunched like he was still carrying the pack, mopping his forehead with a bandanna. "You want me, boss?"

Will pointed to the map. "We're here. All you have to do is follow this trail and you'll hit the roadhead. It's flat and straight, about two miles."

"I told you. I can't read that thing."

"You don't need to read it, just stay on the trail."

"Then why show me the map?"

"Just do it!"

Franco's eyebrows came together. "What are you going to do? Desert us again?"

Will almost hit him, and probably would have if Anita hadn't stepped in.

"Mr. Buchanan?" she said. "I know how to read a map. I'd be glad to lead us out."

Will looked at her. He thought of her screams the first night. "No. Mr. Delacorte will manage." He met Franco's eyes. "It's part of his job."

"I want to do it," she said.

Her insistence seemed odd at first, then it registered that she didn't want Franco to be in charge of anything. "Never mind. I thought I'd get back and help look for Dee, but..."

"You should." Anita held out her hand. "Let me see the map."

Will gave it to her. "Show me where we are," he said.

She oriented the map, found the junction of the Cutoff and Oliverian Brook, and put her little finger on it. "Here?"

"That's right."

"And we just follow the brook out?"

"You've got it."

She looked at Franco, then quickly folded the map. "Cake," she said, and walked back to the group.

Franco shook his head. "From the mouths of babes..."

"See if you can help her out."

"I've got to hand it to you. You've got guts putting a kid in charge."

"I have confidence in her."

Franco smiled. "You're probably right," he said. "At least she'll stay with the group."

WILL MADE GOOD TIME without the burden of his pack on the way back up to Camp Rich. He tried not to think about the girls and Franco. They would be all right. Search and rescue from North Conway would no doubt use Oliverian Brook as access. The trail would be buzzing with people.

Now that he was alone, he focused his thoughts on Dee and what he could tell the search party. The lack of any signs of struggle indicated she left on her own, or with somebody. Walt

Krieger? He had trouble believing it. He doubted Walt could have known the route. The wind chime kept ringing in the back of his mind, and he thought again about Franco's incessant nagging at him over the issue. He felt in his heart there was a connection with the wind chime and Dee's disappearance, but what would he say about it? That he suspected Franco had something to do with putting it there? Well, so what? What did that have to do with Dee's disappearance? No. It would do no good to talk about it unless he had some hard evidence. He'd relate what happened at Camp Rich and leave it at that.

He met up with three men from the Wonalancet Mountain Club, who were on their way to join the search, at the junction of the Pasaconaway Cutoff and Square Ledge Trail. He hiked with them the rest of the way.

By 2:00 p.m. the North Conway contingent had joined them, along with helicopter support from the National Guard. They split up, scoured the area around the camp, including the trails that led to the summit.

At sundown, the search was called off until the next morning. There was no sign of Dee.

EIGHT

PERRY KNOX SAT behind his desk and made a tent with his fingers. He looked at Will. "I'm trying to get this straight. You were on top of Pasaconaway when Dee disappeared?"

"I went up there to see if I could find something." Will knew this wasn't exactly the way it happened, but it wasn't a lie, either. He had been out investigating, after all. He didn't want to get muddled in some discussion of going up to the summit to get away from Franco—it was best to keep him out of this as much as he could until he could dig into the guy's background.

"What were you looking for?" Perry said.

"I thought we were being followed."

Franco leaned back in his chair and said, "All I know is, when I woke up Will was gone."

"You know someone was tailing us," Will said. "Anita saw the guy."

"But you told her she was seeing things."

"We both heard noises!"

Franco looked away.

Will gripped the arms of the chair and tried to calm himself. He wasn't handling this well. He stared at the old Regulator clock on the wall behind Perry's desk and tried to focus on the pendulum swinging inside the glass door.

"Excuse me," Laurie said. She held a pen poised above her pad. "What noises?"

"A real clanging," Franco said.

"You mean that night?" Laurie asked.

Franco shook his head. "The night before. Will went to investigate. I think he found something, but he won't say a word about it." A trace of a smile played on his lips, then disappeared.

Laurie looked at Will. "Did you find something?"

"No." He had prepared himself for this part. He would tell Laurie later about the wind chimes when he could connect them to Franco. He had planned on the weekend to go back and retrieve the contraption. There had to be fingerprints on the thing.

"Amazing," Franco said.

Will sat forward. "What's amazing?"

"Nothing."

"You're accusing me of something. Get it on the table!"

"It's on the table!"

"All right, that's enough," Perry said. He measured both men. "What's with you two?"

"Better ask Franco," Will said. Damn. He had to control himself better. Franco was pushing his buttons, and it was working especially well because of the guilt he felt periodically as a rush of heat on his neck. There was no way of getting around it: He *had* screwed up and left the group.

Perry stood. What he said didn't help get rid of the guilt: "We don't have time for games. We've got a girl missing." He was about to add something more, but the phone rang. He picked up. "Yeah. Yeah. Okay." He put his hand over the receiver and looked at Laurie. "The press is outside."

"Tell them the case is under investigation," Laurie said. "We'll issue a statement later."

He relayed the message, then put the phone down. "They want me to say it for the cameras."

After Perry left, Laurie said to Will: "Do you think she was kidnapped?"

Will shook his head. "There was no sign of a struggle."

"The dirt was pretty stirred up around her tarp," Franco said.

"Most of that was from the girls. They were in a panic when I got there."

"It took some time to find you. I almost got a heart attack climbing up that thing," Franco said.

Laurie stared at Franco. "Yes, I think we've heard enough about that."

Will sat forward. She had come to his rescue; he was touched.

"Suit yourself. I just wish Will had been there, that's all."

Laurie said to Will, "If she wasn't kidnapped, what do you think happened?"

"She might have run away. I know she hated being at school."

"She told you that?" Laurie asked.

Will nodded. "She wanted to be with her boyfriend."

"Boyfriend!" Franco said, like he didn't believe it.

Will stared at Franco. "Yeah, her boyfriend."

"I never heard her say anything about a boyfriend."

"Mr. Delacorte, please!" Laurie said. "I would appreciate it if you let me ask the questions."

Franco smiled at her, that impish look again.

Will took some comfort in realizing that Franco's attitude was getting to Laurie, but he canned the idea that she was defending him. She was just plain irritated by the jerk. "Anita thought she saw someone in the woods the first night," Will said. "Maybe the boyfriend was following us. I don't think that's the case, but I guess he could have been hanging around the school before we left."

"Why do you say that?"

"Oh, because of some of the stuff that happened."

"What stuff?"

He hesitated. "Nothing. Just some practical jokes, that sort of thing."

"What sort of thing exactly?"

"Oh, somebody split my garden hose."

Laurie made a note of it. "That's all?"

"Some other pranks."

"Like what?"

He felt the rush of heat on the back of his neck again. Why the hell *would* Walt Krieger play games with him? He really was losing it. "Look. I don't know why I said that. Now that I think about it, the pranks probably don't have anything to do with Walt—or Dee."

Laurie waggled the pen between her fingers. "No," she said. "We'll just chalk it up as new discoveries about Will."

Perry came back. "The press are an insistent breed," he said.

Laurie closed her notebook. "And they've just begun to ask

questions.'' She got up out of her chair. ''What we talked about stays here. I'm sure Mr. Knox agrees.''

Perry nodded.

''And you will get asked,'' she said.

''You mean I can't say anything?'' Franco asked.

'''No comment' works well.'' She put the notebook in her hip pocket. ''Just remember this is Jonathan Tyler's daughter we're talking about.'' She glanced at Will. ''The Jonathan Tyler.''

THE SEARCH FOR Dee was ongoing and relentless. State police, Fish and Game, and scores of volunteers combed the area. Will wanted to join them, but Laurie cautioned him not to get involved. He would be hounded by reporters and not much use anyway—so, he sat on his hands and waited for news.

Will was unable to sleep the night after the meeting in Perry's office. At 3:30 he finally gave up and crawled out of bed. He took a Sierra Club poster off his wall that depicted a scene of El Cap, brought it into the kitchen, and laid it out blank-side up on the counter. He made a chart, dividing the days and nights of SMOOT into grids, and, using red ink for the days and blue for the nights, began to list all he could remember about what had happened. The exercise made the time pass, but it didn't yield any new insights into what had happened to Dee.

He sleep-walked through morning classes, especially Freshman Science, vaguely aware of the eager new faces staring back at him and that one of them belonged to Berkeley Hutter. He handed out syllabi without making eye contact. His students sat quietly as he mumbled through homework instructions. He was sure they were all judging him: Here was the guy who had actually lost a student on SMOOT. Whatever you do, don't go in the woods with *him*.

He stayed away from the dining hall at lunch and took a walk along the cross-country running path, but he couldn't get Dee's face out of his head, the picture of her hair over her eyes.

At least his last class was Wildlife Ecology, his favorite. An upper level elective, the course was populated with students he knew well, so when he walked up the steps of Sloan Science

Center he felt ready to face them, but he wasn't prepared for the questions.

He was going over the syllabus when Arnold Reiniger raised his hand.

"Yes, Arnold."

"I don't understand, Mr. Buchanan."

"You mean about the due dates?"

"How could she just disappear?"

Will glared at him. Arnold was a bright but socially inept kid who had the annoying habit of blurting out whatever was on his mind. "I'm sorry. What has that to do with the field project we're discussing?"

"Nothing."

"Then let's continue."

Sally Justin raised her hand.

"Yes?"

"We're all just dying to know," she said. "We want to hear the real story."

"The real story?"

"Some kids are saying you weren't there when she disappeared. That's not right, is it?"

Jerry Santos chimed in. "I told them they were all liars, Mr. Buchanan. They don't know what they're talking about."

Will managed a smile. He would expect nothing less from Jerry Santos. His dorm leader, Jerry thought Will's clothes were cut from celestial cloth. "We really don't have time to discuss this."

"Do you think she was kidnapped?" Sally asked.

Arnold twisted in his seat to get a good view of Sally. "That's my guess."

Will held up his hand. "All right, that's enough." He walked closer to Arnold's desk. "Now, are there any questions about the field project?"

"Will you give us help finding topics?" Sally said.

"Of course."

"Do we have to do it?"

"Yes, Arnold, you have to do it." He walked to the front of

the room and glanced at the clock. "You have your syllabus and reading assignment. If there are no further questions, you're free to go." No one moved. "Well?"

"There are twenty minutes left in class," Sally said.

"I'm aware of that."

"I thought we didn't have time to talk about Dee Tyler," Arnold said.

Will didn't have a comeback. He was aware of the class waiting for him to say something. He walked to the chalkboard and began erasing it. He looked over his shoulder. "I can't believe it, Arnold. I'm giving you twenty minutes and you haven't moved."

Arnold gathered his books. "Hey. You don't have to tell me twice. I'm outta here."

WILL FELT BETTER once he was outside. He looked at the sky: Puffy clouds rode the wind, and when the sun poked through it was warm on his face. He still had a full hour before his woodsman's team activity in the afternoon, so he decided he had time to check his mail.

The mailroom was situated in Larch Hall. To get there he took a short cut through the humanities building. He walked down the corridor past the open classroom doors, and he sensed the energy, the excitement of opening day. He had always liked this time of year, but now he felt oddly distanced, like he didn't belong. He walked faster.

An outburst of laughter came from one of the classrooms near the end of the corridor. He walked by and heard Franco's voice: "...for Spanish is truly the loving tongue. Ever heard the song?"

Will leaned against the wall and listened.

Franco began singing; his voice was a full, rich baritone. He finished the chorus to applause. "Yes, truly a loving tongue, and you must make love to it each time you speak."

"Won't we get busted?"

Will recognized the student's voice: Mike Cruikshank, a real trouble-maker.

"We shall practice it safely," Franco said.

"You mean we have to wear condoms?"

More laughter. Will thought maybe he should get Perry to listen to this.

"Stand up, young man," Franco said. *"¿Cómo se llama?"*

"What?"

"I asked your name."

"Mike."

"Say *'Me llamo Mike.'*"

"Why?"

"Because I asked you to." Will listened for the response, but none came. "Okay," Franco said. "Do you know what's in my hand?"

"Yeah. It's a piece of chalk."

"La Tiza. Chalk. Repeat, please."

"La Titza."

Mike's pronunciation provoked nervous laughter. It didn't last long.

"Not bad," Franco said. "Now watch. See the chalk fly against the blackboard." Will heard the impact. Franco must have really winged it. "Oh my," Franco said. "See the little lump of chalk sticking on the blackboard?" The room was silent. "Do you, Mike?"

"Yes."

"Si Señor Delacorte."

"Si Señor Delacorte."

"Good, Mike! Now, the name for blackboard—*La pizarra!* Repeat."

"La pizzesrra."

"Nice try. You have to roll the r's. Flop your tongue around."

"This is stupid."

"Come on. Remember kindergarten? Make the sound of a truck. Go rrrrr."

"Can I sit down?"

"When I tell you to. Now go rrrrrrr." Mike made the noise. "Great. Now everybody. Make the sound of a truck. Rrrrrrrrr." The class was hesitant at first, but soon came a chorus of truck sounds. "La Piza—RR—a." Franco intoned. The class responded. "The word for railroad: El fe—RR—oca—RR—il!" Everyone tried, but the word fell apart in the laughter. "Well," Franco said. "You really bollixed that one." He paused. "What do you think, Mike?"

"I can't say it."

"Say ferro."

"Ferro."

"Then carril."

"Carril."

"Super. Now put them together." Mike managed a close pronunciation. "Excellent!" Franco said. "You can really do well in this class, Mike, especially when you stop playing games."

"I don't play games."

"Not even 'Test the Teacher'?"

"I wasn't testing anybody."

Someone blew a raspberry.

"Exactly," Franco said. "All of us know what you were doing. But you should know I'm a chalk thrower. From now on my first shot won't be at the blackboard, it'll be at your *cabeza*. You know what that is?"

"My head."

"God. You are quick. *Cabeza*. Say it!"

"*Cabeza.*"

"Come on. Make love to it."

"*Cabeza!*"

The class applauded. Someone whistled.

"You can sit down now, Mike. That was wonderful."

Will walked away, puzzled. Franco had played Mike like a flute. Where was this self-assurance on SMOOT? And his voice! He couldn't recall Franco even humming anything.

NINE

THREE DAYS PASSED AFTER Dee's disappearance, and despite extensive searching there was still no sign of her. A hiker had found a woolen shirt, but it turned out not to belong to Dee.

Will waited in the bar of the Burger & Brew. He glanced at the clock over the cigarette machine. Laurie was twenty minutes late.

The bartender came over and gestured at Will's empty glass. "Another draft?"

"Sure, Howard. Why not?"

Howard Blaisdell reached for a new glass. He tipped it under the spout of the beer engine and pulled the handle. "Waiting for Laurie?" Will nodded. Howard placed the glass on a cardboard coaster advertising Miller Lite. "Maybe she's out on a call," he said.

"How long have you been working here? I thought you were up at The Mill House."

"Still am, sort of. Same owners built this place. You know, them lawyers from New York." Howard ran his finger under his thick mustache. "They wanted me to get the bar up and running."

"Quite a joint."

"They're counting on tourists spilling over from Lincoln."

"That's a ten-mile spill."

Howard winked at him. "Word'll get out, you'll see."

Will finished his draft and was thinking of ordering another when Laurie walked in. She was still in uniform. "I'm late, I know. Don't say anything."

"Let me guess," Will said. "You were held up." She cocked her head but didn't smile. "Sorry. Bad joke."

"I'm not in the mood."

"You look like you could use a drink," Howard said.

"I want food."

The hostess led them to a table in the back by the window which overlooked a duck pond with a fake mill wheel. Laurie ran her hand along the edge of the table, which was oak heavily glazed with urethane. "This is a nice place." She sat back in her chair and read the menu. "Look at this."

"What?"

"They have shrimp."

"In Saxton Mills?"

"What's wrong with Saxton Mills?"

"Nothing." Will didn't look at his menu. He knew what he wanted: a sirloin strip, medium rare.

After they ordered, Will said: "I'm glad you agreed to have dinner with me."

"It's a working dinner." She took a sip of her wine. "So, let's hear the story."

"What story?"

She leaned over the table. "What were those clanging noises? You told me you had something more to say about SMOOT. I'm guessing that's it. If this is another one of your games..." She put her napkin on the table.

"Hold on!" Will said.

She sat back. "Well?"

He ran his fingers up and down the handle of the mug. "I didn't want to tell you in front of Franco."

"Why not?"

"Because he wanted me to. He kept goading me. I didn't want to give him the satisfaction."

"You two are something else."

"I don't trust him."

She slapped the table with her hand. "Listen. If you know something, I want to hear it."

The wind chime tale drew all of Laurie's attention. When he finished, she said, "And what happened after that?"

"I cut the thing down and dragged it off."

She pulled her notebook out and began writing.

"Always working," he said, and picked up his napkin.

"I'll only be a minute."

When she finished writing he said, "So, what do you think?"

"It's interesting."

"I think it's key."

"Could be."

He hesitated. "Wait a minute. You don't think it's important?"

"I have no idea."

"You *don't* think it's important, do you?"

"I didn't say that."

"Didn't have to. I can tell."

She sighed. "Look, I don't know one way or the other. For all I know some kid could have left it there. Maybe a demented artist. I just can't figure out what you were so hush-hush about. And this Franco business..."

"He's involved. I know he has something—"

"Oh, by the way." She pointed her pen at him. "I checked out your garden hose. You were right, somebody did deliberately cut it."

He held the napkin above his lap. "Wait a minute. You walked into the shed and looked at my garden hose?"

"That's right."

He let the napkin drop and threw up his hands. "I don't believe it."

"What's the matter?"

"You could have asked."

"You weren't around."

He leaned forward. "Don't you need a search warrant to go snooping around like that?"

She ignored the remark and closed her notebook. "I'll run this by Lamont. See what he thinks."

"Who?"

"FBI."

"Here?"

"That's right."

"In Saxton Mills?"

"We've got shrimp. Why not the FBI?"

"I don't believe it!"

"Why is this so surprising? They handle any kidnapping. Where have you been?"

"Teaching school for twenty years. I don't get around much."

"No kidding."

"Why are they treating it as a kidnapping? Is there a ransom note?"

Laurie paused. "No."

"I don't get it."

"Look. This is big stuff. Dee Tyler isn't your everyday disappearing act."

"You think it's an act?"

"I didn't mean it that way."

"But if there's no note..." He thought a moment. "I bet Jonathan's behind this."

"What do you mean?"

"It's just like him. He makes a few phone calls, gets an FBI agent to set up shop because he doesn't trust the local constabulary."

"He's that powerful?"

"What do you think?"

"I think you're naive."

"Is that so?"

"This is a kidnapping, Will. The FBI are supposed to be involved."

"I bet he had something to do with them getting on this so fast."

She put her notebook in her purse. "You know him better than I do, remember?" she said in an offhand manner. "My only source is *People Magazine*."

Will drank from his water glass. He downed half of it and wondered where his thirst came from. A waiter came over to refill his water glass. Will watched him as he poured.

"That man who just filled your glass?" Laurie said.

"What about him?"

"He's Vietnamese."

"So?"

"The Methodist Church is sponsoring his family. He was one of the boat people."

"How did the boat get this far inland?" Laurie shook her head. "What's the matter now?"

"Why do you have to be so snide?"

"What do you expect? You mention the FBI's in town like it's some casual thing, then you launch off on the boat people."

"Maybe we shouldn't talk about anything."

"Maybe we shouldn't."

They stared at each other a few moments, then she turned away and looked out the window at the duck pond.

"Okay. New slate." He ran his hand over the table. "Tell me about the Vietnamese family."

She remained facing the window. "You don't really want to know."

"Yes, I do. I'm interested."

"No, you're not. You couldn't be bothered. The waiter has nothing to do with you."

"Now who's being snide?"

"That man," she said gesturing toward the bar, "has gone through more hell than you and I could ever imagine. If you could just get out of yourself, you might be able to show some compassion."

Will sat back in his chair. "Yeah, but has he ever spent a winter in New Hampshire?"

"Damn it, Will!"

He refolded the napkin and flapped over the corners. He spread it out neatly on his lap. "I don't like what's happening to us. I try to think of what went wrong, and I can't."

"It's simple."

"We were going along fine. Then I mentioned I knew Jonathan Tyler. That's when it all changed. Now you treat me like the enemy." His throat felt dry; he took another tug on his water glass.

"God! You're not that dense, are you?"

"What?"

"Jonathan Tyler isn't the problem. If it hadn't been Jonathan, it would have been something else. I can't believe—"

He held up his hand for her to stop. "You know what? Maybe it's me who doesn't know you. I sure as hell don't know how many men you've had in your life."

She brought up her wine glass halfway and stared into it. "You want to know how many men I've slept with? Is that what you want?"

He shook his head and looked down at the table. "You know what I think?" he said.

She took a sip. "I'm not the least bit curious."

"You're not?"

"That's right."

His eyes met hers. "Maybe I should leave."

"Maybe you should."

"Or you should."

"I don't think so. I'm too hungry."

"I was here first." In the silence that followed he had a chance to realize the silliness of what he had just said. Pathetic. Like a kid staking out a seat in a school lunchroom.

She twisted the glass by the stem. She looked out the window at the duck pond. His neck burned. This was going nowhere. She said, "I'll tell you how many men I've slept with."

"Forget it. I'm not interested."

"Let's see, there was Forrest MacArthur in high school, but that was more a dry hump than a real fuck. And Ben Hecht in the woods behind the tennis courts. Now, Ben was a different story...Ben was what you might call 'well hung.'"

"That's enough!"

"But we haven't got to the good parts yet."

He sat back in his chair. "Okay. What about Jack? How was he?" She didn't say anything. "Well?"

She leaned forward. "Look, Will. I'm not going to talk about Jack. Jack's not the problem, you are."

"I'm the problem?"

"You're not up front with me."

"That's not how I see it."

"Really?"

"You're scared of being burned again, that's the problem." She looked down at the table, held her head in her hands. "I'm not your former husband, Laurie. I don't sleep around."

She jerked up her head. "Jack never lied to me," she said. "He just never told me the truth."

"What?" Will started to laugh but caught himself. "Do you know how stupid that sounds?"

"If you think that sounds stupid, then you really have no clue. And since it's obvious you have no clue, I'll explain it to you: I got hurt once for what I didn't know about a person. I'm not ready to let that happen again."

The waitress delivered the meal. They both watched her in silence.

Laurie took off the warming lid and brought her nose to the dish. "Hmm. Smells good," she said. She broke off the tail of a shrimp with her fork, dipped the shrimp in melted butter, ate it.

"So what should I do?"

She pointed at his plate with her knife. "Eat your dinner, Will."

"I mean about us."

"Nothing." She dabbed at her mouth with the napkin.

He sliced into his steak. It was too rare and bled all over his plate. "I guess that means you won't sleep with me tonight."

"What!"

"Just kidding."

She snapped the tail off another shrimp.

TEN

"WILL BUCHANAN?" The man stood tall in the doorway, hands thrust into the pockets of a blue peacoat.

"That's me."

"Jonathan Tyler wants to speak with you."

"He's here?"

"Would you come with me, please?"

Will hesitated. "Just give me a second. I've been cleaning out my cat's litter box." The man followed Will into the kitchen. He studied him at the sink like he had never seen anyone washing up. Will dried his hands on a towel. "Where is he?"

"Outside." The man motioned with his head. "In the limo."

A sharp edge of cold sliced through him as he walked to the car. The full moon was brilliant against a dark sky. It looked like a night for howling.

The man opened the door to the limo. Will could barely make out the dark figure of Jonathan Tyler.

"Come in, Will. Please." A hand gestured, catching the light. "Peter. Take a walk."

Will climbed into the limo. Peter hesitated, his hand on the door handle. "It's all right," Jonathan said. Peter closed the door. The courtesy lights were on, but Jonathan's face was in shadow. "I wanted to make sure I caught you before I left," Jonathan said.

"I didn't know you were in town."

"You're not supposed to. I'm a celebrity, remember. The life of a mushroom."

Will waited, but he didn't continue. "Jonathan, I..."

"No. Don't say anything. I don't want you to say anything." Jonathan shifted on the seat.

Will's eyes began to adjust to the light. He could see Tyler better and noticed that the lines near his eyes were deeply etched.

"I'm sorry," Jonathan said. "I was just thinking about the last time we were together, the night Jeanne died." He slipped his hand through the strap by the door. "They say it gets easier, Will. It doesn't."

Will ran his hand over the plush door of the limo. "Can I say something now?"

"Of course, please."

"I was looking out for Dee."

"I don't doubt that."

"I'm really sorry this happened."

"I'm sure." Jonathan let the words settle. "I know you were away from the scene when she disappeared," he said.

If Jonathan's words had been a fist, he couldn't have stunned Will more. Jonathan Tyler had obviously been doing some snooping. "How do you know I wasn't there? Who told you?"

"I know you, Will. I'm sure you had a good reason for leaving the group."

Will leaned against the door. Then it all came clear. "It was Franco Delacorte, wasn't it?"

Jonathan shifted his position on the seat. "Tell me. You think Dee ran away?"

Will exhaled slowly. Since the Burger & Brew with Laurie, he hadn't been able to think clearly about any of this. He had been so sure the key to unlocking the mystery was connecting Franco to the wind chimes, but Laurie had burst that bubble. Would Franco have been stupid enough to leave his fingerprints? No. Will had nothing to offer his old friend. "I don't know what happened, Jonathan."

"You told some people that Dee didn't like it here."

"She said she wanted to be with Walt."

"Ah, yes. Walt Krieger."

"What's he like?"

"A loser." Will didn't say anything. "I guess it's possible the two of them ran off together," Jonathan said. "Maybe it's that simple."

Will sat up straight. "Do you think Walt could have followed us? I mean, were they that much in love?"

Jonathan let go of the strap. "I really don't know much about him," he said. "Dee started seeing him a few months ago." Jonathan's hand went to his face; he looked like a man suddenly stricken with a migraine. "Let's not kid ourselves, Will. I'm expecting the worst, here."

"What do you mean? What's the worst?"

He paused. "I think she's been kidnapped."

Jonathan said it. What had been sitting between them like a third unwanted guest, suddenly stepped forward. Will felt a droplet of sweat break on his forehead. There was no damn air in this rolling palace.

"You wouldn't believe the weirdoes out there. This celebrity shit isn't what it's cranked up to be."

"But wouldn't we have heard from the kidnappers by now?"

"You would think so."

"So, she probably just ran away. I'm sure we'll hear from her soon." Will could hear the eagerness in his voice. "She's a damn nice kid," he added.

"And you can see Jeanne in her face, can't you? It's not the eyes so much as the way she holds herself. An attitude. Something." The sadness in his voice was heavy. "Sometimes it's hard to look at her," Jonathan said. "You know what I mean?"

"I'm not sure."

"You know exactly what I mean."

The statement caught Will off guard. It sounded like an accusation. Maybe the third unwanted guest sitting between them was Jeanne.

"You'll keep me informed?" Jonathan said.

"Sure. But your best bet is the police."

"They don't always tell the whole truth. I'm counting on you. I want to give you my number."

"I have it."

Jonathan's hand passed through the light. "This is a special one. Call it my red phone."

Will took the card.

Jonathan pushed down on the handle and gave the door a shove. "I thought this would be a safe place for Dee. I guess I was wrong."

Will got out of the limo. "I think we're going to hear from her pretty soon," he said. "If she was determined to run away, you really can't blame the school."

"Maybe not. But somebody's responsible."

THE NEXT AFTERNOON, Will came back from class and found a man in his living room sitting on his couch. "Who the hell are you?"

The man stood up quickly. "Sorry. The door wasn't locked."

"It wasn't wide open, either."

The man smiled. He worked his hands around the brim of his hat. It was a city hat, a fedora. "I'm Terrance Lamont." He reached into the vest of his three-piece suit and pulled out a badge. He showed it to Will. It looked real enough—a fancy embossed seal of the FBI.

"You always let yourself in whenever you want?"

"I didn't think it was a big deal." Lamont put his badge away, sat again on the couch, crossed his legs. "This is a dormitory, isn't it?"

"This is a faculty apartment in a dormitory, which makes it private property."

"Oh. You own it?"

"No."

He looked down at his hat. "You want I should get a search warrant?"

"A search warrant?"

Lamont looked him in the eye. "Yeah. Any reason I might need one?"

What the hell was this? A B-movie? Will finally realized who Lamont reminded him of—his jowl-flapping Uncle Malcolm, his dead father's brother, singular in a family line of loggers for becoming a tweedy research scientist at Dow Chemical, specializing in napalm research in the 'sixties. He didn't like Malcolm, either. "Oh, sure. I'm hiding lots of illegal stuff." Lamont didn't move. "You're not serious, are you?"

Lamont smiled again and straightened his coat. "Kind of touchy about your apartment."

"Look. This is my place. I don't particularly like finding people in it I don't know. What do you want?"

"You can figure it out. You know why I'm in town. Officer Eberly tells me you have a theory about Dee's boyfriend: You think he had something to do with her disappearance."

God, not this again. He wished Dee had never come over that day and rhapsodized over Walt. "I only know what she told me."

"And what was that?"

"That she didn't like the school, that she wanted to be with Walt."

"That's the boyfriend, right?"

"If you've been talking to Officer Eberly you should know that."

Lamont cleared his throat. "Look, Will. I'm going to stay here until you tell me what you know." Will knew he should answer the man's questions—this was the FBI for Christ's sake—but he was still angry over the intrusion. "I just get a little tired of saying the same things."

Lamont shifted his weight on the couch. "We're all tired." His ample rump left a deep dent in the cushion. "You don't mind if I call you 'Will,' do you?"

"Does that mean I can call you 'Terrance'?" He shouldn't have said it. He had better be careful being such a wise ass with this guy.

Lamont didn't seem to notice. "Can if you want. Hate the name, myself." He settled back in the couch and sighed. "Lamont. That's good enough."

Will decided he'd adopt a more congenial tone. "Would you like something to drink? Some tea, perhaps?"

"I always enjoy a good cup of tea." Will made a move for the kitchen, but Lamont stopped him with: "But I don't plan to be here that long. Let's get started." Will pulled the ladder-back chair away from the corner and sat facing him. Lamont took out a cigar from the inside pocket of his jacket. "Mind if I smoke?"

"Yes." Lamont continued unwrapping the plastic from the cigar. "There's no smoking in school buildings," Will said.

"I thought this was your private property."

"It's the law. A fire code."

"I heard you the first time." He stuck the cigar in his mouth and chewed on the end. He yanked out a small notebook from the same pocket and motioned for Will to begin. Will recounted the conversation with Dee in his apartment. He talked slowly, trying to recall each detail. He described her attitude toward the school, what she was like on SMOOT. Lamont rolled the cigar in his mouth and wrote it all down. He stood when Will was finished and pocketed the notebook. "We've got BOLOs out on Krieger now."

"Excuse me?"

"Be On the Lookouts."

"I hope you find him."

"I imagine you do."

"What's that supposed to mean?"

"If Dee's with him, you're off the hook."

"I didn't realize I was on the hook."

Lamont pulled the cigar from his mouth. "Then you're pretty damn green about the ears." Will blinked at him. "I'm supposed to say something more?"

"I would like to hear exactly what you mean."

"Okay," Lamont said. "If she doesn't show up soon, people will want to blame somebody—and that somebody is most likely you."

"Me? But I haven't done anything."

Lamont got up from the couch and looked out the window. "Doesn't matter." He parted his jacket, rested his hands on his hips, and revealed a handgun lodged in a holster on his belt. It looked like a Beretta. "Damn, you've got a great view," he said. "This is a hell of a pretty town. I may retire up here."

"What do you mean, it doesn't matter?"

Lamont put on his hat, adjusted the brim. "You're a teacher, aren't you? You're smart enough to figure that out." He patted Will on the shoulder. "I'll be in touch."

ELEVEN

THE EVENTS OF the past few days had left Will bone-tired, and on Sunday morning he decided to hunker down. Usually an early riser, it was well past nine when he finally stumbled out of bed and opened the front door to see if the *Boston Globe* had been delivered. Outside, the mist was heavy, but it looked like it would burn off. He found the paper wrapped in a blue plastic bag a few feet from his doorstep.

He made coffee and sat on the couch. Butch came out of the bathroom and hopped up next to him. He wedged himself between the cushion and Will's arm and got his motor going. Will drank coffee using his left hand to keep from disturbing the cat, watched the mist brighten through the sliding glass door as the sun tried to poke through.

He sipped his coffee and reached for the paper with one hand to spread it out on the couch. He scanned the front page. There was news of the search for Dee, but nothing had changed—she was still missing.

He found the automotive section, read John White's review of a fancy Jaguar that cost enough for two years of college, and scoured the used-truck columns for a 4x4. His own '79 Dodge pickup had been bondoed and bailing-wired so much he doubted whether it would make it through another winter. He didn't find anything that looked decent.

Butch stirred and stretched, then hopped to the coffee table. With both hands free, Will flipped through to find the sports. Butch suddenly lunged from the coffee table and landed on the paper and Will shooed him off. Parts of the paper fell to the floor and his eye caught a headline in the New Hampshire section: Girl Still Missing from School Camping Trip—and below it, in smaller letters: Exclusive Interview with Teacher.

Will grabbed the section with both hands. He didn't have to guess who the teacher was. Franco's words leapt out at him: *It was a long and grueling trip, fraught with difficulty.*

"'Fraught'?" He read further, scanning quickly.

Franco talked about Dee, his impressions of her, then about himself, how he had never been in the woods before, how awkward he felt. In response to the interviewer's question on the wisdom of a school sending inexperienced people into the woods, Franco replied: *Oh, we had an experienced leader, there's no doubt about that, although I did question his decision-making. He was good at woodlore, that kind of stuff, but he didn't handle the kids very well. He would leave us by ourselves for no apparent reason. One time, he even put one of the students in charge. He was actually away from camp when Dee Tyler disappeared.*

"Son of a bitch!" Will threw the paper on the floor.

Butch jumped off the side of the couch, hit the lamp on the end table, and knocked it over.

Will stormed down the hall and into the bedroom. He threw on pants and a shirt. In the hallway, Butch got underfoot and Will nudged him aside with the toe of his shoe.

Butch raised his back.

"Get out of the way, Butch!" He rolled up the New Hampshire section of the paper, squeezed it under his arm like a swagger stick, and stepped outside. The air had a musty smell; the mist still hung in patches.

Franco's apartment was across campus, about a ten-minute walk. A first-year teacher usually drew assignment in Desmond Hall—aka "The Jungle." Franco had avoided any dormitory responsibility, and Will could just hear him worming out of it during his contract talk. It fueled his anger as he walked. He was sure Perry would regret giving Franco special dispensation.

The apartment had once been a carriage house, part of an estate bequeathed to the school. Will crossed the main parking lot to get to it. Ahead of him, several backboards were set up along the edge of the lot, and he could see someone shooting hoops.

He didn't think much of it at first, then he recognized who it was.

Franco bounced the ball. He pulled up for a jump shot. Swish.

Will stopped, watched him retrieve the ball. Franco dribbled it a few times between his legs like a point guard ready to make his move to the basket. He spun to the left, let go a high arching fade-away jumper that bounced once on the front of the rim and rolled into the net.

Was this the same man who tripped over himself on SMOOT? Will watched him for a few minutes, awed by the grace of his moves, a pot-bellied cat with Shaquille footwork, then put the newspaper on the ground and walked toward Franco.

Franco was in the middle of another spin move when he turned right into Will. "Hello, Franco," Will said. Franco froze. The ball dropped from his hands. "Getting a little exercise this morning?"

"That's right." Franco Delacorte picked up the ball. "I'm not very good at it, though."

"Yeah. It looks that way."

Franco slapped at the ball using the flat of his hand. "I just wish they'd put handles on these things," he said.

"Mind if I join you?"

Franco tossed him the ball. "Here. I've had enough, anyway."

Will caught it. "Ah, come on. Let's play together." He fired the ball at the net. It was short and banged off the front of the rim. He bounced the ball back to Franco. "Your shot," he said.

Franco went to the foul line. He let go a miserable duck that didn't even reach the net. "Guess I still need to warm up." He handed Will the ball. "Here. I bet you can show me a few things."

"Seen the newspaper this morning?" Will tried a foul shot, hit it.

Franco picked up the ball and underhanded it to Will. "Not yet."

"For someone who was supposed to have no comment you had a lot to say." He tried a two-hand set shot. There was little spin on the ball; it rattled inside the rim but dropped through. It bounded off the asphalt and onto the grass.

Franco made no move to go after the ball. "I really have to get back," he said.

"You have to get me the ball. I made the basket." Franco hesitated. "I'm sorry. Those are the rules."

"Of course," Franco said. "Always important to play by the rules." Franco exaggerated a limp as he went to recover the ball. He groaned a little when he bent down to pick it up.

"Still stiff from Orientation, I guess."

"Boy, you've got that right." He tossed the ball to Will. "Just put it on my front porch when you're through."

"You made me look pretty bad in that article," Will said. "I'm amazed how you can twist things."

"I'll have to read it—I was probably misquoted." Franco walked away.

When he reached the edge of the asphalt, Will yelled, "Hey, Franco!" Just as he turned, Will fired the ball at him. Franco caught it, but more with his stomach than his hands. "How about a little one on one?"

Franco held the ball. "I told you. I don't play well."

"I know. And you're a little stiff, too." Franco didn't respond. "I think you're afraid I'll beat you."

"Is that what you think?"

"In a fair game, you'd be dead meat."

"I don't think so."

"Oh. You don't think I'm good enough?"

"No."

"No, you don't think I'm good enough?"

"I think you're a worthy opponent."

"Let's find out."

Franco bounced the ball. "I have things to do."

"Chicken!"

"Well, that's mature."

"Hey! Who's taking his ball and going home?"

Franco bounced the ball again—once.

Will stood toe to toe with the man, just like he'd done on the mountain side. He could smell him. Franco's T-shirt was stained with sweat about the shoulders. He had obviously been working out quite a while before Will's arrival. "You're right, Franco. No more games. Things are getting too serious."

Franco let the ball drop from his hands. "I'd appreciate it if you wouldn't stand so close. You've got coffee breath."

Will poked Franco's chest with his finger. "Don't fuck with me. You crossed the line talking to the press like that."

Franco slapped his hand away.

Will saw red. He punched Franco in the face and he dropped like a log. Will's hand stung, and he resisted the urge to shake it.

Franco struggled to get up. There was blood coming from his nose.

Will was ready for him. "Let's go."

Franco gingerly touched his nose. "Sucker punch," he said.

Will shoved him. "Come on. Fight me, you bastard."

Franco ran the back of his hand over his mouth. "I deplore violence," he said.

The smirk again. Will grabbed him by the front of the shirt and yanked him close. "This is fair warning. I'm coming after you, Franco. I'm going to find out exactly who you are and why you're here."

Franco's face was red around his cheek. He'd have a shiner, for sure. "Name's Franco Delacorte," he said. "I teach at Saxton Mills."

Will pushed him.

On his way backwards, Franco stepped on the basketball, lost his balance, and fell hard. He got up slowly and brushed himself off. He picked up the basketball and walked away. At the edge of the asphalt he stopped and turned. He let fly a one-hander from beyond three-point land. It traveled high in an arc and dropped through the hoop without touching the rim.

ON MONDAY, Will caught up with Perry Knox as he came out of a morning meeting with the business manager. Perry pointed to the rolled newspaper in his hand. "I thought you'd be here to see me."

"You've read it?"

"Yes."

"I've got to talk to you," Will said.

"And I you." Perry glanced at his watch. "I have an appointment in fifteen minutes."

"I'll take what I can get."

"Okay. Let's go for a walk; I need some fresh air."

The wind was blowing hard and leaves spiraled around their feet. Perry pulled up the lapels of his sport coat and shoved his hands in the pockets. "Damn figures make my head spin."

Will didn't understand at first, but then made the connection with Perry's meeting the business manager. He slapped at the newspaper. "You know what bothers me most?"

"I would imagine the whole article."

"Delacorte had to go out of his way to do this."

"You think he called the press and offered to tell his story?"

"It was malicious, Perry. And this after we were supposed to say 'no comment' if anyone asked."

"I don't think you should accuse the man until you find out for sure." He stopped walking. "And I especially don't think you should go around beating up faculty members."

Will flexed his hand. He had a few cuts on his knuckles and he wondered if Franco's teeth were loose. He hoped so. "I don't make a habit of it except when I'm threatened."

"Delacorte was in the office first thing this morning."

"I bet he was."

"He wants to sue your ass."

"Sounds about right for him."

"From the way he tells it, he has good cause. Says you jumped him."

"Sounds about right for me."

Perry hesitated. "You mean he's telling the truth?"

"I punched him."

Perry shook his head. "I must be missing something. We have

Dee Tyler missing, and I have to worry about two faculty members killing each other."

"There's a connection there, Perry."

Perry drew himself up straight. "Well, I want you to stop it right now before it gets worse."

"Get Delacorte off my back."

"He says he's willing to forget everything if you just say you're sorry."

"What!"

"Just apologize, will you?"

"Forget it. I'm not sorry."

Perry sighed deeply. "I guess I just don't get why you hate the guy so much. He was very civil about this whole affair when we talked."

"Civil? I thought he wanted to sue."

"Oh, he mentioned a law suit, but it was in context."

Will raised an eyebrow. "You mean he'll sue if I don't apologize."

"Yes." Will shook his head. Perry put his hand on his shoulder. "Look, Will. I'm sure you two just got off on the wrong foot. Franco's made quite a positive impression since he's been here. The faculty like him, and so do the kids."

"They don't know him, then."

"Please, Will. I can understand your frustration over this article, but—"

"What do you expect? Of course he's going to win friends and influence people. He can suck up to anybody." A gust of wind sprang up and cut through them. "I'm going to call the newspaper," Will said.

"I don't think that's a good idea."

"Maybe not, but I have to do something."

Perry hugged himself against the cold. "I don't want to get into an argument in the middle of the campus, Will. I am very concerned about this, though. I don't think Franco did the right thing, but you're not without blame. You're starting to take this much too personally."

"You think so?"

"I do. And I'm worried it will affect your work."

Will almost told him it already had, but he checked himself.

They walked in silence for a few moments, heading toward the field house. They passed behind the art building that offered temporary protection from the wind, then stopped by an oak tree, the leaves just beginning to turn yellow.

Will broke off a leaf and spun the stem in his fingers. "I guess you don't know Franco like I do."

"True. But continuing this enmity is no good for anybody."

Will took hold of Perry's arm. "Who is Franco Delacorte, anyway?"

"What do you mean, who is he?"

"What do you know about him?"

"I know he's a scholar."

"A Ph.D.?"

"In French. A master's in Spanish and German, and he speaks several other languages fluently."

"What is someone like that doing here?"

"This isn't his first job, Will. He taught at the Ferry School outside of Washington. He just got sick of the graduate bullshit. He wanted to work with kids."

"How did you find out about him?"

"He just showed up."

"You didn't go through an agency?"

"No. He was hired late."

"Jesus, Perry."

"What?"

"Don't you think it's a bit odd? You usually don't do your hiring that way."

"It's not like I didn't check him out!"

A group of students made their way toward them.

Perry stepped off the path to let them by. He smiled and called each by name. When he turned back to Will, the smile faded. "I'm not interested in being grilled further about my hiring practices. If you have something you want me to consider, please tell me now."

Will paused. "I'm not trying to make trouble. I'm just trying to understand what's going on here."

"I'll talk to Franco more about this. Just let me handle it."

"Okay. But I'm not apologizing."

"We'll see."

"I'm not, Perry."

"He's a good teacher, Will. I don't care how he got here. I hired him because he was the best one for the job. He even took a pay cut to come here."

"He took a pay cut?"

Perry didn't answer. The tendon along his jaw line flexed. "I've got to get back, Will."

"How much of a pay cut?"

"I can't tell you that." Perry put his hand on his shoulder. "Now, I want you and Franco to kiss and make up." He walked away from him.

TWELVE

WILL CAME OUT OF CLASS and spotted Lamont down by the pond. He was throwing a tennis ball to a black Labrador that belonged to one of the secretaries. At first, he thought of sneaking back into the building to avoid him, but then recalled how poorly he had handled their first encounter. He decided instead to meet the man head on. He had nothing to hide. He strode confidently to greet him. "Are you here to see me?"

Lamont threw the ball into the pond. The Labrador plunged in after it. "Look at him go."

"Bellboy's a no-brainer," Will said. "I hope you plan to stay a while. He'll drive you nuts."

"His name's Bellboy?"

"When he was a puppy, he got hold of a suitcase and started dragging it by the handle. That's the story."

Bellboy came out of the water and shook himself. Will and Lamont backed away. Bellboy dropped the tennis ball at Will's feet, who picked it up and winged it back into the pond.

"A magnificent animal," Lamont said.

"Dumb. Relentless."

Lamont looked at Will and winked. "Make a good lawman," he said.

Will managed a smile. "You must be here for a reason."

Lamont looked back to the dog, then his eyes shifted across the pond. "This is a beautiful place," he said. "You're a lucky man."

Will nodded. He hated this habit of Lamont's, this avoiding the issue, but he realized it must have come from years of drawing people out. Let them talk themselves into trouble.

Bellboy came back for another round. This time Lamont faked throwing it in the pond and tossed it high in the air in the opposite direction. Bellboy crashed into the water and swam around like a rudderless boat.

Lamont chuckled. "Like you said. More heart than head."

"But he's happy."

Lamont stared at the dog. "Krieger turned up," he said.

"Dee's boyfriend?"

"We found him in Chicago. A Phish concert."

Bellboy came out of the water. He swept the ground with his nose.

"Looks like a vacuum cleaner," Lamont said.

Damn. Come on, Lamont. Tell me what you know. "What about Krieger?"

"He's a granola head." Lamont turned to Will. "He wasn't anywhere near New Hampshire when Dee disappeared."

Will's heart sank. It was the one hope he had clung to. Every morning he expected to hear that Dee and Walt had been found shacked up some place, that it was all a ruse created by Dee to get her father's attention. "He has witnesses, I guess?"

"Yeah. His story's tight as Bellboy's asshole." Lamont pulled out a cigar, stuck it in his mouth and pulled it back and forth a few times to moisten it. He chewed on the end but didn't light it. "I thought you should know," he said.

"Why?"

"It was your theory."

Will couldn't take his eyes off the cigar in Lamont's mouth. It distorted his face. Will suddenly felt sick. "I only told you what Dee said about him," he said. "It seemed logical."

He took the cigar out of his mouth and spat. "That's the trouble with logic," he said. "The major premise gets screwed, the rest goes down the toilet."

This time it was Will's turn to watch Bellboy. The dog was zeroing in on the ball.

"If he'd just look up, he'd see the damn ball," Lamont said.

"What do you want from me?"

"I guess I'm looking for ideas."

Will thought a moment. Right now the only idea he had was that Dee must have been kidnapped. In his mind's eye he saw her shaking her hair, the old habit to get it off her face. "I guess they still haven't found anything." Lamont eyed him curiously. "The searchers."

"No. In fact, they're about to call the whole thing off."

"What?

"It's been a week."

The thought that they would give up looking caught him up short. "If it's a question of manpower, maybe the school can take it over. I know Perry doesn't want to disrupt the schedule anymore than it is, but if you want us to help out..."

Lamont placed his hand on his arm. "Take it easy."

"I wish I could do something, that's all."

"She isn't out there."

"How do you know?"

He turned away from him and spat. "Because we would have found her by now," he said. "They've covered every inch of the area."

"You're sure?"

"With dogs."

Bellboy found the ball.

"Damn. If I had a nose like that," Lamont said.

Bellboy was proud of his find. He swaggered back to them, his tail thrashing the air. He dropped the ball at Lamont's feet.

"It's too bad," Lamont said. "I like it when theories pan out." He kicked the ball into the pond. "Now I have to go to work."

ON FRIDAY MORNING Perry called Will into his office; he figured it was going to be more of the same about Franco, but he simply was *not* going to apologize. But when he saw Perry's face, he realized it must be something more.

Perry looked down at the document in his hand, then his eyes rose above half-glasses. "Jonathan Tyler has brought suit against the school." Will sat down slowly. He waited for Perry to say more. "You're cited for negligence."

Will felt a numbness move up his spine to his neck. His mind flashed to the conversation in the limo, and Jonathan's last words about someone being responsible. "So, what am I supposed to do?"

"The school lawyers are looking into it. I don't want you to do anything until we hear from them."

Both men were quiet.

"I can't believe it," Will said, breaking the silence. "This whole thing doesn't make any sense."

"I have a call into Jonathan."

"He won't return it." Will's thoughts drifted again to the limo and the number for Jonathan's red phone. "Maybe I can get hold of him."

"I told you. I don't want you to do anything."

It hit him then: Perry didn't trust him anymore. All along Will had felt that Perry would back him no matter what. For the first time since Dee's disappearance, he felt completely alone. "If that's what you want."

Perry sighed deeply. "That's what I want."

"I think it's a mistake. We should have helped them look for Dee right from the beginning. I know that area."

"I understand, but—as I've explained before—we have a school to run here. It was best to keep things moving along and you away from the press."

"Someone's setting me up, Perry."

"You mean Jonathan?"

"Could be."

He took his glasses off and twirled them by the stem. "Why would he do something like that?"

"I have no idea."

"How well do you know him, anyway?"

"We met in high school. Things were different, then." He thought of the old band. How excited Jonathan had been when the first record hit big. "I don't think I know him at all, now."

Perry sat back in his chair. "Jonathan's just frustrated. There's no conspiracy here, Will."

"So, he accuses me of being negligent."

"Are you?"

The question hung in the air, and it made Will mad that Perry would even ask it. He considered this might be a good time for a dramatic exit, but he felt stuck to his chair. "Do you think I am?"

"No, I don't."

Will nodded. "I appreciate the speed of your reply." He almost added, "But I don't believe you," but checked himself.

"It doesn't mean that others won't."

Will felt his anger building and pushed his chair back, finally getting himself unstuck. "It stinks!"

Perry studied him. "You really think someone's out to get you?"

"That's what I think."

"If not Jonathan, then who?"

"You don't want to hear it."

Perry threw his glasses on the desk. "Christ. Not Franco Delacorte again." He rose and leaned over the desk, both arms straight.

"All right. You don't want to hear it." Will looked down at his shoes. "Is there anything else?"

Perry relaxed his stance. "I meant what I said: I *don't* think you were negligent. We're going to fight this."

Will suddenly thought of his classes, all the eager faces wanting to know. And what would he tell them? "You still want me to show up for work?"

Perry smiled, but it looked forced. "Of course." He put his hands in his pockets and jiggled his change, and turned to face the window.

Will could feel Perry's agony over Jonathan's suit. He had worked so hard to build this school up, and something like this could tear it apart in no time flat. Will vowed it wasn't going happen. It was time for him to find out exactly what was going on.

"Just look at them out there."

Will knew what he was talking about. He had passed the demonstrators outside the front gate on his way in. "Jonathan Tyler fans are legion," he said.

"But the signs! 'Tyler's Troopers for Justice.' And that one:

'It's late. Do You Know Where the Rest of the Kids Are?'' He turned back to Will. ''The school doesn't deserve this,'' he said. ''Don't they realize we're doing our best?''

WILL DROVE the school's 4x4 up toward a clearing where he had set up targets and heavy-duty sawhorses. In lieu of coaching, his job was to manage the two thousand acres of school woodlands. Four dorms had wood fired furnaces, which meant he and ten students, who opted to help him rather than play a sport, had to do all the cutting and hauling for the heating season.

It didn't surprise him that Berkeley Hutter had signed up for the activity. Since the first day Will had found him dragging his suitcase up the hill, Berkeley had shadowed him and seemed always underfoot. Will didn't mind it much. He didn't know why kids like Berkeley just latched on to him, but he liked the way it made him feel.

Berkeley bounced along in the cab beside Will as the others held on to the stake-side rails in the back. ''I don't understand what we're going to do,'' Berkeley said.

''I want to show you some of the events at a woodsman's meet.''

''Like what?''

''Like ax throwing.''

''Really?''

Will smiled at him. ''Yeah, really.''

''Cool.''

Will gripped the wheel hard and geared down because the logging road was full of deep ruts. The last thing he needed was to jettison a few students off the back—it would be his final act of negligence.

When he reached the clearing, he was surprised to see a woman sitting on a stump. As he drew near, she stood and brushed at her denim skirt.

He stopped the truck, opened the door, and jumped down. ''Something I can do for you?''

The woman reached out her hand. ''I'm Celia Tilden. WTIZ out of Portland.''

Will looked at her hand, but didn't extend his. "This is private property," he said.

She withdrew her hand. "I know you don't want to talk to me."

"I don't have anything to say."

"I understand," she said.

"Then I guess you should leave."

She hesitated. "I thought my viewers would be interested in knowing who you are."

"Forget it." He was aware of his students gathering around, watching. He turned to them. "You guys can get the axes and saws out of the truck. I'll be with you in a second."

When they left, he said, "How did you know where to find me?"

"I looked at the calendar on your desk. You wrote it down."

What the hell is this? "You looked at my desk? You've got some nerve."

She didn't respond, like it was okay to invade another's privacy if it meant a story, and he was a damn fool if he didn't know it. Will studied her. He had seen her before on the newscasts, on the one channel he could get a semblance of reception. Celia Tilden.

"All I want is footage," she said. "A day in the life, that sort of thing. It might help your image."

"My image?"

"What my viewers know is that there's some teacher who lost a kid in the woods."

"I didn't lose a kid."

"Maybe not. But that's what people think."

"And you're going to change that."

"I want to give them a face to the name. I want to show them a teacher who cares about his students."

Will found himself smiling at her. If she expected him to believe that, then she must think him an easy touch. "Is that what you think?"

"You need a favorable press, Will."

"And you're here to help me out."

"I'm here to get a story. It's my job."

The students came back with the tools. Celia turned to them. "Hey! How would you like to be on TV?"

"Wait a minute," Will said. "I didn't say you could film anything."

Jerry Feingold stepped forward. He hooked his thumbs in his jean pockets. "What do we have to do?"

"Whatever your teacher wants."

It was a cheap ploy and Will was pleased his students didn't respond with the enthusiasm Celia expected. Will could see it in her face. On the whole, the kids who signed up for the activity were the shy ones, the nonconformists who didn't want to kick a ball or slam a tackling dummy.

Celia waved her arms. Out of the edge of the clearing stepped two men, one holding a boom mike, the other a TV camera.

"Have they been shooting since we've been here?" Will asked.

She smiled. "It's their job."

The woman was tough. He didn't shake her hand. They must have that on video. He could just imagine how she would manipulate that image to her liking. "Tell him to turn that off for a minute," he said.

"We just want a story, Will."

Will looked at his assembled woods crew; they were watching with interest. He grabbed her arm. "Celia? Can I see you a moment—off camera?"

She stood her ground. "Let go of my arm." He relaxed his hold. "Okay," she said.

They walked away from the group.

"I don't like your tactics," Will said. "You could have asked me to be interviewed."

"Would you have granted the interview?"

"Probably not."

"Then you can understand why I did this."

"You're interrupting my class."

"I don't want to argue. What can I do to make it right?"

"You can leave."

"And make a story out of what I have so far?"

Will paused. "What is this? Electronic blackmail?"

She folded her arms. "I meant what I said: all I want are some visuals of you doing your thing and interacting with the kids."

"What's the copy like?"

"Just do what you planned. Let me worry about the story."

"Why should I trust you?"

She smiled at him. "Because you can't afford not to."

WILL HEFTED the double-bladed ax and led off with a little introduction about what a woodsman competition is, and how he hoped they might be able to work on skills to feel comfortable enough to field a team.

"How do you throw that thing?" Berkeley asked.

"You want to try it?"

Berkeley looked at the target. It was a slice of tree trunk mounted on a tripod of heavy-duty poles. "Kind of far away, isn't it?"

"Think I can hit it from here?"

"No way."

"How 'bout the rest of you?"

"You've got to be shittin' me," Callie Overhill said. The only female in the group, Callie was into punk. She looked out of place with her black leather jacket and high-laced Doc Martens.

"Excuse me," Will said to her. "You're on camera."

"I meant 'kiddin' me.' Sorry."

She wasn't sorry and Will knew it. She pouted at him, her blue lipstick making her look cadaverous.

He faced the target and estimated about twenty yards. He could feel their eyes on him, but he wasn't nervous. He raised the ax above his head and let fly. It tumbled end over end in a smooth arc and landed with a satisfying chunk just above the bull's-eye.

He turned back to them. "Well? Who wants to be first?"

The next evening, Will fiddled with the rabbit ears and managed a snowy reception of the news out of Portland. And there he was, giving his little lecture on woodsman competitions, followed by film of the ax toss. He enjoyed seeing Berkeley Hutter's mouth drop open when he hit the target, something he'd missed with his back turned. Then the inane questions. Yes, he had been involved in competitions since he was a boy. He also liked the two-man cross-cut event, but he supposed the ax throw was his favorite. Did he like to throw other things? Well, he was pretty good with a knife.

Will expected the feature to end after Celia's interview, but she kept on talking. Suddenly, Jonathan Tyler's face appeared on the screen. Will turned up the volume. "And what is the connection between a quiet, ax-throwing man from New Hampshire and this famous singer? Neither would talk to us about it, but our crack investigative team has unearthed some interesting facts. Here's a picture of Jonathan Tyler's first group. Now look carefully at who's playing bass..."

Will watched in silence. When the feature cut to commercial, he rose from his chair and slapped the Off button.

Celia Tilden had dug up information he had said nothing to her about, and it was personal stuff she couldn't get from reading notes. She had to have talked to someone close to the group. He doubted whether Jonathan had told her anything unless he thought it somehow might help his suit against the school. But he was sure Jonathan's lawyers wouldn't want him to say anything, especially to some podunk TV station—if Jonathan wanted to spread the word, he could go national at the drop of a hat. As he thought about it, there was only one other person who could have revealed the inside information about the group that appeared in Celia's special—Laurie.

He had to find her.

THIRTEEN

LAURIE SAT AT HER DESK in the police station talking on the phone. She glanced up at Will when he walked in, then turned her attention to a note pad.

He leaned over the counter. "I have to talk to you."

She motioned for him to be quiet and swiveled in her chair so her back was to the counter. She continued her conversation.

Will checked the back room next to the holding cell. She was by herself. Ray must be out on a call. He returned to the office, put his hands on the counter, and vaulted over it. He stood next to her.

She said into the phone, "Something's come up, I'll have to call you back." She slammed the phone down. "This had better be good."

He took hold of her elbow, urged her up from the chair, and steered her toward the counter. "Let's talk in the back room."

She pulled away. "Have you gone completely nuts?"

"It's about Jeanne Tyler," he said. "Have you seen the news?"

"No." She walked to the counter and lifted the hinged top.

He followed her to the back room. The glass in the door rattled when he closed it. She stood in the corner, her arms folded.

"They had this thing about me on TV," he said. "It went back to my early days with Jonathan; they ran some old footage of the band."

"The band?"

"Waggoner's Lad."

Laurie relaxed her arms. "Oh yes," she said. "The band."

She grew silent and Will guessed she was remembering what he had told her about Jonathan the last night they'd slept together.

"I guess you're getting to be front page," she said finally. "You have to expect some of this scrutiny, you know."

"I know. I'm not that naive." Laurie didn't look too sure. "The point is they aired information I didn't give them."

Laurie raised her hand. "Whoa. Wait a minute. You talked to the press? What exactly did you say?"

He relayed the story of Celia Tilden showing up for his woodsman's activity and how he mollified her with the ax-throwing footage.

Laurie laughed.

"This is funny?"

"I'm sorry, Will. I'm trying to imagine the scene." She smiled at him. "You couldn't resist the urge to show off, could you? Celia Tilden sure had you pegged."

Her remark stung, and he felt that familiar rush of warmth on the back of his neck. "I was just doing it to get rid of her," he said.

"Of course." She placed her hands against the back of a steel folding chair. "What exactly did you tell her?"

"That's just it. I didn't tell her anything about the band."

"So she did some research. She's a reporter."

Will jabbed a finger in the air for emphasis. "She didn't get it from reading old record reviews, I can tell you that. The only way she could have found out the stuff is from somebody who knew us back then."

Laurie paused. This seemed to have spurred her interest. "Tell me what she said."

He ran his hand through his hair. "She talked about Jeanne and me—about Jonathan and how the band broke up because of our rift. Stuff like that."

"You think Celia Tilden interviewed Jonathan?"

"I don't know." Will looked her in the eyes. "Something's going on, Laurie. I don't know what it is, and I don't like it."

Laurie sat down at the table. "Did she make some sort of point? I mean, what was the reason to dip into the past?"

The room was often used for interrogation and it felt stuffy, like it was closing in on him. "This is all tabloid stuff. Anything goes."

"Tell me more about Jeanne."

The shift in Laurie's questioning caught Will by surprise. "What do you want to know?"

"She couldn't have loved you very much if she dropped you like a rock."

Will thought a minute. "There was more to it than that. It didn't happen overnight—Jonathan took his time and he lured her with promises he couldn't keep."

"Like what?"

"He told her he'd help with her singing career."

"He was going to make her part of the group?"

Will shook his head. "She was a lounge lizard. Sang a lot of cover stuff. Show tunes, that kind of thing."

"You mean not star material?"

Will nodded. "And Jonathan knew it. He just wanted her. I could have killed him."

"God, Will."

"What's the matter?"

"Don't say things like that."

"Ah, come on Laurie, I wasn't being literal."

"I know that, but others might not."

"Give me a break."

"You've got to be careful what you say, especially now."

Will walked to the window and looked out. He had a view of the parking lot and his truck tucked next to Laurie's cruiser. "Especially now, what?" he said, slowly turning back to her. She looked down at her hands. "Now that I'm a suspect? An ax murderer? The tooth fairy?"

"Let's stay focused, Will. You came here for a reason."

"Especially now, what? I want to hear what you were thinking."

She sighed and turned her gaze to the table. "I just meant that you have enough troubles without saying something you might regret." She looked at him. "That's all I meant."

The tone in her voice was genuine concern, and it caught Will off guard. Maybe she really did care for him, after all. He turned back toward the window, placed his hands in his back pockets.

"What about that other member? Grace?" Laurie asked. "Could she have anything to do with this?"

Grace Diccico? Huh. But how could it be? She was long gone in the past. He left the window and joined Laurie in a chair opposite her at the table. "I doubt it. We haven't seen each other since those days in the band."

"She's another one who knew you then." Will's mind flashed a memory of Grace in front of a microphone, her dark hair hanging over her eyes, her voice throaty and sensual. "What was she like?"

"Kinda moody. Hell of a singer, though."

"What was she doing while all this intrigue was going on between you, Jonathan, and Jeanne?"

"Getting more and more pissed off. And when I split, we had a hell of an argument about it. She seemed to think I was deserting Jonathan. I guess she had good reason."

"She didn't do any music after that?"

"Not that I know of. Maybe nobody else wanted to hire her."

"Seems odd. I mean bands split up all the time; wasn't she good enough for another group?"

"I think it was more than the music. I think she had a thing for Jonathan, and if she couldn't sing for him, she wouldn't sing for anybody else."

Laurie leaned back in her chair. "It just gets better and better, doesn't it?"

"Oh, she would never admit it. It was the way she looked at him sometimes. You know how it is between people. You can tell."

Their eyes met and Laurie looked down. "What do you want me to do about this?" she asked.

"What?"

"Why did you come down here?"

Will shifted in his seat. "I just had to be sure about a few things, that's all."

"Wait a minute." Laurie rested her elbows on the table. "What exactly did you have to be sure about?"

"Forget it, Laurie. Can't we just keep talking? I've missed being with you."

She got up from her chair. "Oh, I think I get it." She knocked her fist lightly on her forehead. "Of course. You think that I'm the one who leaked the information to Celia Tilden."

"No, I don't."

"But you did when you first came in."

"I didn't know. I had to find out."

She put her hands on her hips. "So that's what you think of me."

Oh, Christ, he'd managed to piss her off again. "I was being stupid. I see that now."

"I'm a cop, damn it. How could you think that?"

"It was a mistake, all right? I said I was stupid. What more do you want?"

She exhaled slowly. She looked like she was counting to ten. "Nothing, Will. I don't want a thing from you."

They were silent a few moments. "I'm just trying to understand what's happening to me," Will said, finally.

"So, how come you're so sure I didn't speak to Celia?"

He looked at her. Her eyes were angry. "You know how it is between people. You can tell."

"Maybe I should just arrest you, stick you in jail for your own safety. Put you out of your misery."

"On what charge?"

"Assault and battery."

"What?"

"I had a visitor today. One of your favorite persons. Says you attacked him."

Will sank back in his chair.

FOURTEEN

FRANCO HAD LEFT SCHOOL. Perry said it was personal business, and he'd be back in a few days. Will waited until the sun was almost down, pried open a window in the back of Franco's apartment, and climbed through it.

The light from the west cast an orange glow in what Will took to be Franco's bedroom. It looked as if it hadn't been lived in, something out of a New England Inn with a four poster bed and a ceramic pitcher and basin on an oak night stand. Will opened the door to the walk-in closet built under the eave of the roof. He shut the door part-way and snapped on his flashlight. Franco's clothes, what there were of them, hung lifeless on wire coat hangers. Will's foot hit a small suitcase. He stooped and flicked the locks open. It was clean—no ticket stubs, matchbooks, flyers—nothing, not even in the cloth lining.

He returned to the bedroom, knelt and beamed the light under the bed. Dustballs and a duffel bag. He opened the zipper, found more clothes, flannel shirts and jeans, but they looked too small to be Franco's. Did Franco have a partner? He thought about the night on SMOOT when Anita claimed she saw someone in the woods.

He dug deeper and touched something that felt like a book, pulled it out. It was the Holy Bible, RSV. He thumbed through it. There was no name inside, but the pages in the back were dog-eared. In the Book of Revelation, he found two starred passages.

The first, in Chapter Two, verse 10 of the writings to the angel of the church in Smyrna:

Do not fear what you are about to suffer. Behold, the devil is about to throw some of you into prison, that you may be

*tested, and for ten days you will have tribulation. Be faithful
unto death, and I will give you the crown of life.*

And the second starred entry, verses 22 and 23 of the same
chapter regarding the temptress Jezebel:

*Behold, I will throw her on a sickbed, and those who commit
adultery with her I will throw into great tribulation, unless
they repent of her doings; and I will strike her children
dead.*

He put the Bible back in the duffel and zipped it shut. He
made his way into the living room. Books were strewn on a
coffee table. A roll top desk sat in the corner near the wood
stove. He headed for the desk. He yanked up the hood of the
roll-top desk and it stuck halfway up. He had to force it open—
inside, a few circulars announcing sales, a receipt from Milt's
Laundry for cleaning two sports coats and a pair of slacks. No
personal mail. No bills.

He rummaged around on the coffee table. A large, green cloth-
bound book was open, a ribbon marking its place: the Third Act
of *Othello*. He looked for papers, notes, any insertions. He
searched other books: *The Iliad*, not in translation. *Madame Bov-
ary* in the original French. At the bottom of the pile lay a recent
issue of *Paris Match*.

He sat on the couch and thought a moment. He had discovered
little, yet it seemed to confirm his suspicions. Franco traveled
light. Why?

He tried to arrange the table back to the way he'd found it.
As he fumbled with the books, lights from a car washed through
the living room. He hit the floor and listened as a car engine cut
off. He edged toward the window and looked out. He could only
see part of the porch, since the view of the front entrance was
blocked by a pillar.

There were footfalls on the porch. He squatted at the side of
the desk.

A key turned in the lock. The door swung open, and the hall light came on.

Will pressed his cheek against the side of the desk. He should have gone out the back way as soon as he heard the car. What was Franco doing back at school? If he came into the living room, if he sat down to read...

Franco made rustling noises like he was looking for something in the hall closet.

Will rose, his back pressed to the wall. The closet door opened toward the living room. He could only catch glimpses of Franco as he moved stuff from the closet, but it was enough to make him realize his hunch was wrong. It wasn't Franco.

The figure was slight and wore a watch cap pulled down over his ears. Will didn't get a good look at his face because he moved fast, but he guessed that the clothes he had found in the duffel would be a perfect fit. The figure slung a climbing rope over his shoulder, and gathered some other things Will couldn't make out. He turned the hall light off and shut the door.

Will listened to the stranger's footsteps disappear off the porch. The car started, the lights sprayed across the mantelpiece and vanished.

TWO DAYS LATER, Will picked up the phone. It was Laurie. "We just received a ransom note," she said. "They want a million dollars."

"Then Dee's still alive."

"It's handwritten. We think it's her script. We're sending a copy for Jonathan to confirm."

"They forced her to write it?"

"Could be."

"Could be?" Will paused. "You think she's in on her own kidnapping?"

"We can't dismiss it."

Will ran his hand through his hair. "That's crazy. She wouldn't do that."

"You sure? That's why I called. I wanted your read on this."

"I just don't see it."

"She wasn't getting along with her father, right?"

"Or with anybody."

"But you don't know her that well, do you?"

"Enough to know she couldn't pull it off."

"And you're sure about that."

"She didn't have herself together. She was a mess."

"Any idea who it could be?"

"Jonathan has enemies," he said.

"I figured you know about them."

Will hesitated. "It's ancient history."

"Never mind. Give me some names."

The line hummed.

Will leaned against the wall. "All right. Let me think about it, see what I can come up with."

"This should make you feel better, anyway," she said. "It's a good sign. How could you know she was going to be kidnapped?"

"What about Lamont? What does he think about the note?"

"I don't know," she said.

"When do you have to come up with the money?"

"There's supposed to be a second note with instructions."

"I'm guessing the press doesn't know about this."

"That's all we'd need."

"And Lamont doesn't know you're talking to me?"

There was a pause at the end of the line. "That's right," she said.

A YEAR BEFORE, a chain saw took a bite out of Will's foot, and he'd almost lost a toe. He remembered needing an insurance ID number from his folder, and how Hilda, Perry's secretary, pulled the key to the file cabinet out of a drawer in her desk.

It was nearly 3:00 in the morning when Will stuck his master key into the main door of the administration building. The same key got him into Hilda's office. He waited a moment for his eyes to adjust to the darkness. He had resisted this move, thinking about how he was almost caught in Franco's apartment. But since the day Perry had told him Franco had taken a pay cut to teach at the school, his curiosity gnawed at him. He had to know what was in the folder.

As long as the main doors were locked he doubted Sherman Doyle, an elderly security guard who used a hearing aid in each ear, would stroll through the building on his rounds. But he didn't know that for sure, so he had to be careful.

Will took a penlight out of his pocket, opened the top drawer of Hilda's desk, and searched it. Nothing. He checked the other drawers, feeling more than seeing what was in them. In a cubbyhole where Hilda kept nail polish, butterscotch candies, and bottles of white-out, he picked up a box that had once held paper clips and something rattled inside. He dumped out a single key into his hand.

He slowly closed the drawers of the desk and sat a few moments, listening. The wind moaned through the eaves of the roof.

The key went into the lock of the file cabinet smoothly—the steel cylinder popped out. He had no trouble locating the folder.

Two sheets of paper—a one-page résumé and a letter of recommendation from the Headmaster at the Ferry School. That was it. There was a note attached to the résumé in Hilda's handwriting that looked like a reminder to herself that records would soon be forthcoming. The note was dated a few weeks previously, August 22.

Franco's academic credentials were impressive, if they were real. He received his Ph.D. at Yale and did postdoctoral work at the Sorbonne.

Will read through the laudatory recommendation explaining how Franco was an excellent classroom teacher, and how he had made a difference at the Ferry School. The closing paragraph drew Will's interest. The headmaster expressed his regret over losing such a good teacher and mentioned he had not been prepared for Franco leaving. There apparently had been a contract talk and they fully expected he would return in the fall. Franco, however, had never signed the contract.

Will scanned the résumé again with his penlight. He remembered the day he overheard the Spanish class, but there was no mention of his expertise in that language in the report, nor was there any reference to his knowledge of Japanese. Also, there was nothing about Franco's experience before the Ferry School.

He closed the folder. Franco liked to travel light on paper, as well.

HAD FRANCO REALLY taught at the Ferry School? Did he have a Ph.D. from Yale? Postdoctoral work? Will didn't believe any of it. The next morning he placed a call to the Ferry School. "I'm trying to locate Franco Delacorte. I understand he's a teacher there."

"He no longer works for us."

"Do you have a forwarding address?"

"He's someplace in New Hampshire."

"But you don't know where exactly?"

"I'll have to look it up."

"I'd appreciate it."

Will waited a good five minutes before the secretary picked up again. "I'm sorry. I don't seem to be able to locate that information right now."

"Why not?"

"Uh, his file seems to be missing."

"Missing!"

"I'm sure someone just borrowed it. If you would like to leave your name, I'd be happy to call you back."

"No. That's all right."

"Are you sure?"

"Look. I guess I'm a little confused. Why should someone just borrow his file?"

"I don't know. Perhaps the headmaster has it. If you'd like to talk with him, I can put you through."

"No. That's okay."

"If you just leave your name and number..."

Will hung up the phone.

LAMONT WAS AT Laurie's desk, staring at the phone. He looked up when Will walked in. "What are you doing here?"

"I came to see Laurie."

"She's busy." Lamont rose from his chair.

"It's okay. I'll wait."

"I don't think so. This isn't a good time."

"I have a right to be here. I pay my taxes."

"What do you want?"

"Laurie asked me to come down."

The bathroom door opened and Laurie stepped out. She stopped when she saw Will. The pipes in the bathroom hissed behind her.

Lamont glanced at Laurie. "She did?"

"I did what?" she asked.

"You called me last night wanting names."

"And you have some?" she said.

"Maybe."

"What the hell's going on?" Lamont asked.

Laurie stepped closer to the counter. "I told Will about the ransom note."

"You what!"

"I thought he might have some ideas about who kidnapped Dee." Lamont sat back in his chair. "What he knows about Jonathan may be key here," she added.

"That's not the point; you should have let me know."

Will leaned over the counter. "Hey, where do you get off, Lamont?"

"I'm in charge of the investigation, pal."

"So, what does she do? Clean your bathroom?"

"Shut up, Will!" Laurie said.

Lamont glared at Will. "I'll discuss this matter further with Officer Eberly at another time," he said. He took out the notebook from his coat pocket. "Now. What names do you have?"

"Actually, only one." Lamont clicked his ball-point and waited. "Franco Delacorte." Lamont threw the pen down. He got up from his chair and stormed to the counter. Will stepped back. "You could at least run a background check on him," he said. "I'm sure Jonathan's name will pop up somewhere."

"Probably on a lawsuit," Lamont said. "I guess he doesn't like you beating on him too much."

"He deserved it."

"Have you apologized yet?"

"No. Have you received the second note yet?"

Lamont shook his head. "I want you to get out of here before I get angry."

"I'd like to stick around."

Laurie took Will by the arm and led him to the door.

WILL GOT IN his truck and started driving. He knew he'd lose points with Laurie by coming down to the police station, but it accomplished his purpose: to stir things up. She had taken a chance telling him about the note, but he also knew it wasn't all charity. She wanted names. He was determined not to sit back anymore—a bull in china shop approach may not be the best, but at least he wasn't at home talking to Butch waiting for things to happen to him. He would badger Lamont about Franco until exasperation forced him to look into his background.

He passed the police station several times as he meandered the back roads of Saxton Mills. After midnight, he didn't see any cars on the road, but the lights still burned in the police station. Around 2:00 he pulled the truck into Laurie's driveway. She finally showed about 3:30. He flicked on his parking lights when she got out of her car.

She ducked behind the fender and leveled the Smith & Wesson over the hood. "Hands where I can see them!"

"Hey! It's me." Will stepped out of the truck. "What are you so jumpy about?"

"You've got your nerve after the stunt you pulled with Lamont."

"Take it easy. I just want to know about the second note."

She came out from behind her car. "The hell with arresting you. Maybe I should just shoot you and get it over with."

"What about the second note?"

"It's none of your business."

"Come on, Laurie. I'm not going to go away until you tell me."

She put her pistol back in the holster. "It never came."

"You're kidding."

"Right. I enjoy pulling your leg at three in the morning."

"So, what happens now?"

"I don't know."

"You mean you're not going to do anything about it?"

"Just what do you propose I do?"

"I don't know. You're the cop."

She hooked her thumbs in her trouser pockets. "That's right. And from now on, no more favors."

"I wouldn't expect anything less."

"Thanks for hanging my ass out to dry with Lamont."

"I was just covering my own. I'm the one who's suspect here, the one who's 'negligent.'"

She took a step closer. "Look, Will. Take my advice. Let us do our jobs. You don't want to alienate Lamont."

"What's he done for me lately?"

"He might just think you're telling the truth, Will."

She was so close. He wanted to reach out and stroke her hair. "Tell him to investigate Franco Delacorte."

"I'm sure he already has."

"Then he's done a lousy job."

"Give him time."

"I haven't got time. Delacorte's got a plan and it's to set me up. I wouldn't be surprised if he's behind the ransom notes."

"I'm going to bed."

He placed his hands on her waist. "I don't suppose I could scrounge a cup of coffee," he said.

She pulled away from him. "Just go, Will."

FIFTEEN

IT WAS RAINING. Franco was rumored to be back in town and Will went looking for him. Since searching Franco's apartment, Will had kept himself awake at night trying to figure out who that was who'd pulled a climbing rope from the closet. A climbing rope. What could that mean? A friend was borrowing it from the non-adept Franco to do some rock climbing? Why would Franco even have such a thing? He knew there was only one way to find out: get Franco talking—maybe he'd leak something.

He checked Franco's apartment, but he wasn't there. He drove around and eventually spotted Delacorte's Tercel outside the Burger & Brew.

Franco was at a table by himself, nursing a Guinness. He looked as if he had just blown in off the street, his hair sticking up on one side, his tie askew.

Will came up to his table. "Mind if I join you?"

Franco looked up at him, and his jaw dropped. "You want to sit with me?"

Will didn't wait for permission. "Let me buy you a drink."

"Why?"

"Because I feel like it."

"You feel like it?" He smiled. "You expect me to believe that?"

Will ignored him and waved the Vietnamese waiter over to the table. He ordered a Guinness for himself and another for Franco.

Franco's muddy eyes followed the waiter to the bar. "What do you suppose he thinks about?"

"The waiter?"

"Must be quite a change. From jungle to tundra."

Will rested his elbows on the table. "How do you know he's from the jungle? He could have lived his life in Saigon."

"Yeah?"

"Yeah."

"You're wrong."

"What makes you the expert?"

Franco leaned forward. "I know because he told me. I eat here every day."

"I see." Will drew himself up straight in his chair. He knew exactly what he wanted to say, had rehearsed it several times, but the words wouldn't come out.

"What's the matter with you?"

"What do you mean?"

"You look like you're constipated or something." Franco drowned the dregs in his glass.

"I guess I need to apologize to you." There, he said it.

"You guess? You mean you don't know?"

"No. I mean I apologize for punching you. I shouldn't have done it."

Franco squinted. "How do I know this is sincere?"

He wasn't going to make it easy, Will knew. He was prepared for it, though, and resolved to keep his cool. "I guess you'll just have to take my word for it."

"Any reason I should?"

Will smiled at him. "Look. You wanted an apology and you got one. Let's just leave it at that."

"I should sue your ass, anyway."

"Maybe you should."

The waiter returned with the beer. "Thank you, Thành," Franco said.

The waiter smiled broadly, bowed, walked to a nearby table and began wiping it down. Franco took a deep swig of stout. He held the mug to the light before placing it on the table, smacking his lips. "Good stuff." He grinned at Will. "I bet you really missed me, eh?"

Will looked across the table at him. He didn't return the smile.

"I know your students did. In just a few weeks you've made quite a name for yourself as a teacher."

Franco dismissed the compliment with a wave of his hand. "Ah, well. Those who can..."

"I trust you were able to take care of your personal business?"

Franco squinted at him. "You could say that." He gave the impression he was thinking hard about something. "I hate funerals, though."

"I'm sorry." Will ran his hand along the edge of the table. "A death in the family?"

"Tragic, really. A niece." Franco sighed. "So young."

"How did it happen?"

Franco held up his mug and glanced over the top of it. "Kidnapped."

"What?"

"They found her body in a ditch." He drank and brought the mug back on the table with a thud. He wiped his mouth with the back of his hand. "She'd been raped and bludgeoned to death."

Will looked at Franco's eyes. Was this the truth? "How awful."

"Words fail."

"Did you know her well?"

"No. But each death diminishes us, don't you think?"

Will gripped the handle of the mug but didn't drink. "I don't remember reading anything about it in the papers," he said.

"Oh, it was there. Maybe not this far north, though. When does the next dog sled arrive?" He chuckled.

"It's not that isolated up here, Franco."

Franco frowned. "You think I'm lying to you?"

"I don't remember reading about it, that's all."

"You do think I'm lying. I'm surprised you could be so heartless."

"Heartless!"

"First you beat the shit out of me. Then you desecrate the memory of my niece."

"Come on. I didn't mean anything by it."

"No?"

"No!"

Will locked on his eyes and refused to look away. He tried not to blink but he only succeeded in making his eyes begin to tear. After a few moments Franco broke the eye lock and looked down at his beer. "Ah, let's not argue. Life's too short."

Will kept his grip on the mug and didn't say anything.

Franco sighed and craned his neck toward the ceiling. "I've been hanging around this dump too long. It's starting to get old."

Will cleared his throat. It was dry and tight. "Closest thing to cosmopolitan in Saxton Mills."

Franco laughed out loud. "Cosmopolitan? Boy, that's a hoot."

"It isn't that funny."

"You're right. It's funnier." Franco drank again. "Yeah. I'm afraid I'm not long for this burg."

"You're thinking of leaving?"

"If I could get out of my contract, I'd be gonzo."

Will brightened at the prospect. Perhaps he could talk to Perry.

"I won't be back next year, I can tell you that," Franco said. "I don't know how you people stand living up here. All you can talk about is how high the wooly caterpillars are on the tree trunk."

"A little harsh."

"Why don't you just tell me I'm full of shit."

"All I said was..."

Franco leaned forward again. "Hey, Will," he whispered. "This is me, Franco. How come you're trying to suck up to me all of a sudden?"

"I'm not sucking up to you."

"You're trying to be nice. I don't like it. It's no fun."

Will paused. "You don't want me to be nice to you?"

"Why should I? You've lost your edge, there's no witty badinage. In a word, you're boring."

"I'm boring?" The mug suddenly felt light in Will's hand. He drank.

"Insufferably." Franco downed his glass and slammed it on the table. "I don't want to be your bloody friend."

"What do you want to be, Franco?"

"I want to be a bird." He flapped his hands. "So I can fly away."

"If you need my help building wings..."

Franco clapped his hands together—once. "That's it. Much better. Even a snide Icarian reference."

"A what?"

"Icarus. Jesus. You've been reading too many tree books. Come on. Throw another one at me."

Will took a long tug on his glass. He put his mug down gently. "I think you've had too much to drink."

"You want to buy me another one?"

"It's your turn to buy."

"Sorry. That would mean I'm trying to be nice."

"We wouldn't want that to happen."

"I think you're catching on."

Franco gestured to Thành. Still wearing a large smile, Thành made his way through the crowded restaurant weighed down with a tray full of empty glasses. As he approached the bar, a heavy-set man wearing an orange hunter's cap stood.

Will could see it coming and rose from his seat, called out to Thành, but it was too late. The man hit Thành's arm and the tray went flying. Glass crashed on the floor. Some of it splintered on the bar, then showered the man's jacket.

Will pushed his way to the bar. Franco followed.

"You stupid chink!" the man said. He grabbed Thành by the front of his shirt and raised his fist to strike him.

Will clutched the man's arm and hung on. Thành backed toward the bar, hands over his head, trying to protect himself.

The man flung Will around, and he crashed against the bar, his side hitting the rail. "It was an accident," Will said. "Leave him alone."

"Maybe you want some of this," the man said.

Suddenly Franco was between them. "You don't want to hit him. You're just angry."

The man stopped. "You're right. Maybe I want to hit you."

Franco held up his hand—which held a crisp fifty dollar bill.

He snapped it a couple of times. "This should take care of any damages."

The man didn't hesitate. He snatched it away, held it to the light. "Got any more of these?"

"Excuse me?" Franco said.

"Couple more and we'll call it even."

"You want a hundred fifty bucks for causing an accident?"

"The chink got in my way."

"He's not a chink."

The man's eyes narrowed. "The nip, then."

"He's neither chink nor nip. Jeez, it must be lonely inside that head of yours."

The man raised his fist again. "Have it your way, then," he said. "Your face is going to look like a hamburger."

"Okay. Just hold on." Franco reached for his pocket, but instead, in one swift motion, he dropped down and drove upward with his fist into the man's groin.

The man's mouth made an O. He slumped forward, holding his crotch. Franco caught him on the way down with one flash of his foot. The man's head snapped back, but his momentum still pitched him forward. His face hit the floor first.

Franco found the fifty dollar bill. He put it in his pocket and faced Will. "You okay?"

Will nodded. He looked at the floor. The man didn't move.

Franco went over to Thành. He put his hand on his shoulder. *"Cai dó không phai lá lôi cua anh,"* he said. *"Du 'ng lové chuyên dó."*

THE BARTENDER CALLED the police. The Saxton Mills F.A.S.T Squad showed up first. The heavy-set man regained consciousness just as they finished collaring and boarding him. He wore his nose on the side of his face. He swore, his words slurred. He fought his restraints as they rolled him out.

Laurie wrote notes for the report. After the bartender corroborated Will's and Franco's stories, she motioned for Will to follow. They left Franco sitting at a table having coffee, talking to Thành.

In the cruiser, Laurie said: "Anything more I should know about this?"

"I don't think so. That's pretty much the way it happened."

"Tell me about Franco."

"What do you want to know?"

"What are you two doing together, for one thing."

"We ran into each other, that's all." Laurie wrote something on her pad. "You think that's important?" Will asked.

"You never know."

Will thought of Franco's leg shooting out, catching the man's head, the crack of the nose. Then he remembered his own fight with Franco. He had felt so smug about decking the jerk so easily when all the time Franco could have had him for lunch. He would still be in the hospital if Franco had retaliated. "I'll say it again: I think you and Lamont should look into Franco's background."

Laurie looked up from her pad. "Why doesn't that surprise me?"

"He's not who he says he is. Things don't add up."

"Like what?"

"His physical ability, for one. He just did a number on somebody twice his size. On SMOOT he kept falling over himself. I caught him playing basketball like Michael Jordan, but when I challenged him he couldn't hit a thing."

"What does that prove?"

"Did you see him talking to the waiter? Where did he learn Vietnamese? On SMOOT he spoke Japanese. There's nothing in his file about any of this."

"His file! What do you know about his file?"

Will hesitated. "Never mind how I know," he said.

"You looked at it, didn't you?"

"I plead the Fifth."

"Damn it, Will. Why can't you just let well enough alone?"

"Because I'm sure he knows what happened to Dee."

Laurie stared at him. "You'd better be careful. You're so pissed off about the guy you can't see straight."

"Think about it, Laurie."

"You think about it. He was with you. How could he have kidnapped Dee?"

"What did he do while I was on top of Pasaconaway? Everybody blames me for being away. But what about him?" Will felt hot. He ripped down the zipper of his jacket.

Laurie sighed. "Did you break into the office to look at his file?"

"No. I had the key." Laurie wrote on her pad. "I did break into his apartment, though." Laurie shook her head and placed her pen on the pad. "I actually didn't break in. The window was open in back. I sort of stepped in."

She put her hands over her ears. "I don't want to hear this."

"I think you do. Franco's a transient, Laurie. He lives like he's on the lam."

"The last time I checked that wasn't against the law."

"He came here knowing he wasn't going to stay."

"You're telling me you didn't find anything."

"I'm telling you the man is suspicious enough to investigate. When I called the Ferry School, they couldn't find his records."

"You called the Ferry School? Boy, this just keeps getting better and better."

"Somebody has to do the digging, and I sure as hell am not getting help from the police."

She sighed. "You don't have any evidence linking him with Dee."

"No. But I'm going to find it."

She jabbed a finger at him. "Not on my beat."

"Come on, Laurie. Why can't you just hear me out?"

"I've heard enough."

"Listen to me. Something weird happened while I was in his apartment."

"Something weird?"

"Somebody came in. It wasn't Franco. He pulled a climbing rope out the closet and left. What the hell is Franco doing with a climbing rope in his apartment?"

"Gee, I don't know. Maybe he likes to rock climb."

"Franco? Come on Laurie. Does he look like a rock climber to you?"

She threw her pad on the dashboard and stuck the pen in her pocket. "Thanks for the information. You're free to go."

"You're dismissing me again?"

"Unless you've got some more weird things you want to talk about."

"I take it you're not going to investigate him?"

She punched him on the shoulder. "That's a take, Will."

He stared at her. "I don't believe your attitude."

"My attitude! You sit here telling the chief of police about breaking and entering and expect her to investigate somebody's climbing rope?"

"Maybe you should arrest me."

"Maybe I should."

"Naw." Will smiled. "You need evidence for that." He opened the car door. "All you have is the testimony of a raving lunatic. It'll never stand up in court."

He made a point to close the door softly before he walked away.

SIXTEEN

WILL COULDN'T GET Franco's niece out of his head. At times, he was convinced the funeral story was the truth, but another thought kept nagging at him: Franco was really talking about Dee, that he knew where she was, and she was dead. Will kept thinking of the Bible sitting in the duffel bag under the bed in Franco's apartment and the starred line: "...and I will strike her children dead."

He spent the morning of the next day in the town library reading the *Book of Revelation*. He was never very good at understanding any of it. The language was dense and off-putting. All he knew when he sat down in a sun-drenched carrel was that the book somehow dealt with the Apocalypse. He worked his way through the messages to the various angels, the pale horse and rider, the many plagues that would bring us all to our knees. When he finished he wrote down his immediate impressions: *Lots of numbers. Fours and sevens.* He pondered this for a moment, but didn't think it had any significance.

He looked out the window at the passing cars. His seat offered a good view of the main intersection in town that boasted one traffic light. He turned back to the sheet of paper and wrote the word *Power* and underlined it.

Yes, that's the message—the final division of the haves and have nots. He skimmed through some passages again. He was struck with the guarantee which seemed to translate into something like: "if you follow me now, believe in me, and prepare for the end, I will make it worth your while."

In Chapter Two, the same one where he found the starred passages, he read in verses 26-28:

He who conquers and who keeps my works until the end, I will give him power over the nations, and he shall rule them with a rod of iron, as when earthen pots are broken in pieces, and even as I myself have received power from my father; and I will give him the morning star.

The morning star? That's pretty good. And in Chapter 3, verse 21:

He who conquers, I will grant him to sit with me on my throne, as I myself conquered and sat down with my Father on his throne.

Will closed the book, shut his eyes and tried to recall the dark figure dragging the climbing rope out of the closet. The clothes in the duffel bag had to belong to him. His build was lithe, like a teenage boy. Was Franco and another student working against him? Maybe Franco was a pedophile.

Suddenly, an image loomed of Dee's body lying near a tree. His eyes flicked open, but her presence remained and seemed to be calling him back to the woods. He shook his head to clear it, but it left him only with the nagging sense that he should go back into the Whites, that he would only find the answer to what happened if he looked for it. And the wind chime. He hadn't thought about it since Laurie had downplayed its significance. Could it still be there?

Will called Laurie at the police station, but she was out. He left a message on her home answering machine that he was going camping. He didn't have to cover the dorm this weekend and the forecast was for clear weather—Whiteface and Pasaconaway should be beautiful. Would she like to go with him? He stayed at home all evening waiting for her answer, but it never came.

He left early Saturday morning, driving the Dodge out of town, heading toward the Kancamagus Highway. In a way, he was glad she wasn't with him. He needed time by himself.

When he reached Lincoln, the town was choked with leaf peepers. He had to wait in traffic behind a tour bus, drumming his fingers on the steering wheel. His idea was to retrace his steps on SMOOT, and he was anxious to get started; tourist hold-ups hadn't been factored in.

He finally parked the truck at the Greeley Ponds Trail, threw his pack on, and began walking. It felt good to stretch his legs. Setting a fast pace, he didn't stop until he reached the first of the Greeley Ponds. If he kept it up, he would make it past the first SMOOT campsite, push up the South Slide of Mt. Tripyramid, and reach the Downes Brook area by nightfall.

It was a brisk day, and the sky was deep blue against the green of conifers. Near the edge of the pond, the swamp maples were flagrant red. Just past the last Greeley Pond he found fresh moose tracks in the mud on the trail.

By noon he made it to the bottom of the South Slide, and stopped to have lunch at a clearing. It was a high-impact area with a fire pit and pieces of iron strewn about that looked like they'd once been part of an old stove. One of the pieces served as a grate for the fire pit. Will sat down and leaned his back against a rock. He sliced some pepperoni and Vermont cheddar— extra sharp. He drank iodized water.

A few chipmunks gathered, curious over his lunch. He threw a few pieces of cheese at them. He tried to coax the ringleader to eat out of his hand, but its courage faltered when he got too close.

As he was packing up, he thought he heard someone coming down the trail from the slide. He got up and put his pack on. He waited for the hiker to emerge out of the trees, but the sounds of approach had stopped. He listened, but the only noise came from the scavenging chipmunks and the shriek of a black bird above his head. He began walking, stopping every now and then to cock his head and listen for a follower. Nothing. Maybe the sound came from the moose that belonged to the tracks on the trail.

The South Slide opened up before him. The act of climbing forced him to focus. As he gained elevation, the sky yawned wide. He had magnificent views to the southeast of Sandwich

Mountain. He remembered how socked in it was on SMOOT, how the group had separated in the fog.

When he hooked up with the junction of the Sleeper Trail he paused to take in the view. At 2:30 in the afternoon, the angle of the sun hit him directly in the eyes when he faced west. He wanted to stay longer, but to make Downes Brook he would have to get moving. With a reasonable, steady pace over the rolling Sleeper Trail he should arrive with an hour of light remaining.

He pushed on. So far, he had not met anyone else on the trail. That wasn't surprising, given the time of year. But the incident at lunch had left him spooked, and he began to see forms in the shadows. He continually checked behind to make sure he wasn't being followed.

At the campsite near Downes Brook he dropped his pack. The sun had long since fallen over the ridges to the west and he was left with a gray half-light. He took the time to pitch his tent and roll out his sleeping bag. He pulled out his stove and food.

Armed with his flashlight, he made his way to where he had found the wind chime. His familiarity with the area helped, and it didn't take long to find the spot. He aimed the flashlight upwards and identified the limb where the shell casings had been suspended. Part of the rope was still attached. He walked slowly over the small rise where he had dragged the thing after cutting it down. He sprayed the area with light. The wind chime was gone.

What he did find, though, were footprints. Lug soles. They looked old, but he followed them anyway. They led him toward Downes Brook.

He heard the brook rushing hard because of the recent heavy rains, before he saw it. The footprints disappeared at the brook. He hoped to find them again on the other side. He turned off the flashlight and was about to cross when his eye caught a figure upstream in the shadows. He ducked down into the ferns that lined the brook. He thought at first it might be an animal, a deer perhaps, but then he heard the metallic bump of a pail on rock. As his eyes adjusted to the light, he could make out a human form stooped over the water.

He doubted whether he had given away his approach. The sound of the rushing water would have covered his footfalls, and he had been just below the figure when he shut off the flashlight.

He could feel his heart thumping. Maybe this was it. He had come back into the woods, and his good fortune had brought him to this place. His mind raced, remembering lunch and the sound of someone approaching, then disappearing. He had been followed. The person had come up from behind, found the tent but not him, and, because he had been out investigating the wind chime, he had unknowingly put himself in a position of strength.

He wasn't going to blow it. He backed away to the shelter of the trees and began to move upstream. When he was above the figure's position, he crossed over, hopping rocks. He came up behind just as the figure stood with two pails of water in his hands.

"Hold it right there," Will said. "Don't turn around until I tell you."

The figure didn't move.

Will walked up to him. He patted him down to see if he was armed. He wasn't. He flicked on his flashlight. "All right. Let me see your face."

The man shifted around slowly, still holding the two buckets. Will aimed the flashlight.

The man squinted. "Not in my eyes."

Will almost dropped the flashlight. "Uh-oh."

"Aim that thing away from me, will you?"

Still in shock, Will couldn't move. The ranger dropped the pails. "What the hell is wrong with you, anyway?" He ripped the flashlight out of Will's hand.

"I'm sorry," Will said.

"Do I know you?" This time it was the ranger's turn to shine the light. "Oh, yeah. I guess I do." He turned the flashlight off and handed it back to Will. "You ought to have a license to carry that thing."

Will was glad for the darkness, he wanted to hide his embarrassment. "I thought you were someone else," he said.

"Who?"

"I don't know. I was pretty sure someone was following me."

The ranger eyed him suspiciously. "Isn't that what you thought the last time you were out here?"

Will suddenly felt hot. "I think he picked me up just below the South Slide."

"Well, it wasn't me." The ranger was silent for a few moments, then he said, "Christ, I almost shit the bed." Will didn't know what to say. "Your name's Will, isn't it?"

"That's right."

"You say you saw this guy following you?"

"Heard him. I picked up some footprints back there, but they looked old."

The ranger didn't respond immediately. Will was conscious of the water rushing in the stream. "Why the hell would someone be following you?" the ranger finally asked.

"I wish I knew. I don't suppose you've seen anyone suspicious, have you?"

"Suspicious? What the hell is 'suspicious'?" The ranger spat. "I think you're whacked."

"Anybody dressed in camo gear?"

"Look, buddy. You just scared the living bejesus out of me. I'm in no mood to answer any of your lunatic questions."

"Lunatic!"

"Let me tell you something. I'm doing some trail work, and I'm camped this side of the brook just beyond the trees there. Stay the fuck away from me!" The ranger turned. He picked up his buckets. "Fuckin' lunatic."

IN THE MORNING Will took the Rollins Trail over to Pasaconaway. The sun worked hard to break the dawn chill. He stopped when he came to an overlook. Below him was a depression called The Bowl. It was unusual to see it clear of fog. He sat, dangled his feet over the edge, and listened to nit-picking jays in a tree close by.

He tried to relax, but he couldn't stop thinking about the ranger. His face burned when he recalled the confrontation. Grandpa Hank would have laughed himself silly.

Will leaned back and closed his eyes. His thoughts drifted to the fishing camp on Denuve Creek in Quebec. Grandpa Hank was giving him a fishing lesson: "Willy, you've got to keep your ears cocked. Use your senses as a sponge." The old man walked upstream, the water swirling around his boots. "Trouble is," he said. "You keep making too much noise. The fish know where you are."

The memory was pleasing. Will saw himself, a skinny kid with a bad case of acne, standing on a rock in the middle of the stream, feeding out some line, then letting the fly whip above his head while he tried to keep his arm stiff.

"That's it," Grandpa Hank said. "Think of a clock. Keep it between ten and two." Will released the line, and followed it with his arm. The fly hit the water but the line coiled behind it. "Nice going, Willy. You got it out there." He knew Grandpa Hank was being nice; his presentation of the fly was horrible. "You ain't gonna catch fish that way, though." Will checked the position of the fly rod, trying to figure out what he had done wrong. "Focus. Stop the chattering inside your head." Will looked at his feet, at the fly drifting with the current. "I see a monster!" Grandpa Hank said.

"What?"

"Big ugly thing, hanging over the water."

"Where?" Then he realized he'd stood on the rock with the sun behind him and his shadow waved on the water. He had looked for everything but the most obvious.

It seemed like Grandpa Hank had been an old man all his life. He had outlived two wives. When Will's mother died and his father skipped town, it was Grandpa Hank who took him in and raised him. Now all that was left was a fishing camp on Denuve Creek. Maybe he should go up there. Just disappear.

He got to his feet and brushed the seat of his pants. Grandpa Hank was right. He had to empty his head, become part of the woods. The answer to what happened to Dee was out here, he just had to find it.

The wind was still. He looked at his boots, then at the cleated trail he had left behind. He hadn't picked up any footprints this morning, but now that he examined his own more closely, he could see faded ones nearby, probably made from a light hiking boot about size six. He knew they could belong to anybody. It proved nothing other than he was learning to see again.

To his right, a piece of wood drew his attention. He picked it up and turned it side to side. It looked like an eagle, wings spread, soaring into the wind. "Thanks, Grandpa Hank," he said, and stuck it in the pocket of his anorak.

Will figured if he got to Pasaconaway by mid-afternoon he would have enough time to investigate and still make the road-head before dark. He'd have to hitchhike back to the Greeley Ponds Trail parking lot, but with the influx of tourists on the Kancamagus Highway, he should have no problem getting a ride.

He arrived at the shelter at 1:30, dropped his pack inside and went directly to where Dee had set up her tarp. He drove a stake in the ground at the center of the site, took some line from the pocket of his anorak and knotted it in foot long intervals, tied one end of the line to the stake, and holding a stick against the first knot he began to scribe a circle. He did the same with the next. And the next. The idea was to construct a concentric matrix.

When he finished making the lines, he went back to the center. On his knees, he began sifting through the duff, unearthing foil wrappers, a hair tie, rusted tins. He kept hearing Grandpa Hank's words: "Use your senses as a sponge."

On the eighth tier, the arc led him to a large rock. He stood up and tried to kick the stiffness out of his legs. He leaned against the rock, pulled a handkerchief out of his pocket, and wiped his forehead.

So far he had found nothing. But maybe he was missing the big picture, focusing too closely on the fly rod while the monster of his own shadow loomed.

He climbed up on the rock, watched and listened. Leaves from a birch tree rustled as they fell; the sun sent shafts of light into the tent site, then he saw something glimmer, catching the light near the edge of the clearing toward the southeast. It seemed to come from the tenth tier.

He stepped off the rock, moved up two tiers, and followed the arc. Partially hidden by the leaf of a pin oak, he found a gold earring bent in the shape of a heart.

LATER THAT NIGHT in his apartment, Will sat on the couch and tried to solicit Butch's opinion about the earring. "It doesn't mean anything, right Butch? Some hiker probably dropped it after we got out of the woods."

Butch sat on the floor watching the bottle on the coffee table. He flicked his tail.

"Otherwise I would have spotted it on my first sweep." He looked down at the earring in his hand. The heart-shape intrigued him. "Think I should tell Laurie about it?"

Butch jumped up on the table.

Will opened the bottle. He poured two shot glasses full. He put the cap back on and paused to look at the label. "Can't you just imagine the old Buchanan clan lubricating themselves with this stuff?"

Butch was busy with his shot glass.

"I see them on some dank mead in the highlands sucking it down to keep the chill out of their kilts. What do you think?" He was drinking more lately and it bothered him when he thought about it. But a nightcap helped him sleep and for the past few days he'd needed all the help he could get.

He did a shot and poured another. He picked up the earring again. Such found treasure held strong allure. In high school, Will's nickname was "Pack Rat." He still carried a pocket knife he'd found three years ago on a SMOOT trip.

He tossed the earring into the air and caught it. "Let's play a game, Butch. Let's imagine the woman who owns this. I see her as tall and thin. Definitely with dark hair."

Butch paid no attention to him.

Will downed the shot. "The twisted heart means she had once loved and lost..." He stopped himself when he looked up and caught his reflection in the sliding glass door. He looked pathetic, a grown man talking to his cat.

He put the cap back on the bottle.

Butch meowed a protest.

"Bar's closed." He went to his bedroom and searched for a place to put the earring. He settled on an empty diskette box by his computer.

SEVENTEEN

MONDAY MORNING Will found a note in his school mailbox to see Perry immediately. He didn't have a first period class and went directly to his office. When he walked in, he had the feeling Perry had been waiting for him.

Perry came out from behind his desk. "Sit down, Will."

"Good morning to you, too."

Perry stood slump-shouldered. He looked like a man under pressure. "I'm sorry," he said. "Let me start over. How are you this morning?"

Will took a seat in front of Perry's desk. "I've been better."

Perry put his hands in his pockets. He walked to the window and looked out. "I won't waste words," he said. "The board had an emergency session over the weekend." He turned and faced Will. "You've been suspended." Will didn't react. The words didn't seem meant for him. "I fought against it. Our more conservative members thought that for the good of the school..."

"For the good of the school." Will cleared his throat, waited for Perry to say more, but an awkward silence followed.

"You've been suspended with pay, of course."

"Of course." He heard his voice again. The parroting was an embarrassment. He sat up straight in his chair. "What exactly have I done wrong?"

"It's the lawsuit. The publicity."

"Do you think I was negligent? Have you changed your mind?"

"The board felt we had to do something."

"Sure. Suspend the guy. Get rid of the problem."

"It wasn't like that."

"Right. They were more sensitive."

Perry paused. He turned toward the window. "There was no nice way to tell you."

Will watched him. He was chewing on the corner of his lip. He looked thinner. Since school started Perry had become an old man. "You didn't answer my question," he said.

"What's that?"

"Have you changed your mind? Do you think I was negligent?"

"Doesn't matter what I think."

"Does to me."

Perry sat down in his chair. "No. I think the board is reacting out of fear. If it were up to me, I wouldn't suspend you."

"I thought you were in charge."

"I answer to the board, you know that."

Will nodded. He did know that. Perry was only doing his job. "What about my dorm?"

"It's taken care of."

Will lowered his head, stared at his shoes.

"This is really hard for me, Will."

Will looked up. Perry colored and turned away. He figured Perry was embarrassed by how inane his statement sounded. Of course it was hard for him. Briefly, Will forgot he was the one in trouble and was overwhelmed with sorrow for his old friend whose school was going down the tubes—all because of him. He grabbed the arms of the chair. "I won't make it harder. Catch you later."

"If you need help moving, I can arrange it."

"No thanks. Appreciate it." Will pushed himself to his feet. He turned to leave.

"Will?"

He looked back at Perry. "What?"

"I insisted you get paid. I did fight for you."

Will put his hand on the doorknob. "I know you did."

LAURIE WAS OUT of uniform, dressed in a white blouse and tight-fitting jeans. "I just heard."

"You've come to pay your respects?"

"I wanted to make sure you were all right."

"I didn't think you cared."

Her eyes were tired, worn-looking. "I probably shouldn't have bothered." She turned to leave.

Will took hold of her arm. "No. Please."

"You don't want to see me."

He didn't let go of her arm. He couldn't take his eyes off her. "I need to talk to somebody besides Butch."

"You've been talking to Butch?"

"Yeah. He doesn't say much."

"How long has this been going on?"

"Too long."

She hesitated. "Maybe I should stay. Just for a while."

He let her in. They picked their way past stacked cardboard boxes to get to the living room. He moved some clothes off the couch and they sat next to each other.

She looked at the clothes. "You're not wasting any time, are you?"

"What do you mean?"

"Moving out."

"Perry said immediately. I assume he meant it."

"But you only found out today."

"Maybe I just want to get out of here. Tito Marchesi has an empty apartment so I jumped at it."

"Marchesi Meadows? You're going to live there?"

"It's cheap. A place to keep my stuff. I'll probably camp out in the woods for a while, anyway."

She got up from the couch and stood near one of the boxes. The damn jeans. She didn't have to wear them so tight. He ached for her. It had been too long since they slept together. "Did you go into the Whites this weekend?" she asked.

"Yeah, I did."

"It must have been beautiful."

He nodded. "Thanks for returning my call."

"I didn't want to complicate things," she said.

"I'm sorry?"

"Maybe if I wasn't the cop in this..."

Will waited. "Finish your sentence."

"You know what I mean."

"You mean it's hard for the chief to love a cat burglar?"

"Something like that." She leaned against one of the big boxes. "I came over to see if I could do anything. Can I help you pack?"

"Can if you want. I'm almost done."

"I think it's rotten, Will. They have no proof."

"Doesn't matter."

"How can you say that?"

"Not my words. A direct quote from Lamont."

"He told you that?"

Will nodded. "The first day I met him."

"That's hard to believe."

"The day I found him sitting on this very couch."

She looked at the couch, then brushed at the cat hair on the front of her jeans. "Guess who told me you'd been suspended?"

Will didn't have to guess. "Lamont is everywhere," he said. "He's like the fucking air we breathe."

"He's a good investigator."

"You can say that after putting up with his crap?"

"I'm speaking professionally."

"I hate it when you do that."

"How do you want me to speak?"

"Oh, I don't know. How about emotionally?"

"Oh, yeah. Right. That's something you're good at."

Will got up from the couch. "You ought to try it sometime."

"What's that supposed to mean?"

"It means you should try complicating your life. You didn't want to go into the woods with me because you're afraid of your emotions."

"Don't start with this."

"Why did you come over here?"

"I told you."

"Does that mean you care about me?"

She made a move to go, but Will grabbed her by the shoulders. "Why can't you just let yourself love me?" She pulled away and headed toward the door. "Wait a minute!" He caught up to her and placed his hand on the door, held it closed.

"Let go of the door, Will."

"Just a minute."

She reached for the handle and yanked on it.

Will slammed the door closed again. "This isn't about us, okay? It's about Lamont."

"What about him?"

"I think he's been nosing around. I noticed some things were out of place. You might mention that if I catch him anywhere near my new apartment without a search warrant I'll deck him."

"You'll deck him? That's the message?"

"You heard me."

She opened the door. "I'm afraid that's one you'll have to deliver yourself."

WILL FIGURED it would take three trips in the Dodge to move into his apartment at Marchesi Meadows: one for the furniture, two for the cartons stuffed with clothes and "found art," and a third for his bass fiddle.

When he took the bass fiddle out of the closet, the cover was coated with dust. During his suspension he would have time to practice, but playing bass by himself always made him feel more isolated—it is an instrument that yearns for company. It was worse than drinking with Butch.

Will started moving his stuff early the next morning. He wanted to leave before word of the suspension got out. He made the first two trips before the dorm began to wake up, but when he lifted the bass fiddle into the bed of the truck, he turned and found Berkeley Hutter watching him.

Berkeley was in his bathrobe, a striped affair and much too big for him. "So, it is true," he said.

Will ran a piece of rope around the neck of the bass and hitched it to a cleat on the side rail. "It's only temporary," he said. "I'll be back before you know it."

"But who's going to take care of us?"

"I'm not sure."

"Jerry Santos thinks it's Mr. Malboeuf."

"Jerry should know."

"But we hate Mr. Malboeuf. He's got bad breath."

Will finished tying off. He smiled at Berkeley. "Mr. Malboeuf is a nice man, you just have to keep your distance."

"I don't want you to go, Mr. Buchanan."

Will opened the door of his truck. "You'd better get ready for class. You don't want to be late."

As he drove away he watched Berkeley in the rearview. Seeing the kid had brought it all home. He had lost his job, and for what? He swore and pounded the dashboard—once. He checked the mirror again and Berkeley hadn't moved. He just kept getting smaller and smaller.

WHEN HE PULLED into the driveway of Marchesi Meadows, he found Lamont sitting on the doorstep reading a newspaper. Will turned off the motor and opened the truck door. He didn't acknowledge Lamont, simply began untying the ropes that held the bass fiddle.

Lamont approached the truck, paper in hand. "Hello, Will." Will didn't respond. "You're becoming quite famous, you know? You made *The Globe* again this morning."

"I have a new policy, Lamont. I've decided to ignore you."

"Well, that's not very nice." He tucked the paper under his arm. "Say, can I give you a hand with that thing?"

"I'd prefer you didn't touch it."

"Of course. Probably a good idea. My wife won't let me near her flute, either." He held up one hand. "Stone fingers."

"They match your personality," Will said.

"An unkind cut."

"I would prefer it if you'd just go away."

He sighed. "You know, I'd like that, myself. Maybe take in a symphony, see my wife."

"It might be a good idea to hang around people who can tolerate you."

"Oh, I agree. It's just that these questions keep popping up."

"What questions?"

"Do we have to talk out here? It's a bit nippy."

Will threw the end of the rope over to the other side of the truck. "Look, Lamont. I'm not in the mood for trading words. If you have something to ask me, do it."

Lamont studied Will. "I was just curious. Why did you go up to Pasaconaway this weekend?" Will didn't answer him. He coiled up the rope and threw it into the truck bed. "You can't ignore me forever."

"How do you know where I went?"

"Just answer the question."

"I needed to get away."

"That's all?"

"That's your answer." He lifted the bass fiddle up out of the truck bed.

Lamont smiled. "You'll have to play for me some day. You must be quite a musician if Jonathan Tyler wanted you."

AFTER LAMONT LEFT, Will moved most of the boxes into the spare bedroom. He spent the rest of the day unpacking. As the hours passed his anger grew—the only explanation for Lamont knowing he went to Pasaconaway was that Laurie told him. She was the only one who could have known, and maybe his first hunch about her leaking information to Celia Tilden was also true. It left him feeling like he had swallowed a rock.

He arranged his living room, what there was of it. The couch and overstuffed chair swallowed up most of the space. He skipped dinner. He wanted a drink, but he couldn't remember where he had packed the bottle. Butch was already asleep in his cat bed. He felt like calling Laurie, but the phone wouldn't be installed for a couple of days.

Finally, around 11:00 in the evening, he got into his truck and started driving. It at least created the illusion he was doing something, and it helped quell his anger. He knew Laurie was probably making her night rounds. Maybe he could catch up to her.

He roamed through town and out on the road that led to school, but there was no sign of her. A quick pass by the police station revealed the cruiser was gone. He headed out toward Lincoln, but before he got to the town limits, he doubled back on a dirt road. It took him around a gravel pit that had become the subject of a recent controversy because the owner wanted to fill the land back up with sludge imported from Maine. Will had written impassioned letters about it to the town fathers, decrying the environmental impact on the ground water. Now the problem seemed small and inconsequential compared to what he was facing. He was in a fight for his life—his honor, his job—and he had no idea who he was fighting.

He slowed down to the speed limit when he got close to Saxton Mills again. He crawled past the abandoned drive-in theater. The main street was almost empty. He finally spotted the cruiser near LaPierre's Market. He parked next to it and waited.

In a few minutes, he saw Laurie walking down the street, shining her flashlight at the store fronts. He got out of the truck and leaned against the front fender. It was cold, and he pulled his collar up.

She approached and aimed her flashlight at him. "I thought it was you," she said.

"I couldn't sleep."

"You're all moved in?"

"Yeah. Listen. I'm sorry about last night. I wasn't very civil."

"I know."

"I'm not making excuses. I'm just going to try not to hurt people who care about me anymore."

She turned off the flashlight. "That's a good place to start."

He could see her better now, but the glow from the street light made her look icy and cold. "You once told me you loved me."

She sighed. "What do you want, Will?"

"Why won't you let me talk to you?"

"Talk all you want."

"I mean about us."

She looked down at her shoes. "Just give me some space. Space and time."

"Sounds cosmic."

There was a trace of smile and then it faded.

"Anyway. I just wanted to say I was sorry."

"I accept your apology."

"Thanks." He walked back and opened the truck door. "Oh, by the way. Did you tell Lamont I went up to Pasaconaway?"

She hesitated. "No. I didn't tell anybody."

"Good." He got in the cab, closed the door, and started the engine. He backed out and drove away. He felt something rise in his stomach and it took a few miles to settle back. It was the hesitation that did it: She had lied to him. Right to his face.

EIGHTEEN

MARCHESI MEADOWS HAD a hook-up to a roof antenna, so Will parked himself in front of the TV and watched game shows and soaps. He drank beer and ate peanut butter sandwiches.

After two days of this—when the case was full of empties and he couldn't stand the smell of his own clothes anymore—he decided to foray out to the Laundromat and LaPierre's Market.

It was Thursday, almost four in the afternoon, and the town was packed with traffic. Something was going on. He spotted a car with the WTIZ logo heading out toward the school, and he followed it. When he was almost on school property, he turned the Dodge down a dirt road that led around the back where there was easy access to the cross country running trails. He parked and started walking along a path that meandered close by the gym and ended up near the main entrance.

From a distance, he could see a crowd gathering. Will estimated the crowd to be around two hundred and growing, bigger than any Saxton Mills Fourth of July celebration. He recognized a few as being part of the original Jonathan Tyler contingent that had picketed the school. Perry must be going nuts.

When he reached the end of the path, he crossed the street and moved around to the back of the crowd. He could barely see the dais that had been set up in front of the pillars of the main entrance. There was an array of microphones. News trucks sported satellite dishes and clustered around the crowd.

Students were helping to direct traffic around the scene, and he wondered where Laurie was. She probably knew something about this event, whatever it was, and would have to be here, somewhere.

A murmur rippled through the crowd and grew as Jonathan

Tyler walked across the front lawn, through the gates, and on to the dais. Perry Knox was with him.

Jonathan raised his hand for silence. "I want to tell you first that I'm not going to take any questions. I just have a statement." He bent his head over the lectern: "A few days ago, a ransom note arrived at the Saxton Mills' Police Station demanding a million dollars for my daughter Dee's release."

The crowd stirred. Will could see Celia Tilden in the front scribbling on her pad.

"A second note was supposed to follow with details of the exchange. So far, we have heard nothing. The authorities think I shouldn't be telling you this because it might jeopardize her return. I say it's time for action." He turned. A man wearing sunglasses handed Jonathan a briefcase.

Will recognized him: Peter the chauffeur.

Jonathan opened the briefcase and held it up to the cameras. "Whoever has my daughter, I'm here to show you this." Inside were stacks of bills. He paused, then handed the briefcase back to Peter. "And if Dee is returned within twenty-four hours, I'll throw in another hundred thousand." He faced the camera and pointed his finger at it. "Name the time and place and it's yours. I promise you that. Just let Dee go."

He stepped off the dais and moved quickly through the gates. The crowd began to chant. "Let Dee Go! Let Dee Go!" The cameras shifted to the crowd. People shook their fists to the rhythm of the chant.

He had better get out of there. He began pushing his way through the crowd when someone grabbed his arm.

"Hey. Aren't you Buchanan?"

Will turned. The man had a curly beard but no mustache. "Let go of me."

"It is you, you son of a bitch." He dropped the sign he was carrying and threw a punch.

Will dodged it. He pushed his way past others who suddenly took an interest in him. He reached the edge of the crowd and looked back. The curly beard had gathered others, and they were moving in a wave toward him, yelling his name.

Will took off. He hit the cross-country path in full stride and didn't look back.

THAT EVENING Will began working on a bottle of Laphroig with Butch and by three in the morning it was gone. So was Butch. Will carried him to his cat bed. "Butch, the Comatose Cat," he sang. The little ditty began to form in his head.

Back in the living room, Will continued singing: "Even more famous than the Cat in the Hat is Butch, the Comatose Cat." He pulled out his bass from the closet and took the cover off. He tuned it and began plucking the strings with his forefinger.

"Butch went to an AA meeting
And spiked all the coffee there,
Then he hippety-hopped to a second-hand shop
To buy a red cat coat to wear."

He invented more verses, then finished with a flourish:

"Yes, he's Butch the Comatose,
His breath makes you hold your nose
Butch, the Comatose Cat!"

The lyrics didn't scan well, but they amused him. When he tired of singing, he tried to sleep in the overstuffed chair. His eyelids wouldn't stay closed; instead of inducing sleep, the alcohol had wired him. He walked through the apartment.

When the sun came up he considered shaving. Why bother? Where was he going? He sat all morning in his chair watching the sun trying to force its way through the cracks in the window shade.

THE DOORBELL RANG. He found Anita standing on the doorstep, her arms folded against the chill. "I wasn't sure this was the place," she said.

"How did you get my address?"

"Can I come in?" she asked. "I don't want anyone to see me. I'm supposed to be in the library." Will let her in, closed the door. Anita stared at him. "Are you all right?"

Will ran his hand over his face. He must look terrible. "Yeah. I didn't get much sleep, I guess."

"It's not fair. You shouldn't have gotten fired."

"I've been suspended."

Anita looked over her shoulder at the door. "I don't have much time," she said. "I'm here to give you this." She pulled a piece of paper from inside her jacket and handed it to him.

"What is it?"

"A copy of a petition. All the students who signed it think you should get your job back."

Will read the list of names. There were over a hundred. "I don't know what to say."

"We all think you got the shaft," she said. "We just wanted to let you know we're behind you." She stood taller. "I was elected to let you know."

"Thanks, Anita."

"I've got to go," she said.

"How did you find me?"

"School telegraph."

"What's that?"

Anita smiled at him. "You'd be surprised what we know," she said.

Will considered her words. "I suppose I would. A real underground, huh?" He remembered her screams on SMOOT, how she was sure someone had been out there. "Can I ask you something?"

"Uh-huh."

"That first night, when you saw someone—"

"I still get scared when I think about it. It was creepy."

"Is there anything you didn't tell me about it?"

"I don't think so." She thought a moment. "Sometimes I dream about him, though. It's really weird."

"What is?"

"I don't dream about SMOOT. I'm in a war and he's a soldier. He's after me."

"A soldier?"

"He's dressed like he was that night."

"Wait a minute. You saw what he was wearing?"

"He had a mask on. Something covering his face. And a suit, you know, the kind that looks like it's been smeared with dirt."

"Camouflage?"

"Yeah. That kind of stuff."

SOON AFTER ANITA LEFT, Will took a shower. He shaved and got himself looking halfway decent. His phone still hadn't been installed, so he drove the Dodge into town. He used the public phone in a booth outside LaPierre's Market. Laurie picked up.

"Is Lamont in the building?"

"That's right."

"Can you take a walk? Meet me down by the market?"

"Why?"

"I have some new information."

He waited with the truck running. The heater clipped along, the fan making a clacking noise.

It took her less than fifteen minutes to get there. He reached over and opened the cab door to let her in. "Thanks for coming."

"What's with you, anyway? You think you're the KGB? Prowling around at night, meeting in parked trucks."

"I didn't want to run into Lamont."

"Probably wise. He's not in the best of moods."

"Jonathan Tyler pulled a fast one on him, huh?"

"Lamont let him have it, but I don't think it did much good. Now there's no living with the man."

"What's he up to?"

"He's turned it up a notch. Spends hours on the phone. The fax is constantly running."

"What sort of information is he gathering?"

"I don't see much of it, but it looks like a lot of research on Jonathan. Jonathan's developed quite an empire, you know."

"You think Lamont's discovered anything?"

She pulled her coat tighter. "Could be." The fan was laboring and the hot air just sat above the dashboard. "What about you? What's this new information?"

"I'm convinced more than ever that Franco's behind all of this, and he's not working alone." He told her about Anita and the camouflage gear.

She listened patiently until he finished, then reached for the door. "Okay, thanks."

"Where are you going?"

"Back to the station."

"That's it?" he said. "You have nothing to say to me?"

"What do you want me to say?"

"I just gave you a valuable piece of information."

"I'll see what I can do." She slid across the seat.

He grabbed her arm. "Wait a minute."

She pulled away, got out of the truck, and walked toward the curb.

He called after her. "Don't you see the connection? The guy I saw in Franco's apartment wore camo gear."

She turned back. "You want me to shake down every bow hunter? Is that what you want?"

NINETEEN

"I'VE BEEN DOING some thinking," Lamont said. "Maybe we should go up to Pasaconaway."

"Why?"

"I want you to show me the tarp site."

"There's nothing up there, Lamont."

"Humor me." Lamont coughed on the other end of the line. Will hesitated. "Has Laurie talked to you?"

"She talks to me all the time."

"You know what I mean. Did she tell you about the guy in camo gear?"

"She mentioned something about it. I'm afraid there's not much to go on."

"But Anita did see someone. A real person was following us. She dreams about him."

"Maybe we can scare him up when we go to the mountain tomorrow. It's supposed to be clear."

"I don't feel like going."

"I'll pick you up at eight. We'll have breakfast. Have a great time."

"I have other plans. Have fun, Lamont."

"But you have to show me the way."

"Why don't you get Laurie to take you?"

"Look: I guess you don't understand: I'm not *asking* you, you are going with me."

Will twisted the phone wire. "Something's happened. What is it, Lamont?"

"Just be ready by eight."

The idea of hiking up to Pasaconaway with Lamont was about as appealing as taking Franco on a mid-winter traverse of the

Presidentials. But then again, it would give him a chance to pick Lamont's brain.

"Pick it like a lock, right Butch?" Butch came over and rubbed his leg. "Forget it. Moscow Rules. No drinking 'til four."

LAMONT SHOWED UP right at 8:00 looking as if he had just stepped out of an L.L. Bean catalogue. His hiking boots were fresh out of the box, and he was Polartec from neck to ankle. He wore a felt fedora, the brim flattened toward his head so that it gave him an odd Teddy Roosevelt Rough Rider look.

"The quintessential hiker," Will said.

Lamont colored. "You don't have to make fun of me. It's not like I've never been in the woods."

"Right. But how much hiking have you done lately?"

"I'll be able to keep up."

Will smiled. "If you say so."

"Can we get up and back in a day?"

"I could. Depends on how much poking around you want to do, but I think we should plan on an overnight."

"I just want to see the place, that's all."

"Why?"

He tapped his head. "So I can have a reference when people start talking."

"But why now? I mean, shouldn't this have been one of the first things you did?"

"Are we going, or what?"

They stopped at LaPierre's Market for supplies on the way out of town. Will tried to engage Lamont in conversation on the road to Lincoln, but he pulled his hat down over his eyes and leaned his head against the door.

Will drove up the Kancamagus listening to a tape of Cat Stevens telling his baby it's a wild world. He pulled into the parking lot of the Oliverian Brook Trail where Anita had led the group out of the woods. It was the quickest access to Pasaconaway. He stopped the truck.

Lamont sat forward and straightened his hat. "This the place?"

A stupid question and Will didn't respond. He pulled his pack out of the truck bed and put it on. He waited while Lamont struggled with his—a new Kelty that still had the store tag on it. "One of your shoulder straps is twisted," he said.

Lamont fumbled with it, but couldn't get it straight. "Fuck it. Let's go."

"I'd take off a layer, too. Why don't you just start over?"

"I'm freezing as it is. Come on."

A few hundred yards down the trail and Lamont was sweating in a Polartec sauna. Will could hear him huffing behind him, but he didn't slow the pace down. After a mile or so, he could tell the distance between them was growing.

"Hold it up, Buchanan."

Will stopped, turned and waited.

Lamont trudged toward him. His face was red, and he walked like there were shards of glass in his boots. When he reached him, he threw his pack down. Will watched passively as he took off his jacket. Lamont pointed to his pack. "Aren't you going to help me with this?"

Will took a step away. "No."

"What?"

"You're the FBI. You can take care of yourself."

Lamont forced a smile. "You're enjoying this, you son of a bitch."

"Actually, no. I don't like being in the woods with people who are dangerous."

"I'm dangerous?"

"You need me out here, Lamont. Right now I'm guessing you've got hot spots on your heels. If we don't tape them, they'll be full blown blisters before you know it."

Lamont didn't move. He looked down at his boots. "It's like they were made out of cement."

"I'll take you up to Pasaconaway, but I'm not a ferry service. You're not going to make it unless you do what I say. Clear?"

"I guess I don't have much of a choice."

"You can also leave that attitude at the roadhead." Will dropped his pack. "Now, I want you to ask me nicely for help."

"This is stupid."

"For once, I'd like to hear you say something that isn't sarcastic. I don't think you know what an overbearing shit you are." Lamont opened his mouth but closed it quickly. "Can't do it, can you?"

"Just help me with the boots."

"Ask me nicely."

"Look, Buchanan. I need your help out here, but I'm not going to play your games."

"Maybe we should go back."

"You'd better do what I say."

"And if I don't?"

"You may need my help sometime."

"I doubt it."

"And sooner than you think."

Will hesitated. He took a step toward Lamont. "What do you mean by that?"

"I thought you were the smart one. Go figure."

Will got Lamont's hot spots taped and adjusted his pack. "You should be fine, now."

"When does it start going up?"

"A mile or so."

They reached the Pasaconaway Cutoff in another half hour. The pace was slow, but with the weight of the pack on his hips instead of his shoulders, Lamont was able to keep up until they reached the junction of the Square Ledge Trail. When the trail broke right and ascended sharply up a stream bed, he had to stop every five minutes to catch his breath. Will found him a walking stick, but it didn't help much. They finally arrived at Camp Rich with less than two hours of daylight left.

As Will suspected, the shelter was empty. He started the stove and got some tea water going.

Lamont rolled out his sleeping bag and pad. He took the cup that Will handed him, sipped tea. "Damn, that tastes good. Thanks."

"No problem."

He stared at the ceiling. "This is the shelter where the Wallaces were?"

"That's right," Will said.

"Too bad you couldn't have stayed here that night. Dee might still be around."

"I doubt it. They would have taken her some other time."

"Who's they, Will?"

Will hesitated. "You really think I know?"

Lamont smiled. "I was being rhetorical."

"Didn't sound that way."

Lamont took another sip. He stepped out of the shelter. "Let's take a walk."

"Now?"

"I'm curious."

"Why don't you finish your tea?"

"I can drink and walk at the same time."

Will smiled. "Amazing." He led him away from the shelter.

"You say your tarp was about here?" Lamont asked. He let the cup warm his hands.

"That's right."

"And you got up in the middle of the night?"

"This is tiresome, Lamont. We've been through this before."

"I'm trying to understand what happened. Maybe by going over it again we'll discover something we haven't thought of."

"Like what?"

"How do we know until we do it? Now, you got up in the middle of the night because you wanted to get away from Franco."

"He kept bugging me about the wind chime."

"Ah, yes. The wind chime."

"That's what I said. I guess you still don't believe the contraption was there."

Lamont didn't answer him. He paced off an area the approximate size of the tarp. He set his cup down and pulled out a pad from his pocket, took notes. "Then where did you go?"

Will showed Lamont the rock he had sat on.

"This is the part I don't get," Lamont said. "Why would you leave camp?"

"A whim, that's all. I felt it was safe to leave the group because the ranger was around."

Lamont tapped his pad with his pencil. "Okay. Where did you go from here?"

"I went up that trail," Will said, pointing east of where they were standing.

"Let's go."

"You sure you want to? Not much light left. Besides, it's pretty cold up there."

"I'm here to retrace your steps, remember?"

"There's snow on top."

Lamont hesitated. "How do you know?"

"You could see it from the Cutoff."

Lamont stuck the pad and pencil in the flap pocket of his jacket. He found his gloves in another pocket and put them on. "In the morning, then."

AT DAWN, on the way up to the summit, Will showed him the water source where he had stopped that night to get a drink, breaking a thin skin of ice with a stick. They moved on. Will had to slow down several times to wait for Lamont.

"How could you have managed this in the dark?" Lamont asked. He used a tree as support while he caught his breath.

"I've been coming up here since I was a kid. I know it like the back of my hand."

"And that's why you were so sure Dee wasn't above you. Why nobody searched up here."

"Just take a look around. Dee would never have chosen to go up, believe me. She was content with downhill or flat."

"But she didn't have a choice."

"Would you want to drag somebody up here? It's too steep. You can barely make it yourself."

Lamont adjusted his hat. "I think you could be a little kinder," he said. "Not all of us are mountain men."

"You're beginning to sound like Franco."

"You've really got it in for the guy, don't you?"

"He's two-faced. Even Bellboy could figure that one out."

Lamont ignored the comment. "You sure you didn't know him before he started teaching here?"

Will shook his head. "It just feels like I've known him all my life."

Up one more switchback and they reached the snow line. The spruce trees wore a mantle of white, the trail slippery underfoot. On the last part of the ascent, Will had to reach back and pull Lamont up over a boulder lodged in the center of the trail. "It gets easier from this point on," he said.

"I hope so."

"We're actually on the summit. The trail flattens out in another hundred feet."

"Doesn't look like the top of anything."

"Wait'll we get to the overlook."

Lamont stared at the trees, then at the sky. "It's beautiful," he said. "Hard to believe it's winter."

"It's too early for the snow to last."

"Too bad."

"We still have a stretch of Indian Summer coming."

"I can see why you like it up here."

Will turned. "Does that mean you understand now why I left the group?"

"I didn't say that. But it is pretty."

"You should be careful, you might turn into a mountain man."

"It's pretty. But it's also pretty cold." Lamont flapped his arms against his jacket. "Let's go to this overlook thing and get back down."

Because the sky was overcast, Will didn't expect to see much. He doubted whether Whiteface would be visible at all. The trail opened onto the overlook.

DEE TYLER'S nude body lay on the rock face of the overlook. Her skin was smooth and cold, like a China doll. She held a bouquet of flowers in her hands in prayerful attitude over her middle—daffodils, jonquils—that looked surprisingly fresh. Her long hair was arranged so it fell softly over one breast. She wore a single earring, like a helix, a misshaped gold heart.

TWENTY

LAMONT STAYED WITH the body while Will went for help. By 5:00, Dee's body was in the hands of the State Medical Examiner and was being transported to Concord for autopsy.

Lamont was silent on the way back to Saxton Mills.

Will was, too. He couldn't get the image of Dee's body out of his mind. He kept seeing the earring in her ear. If Lamont knew he had the one that matched it... All he could think of was that while he was away Franco had slipped into his apartment and taken the mate. "Tell me something, Lamont," he said.

"What's that?"

"Did you get tipped off about this? Did someone tell you Dee's body was up there?"

"Let's just say I had a hunch."

"You know more than you're telling me."

Lamont pulled out a cigar, ripped off the plastic wrapper with his teeth. "You've got to have hunches in this business." He crumpled the plastic, dropped it on the floor, chewed the end of his cigar.

"Does Laurie know we went up there?"

"It's none of your business what she knows."

Will wanted to tell him it was his business. He imagined pushing on the end of the cigar and shoving it down his throat.

WILL RUSHED INTO his apartment, Butch at his feet. He tried to ignore him and headed straight for the spare room. Butch trotted alongside and tripped him up. "Out of the way!" Will picked him up and tossed him a few feet down the hallway.

In the spare room he unearthed the carton that contained his computer supplies and rifled the contents. Underneath a ream of paper he found the diskette box just as he had left it. He shook the box and it rattled.

He sat on the floor, opened the box, slid the earring out into his hand and held it to the light. It had beveled edges. The gold heart shape caught the light where it twisted along its arc.

Butch came into the room and nuzzled his head against Will's arm.

Will pushed him back. "Not now. Leave me alone."

The phone rang. Butch hit his arm and the earring popped out of his hand. He fished for it. "Damn it," he said. The phone kept ringing. By the time he found the earring, the answering machine snapped on in his bedroom. Faintly, he could hear Laurie's voice. He ran to the bedroom and picked up.

"Tell me what happened," she said.

"Lamont didn't give you the low down?"

"He didn't say much." She cleared her throat. "How are you holding up?"

"It wasn't pretty."

"Would you mind if I came over and talked about it?"

"You want to come over here?"

"If you don't mind."

"I don't think I'd be good company."

"Listen, Will. You need to talk to someone about this."

"I've got Butch."

"Yeah? What does he say?"

"Not much. Right now he's pissed."

"I'm serious, Will. You might consider getting professional help."

"You mean like you?" He paused. "Professionally speaking, of course."

"Why am I worrying about you? At least your cynicism is healthy."

"And thank God for it."

"I'd like to come over."

"Maybe I don't want you to."

"Why?"

"Maybe I don't trust you." Will waited but there was no response. Butch came to the doorway but didn't venture into the bedroom. He kept his distance.

After a few moments she said, "At least I know where we stand."

"You call up saying you're concerned. I don't believe it. You just want to know what happened up there."

"That's right. But I do care what's happening with you."

"Sure you do. You're just like Butch. Right now he's looking at me with moon eyes and he wants to cuddle because he's hungry. After he gets what he wants, he'll stay away."

"You're putting me on a level with Butch?"

"Remember that night when we had dinner at the Burger 'n' Brew? You said you hated it when people weren't up front with you. Well, I'm the same way. Now, I want you to admit the real reason you called."

He waited.

"It's a professional issue, I admit."

"And that's it, right?"

"I'm coming over, Will. Unless you want me to haul you down here for questioning."

"You'd do that to me?"

"If I had to."

Will leaned his head against the wall. "I was about to make spaghetti. If you don't mind talking and eating."

"I'll be right over."

Will hung up, looked at Butch. "What a bitch! What the hell's wrong with her?" He put the phone down and stared at it for a moment. "What the hell's wrong with me?" He didn't have an answer and neither did Butch. He was left with the overwhelming sense that no matter what he did, he was screwed.

He walked out the doorway. Butch gave him a wide berth, then followed him. In the spare room, Will put the earring back in the diskette box and returned it to the carton underneath the ream of paper. "Come on, Butch," he said. "Chop, chop."

Butch sat on the kitchen counter.

Will opened the refrigerator, hefted the milk container, pinched the wax top and sniffed. It was still good. He poured milk in

Butch's bowl. "Here you go," he said. Butch didn't move. "The hell with you, then." Damn cat! Will checked the cupboards for spaghetti sauce. Butch ambled along the counter and hopped across the stove. He sat near the sink and watched Will. Will pulled out a jar of spaghetti sauce. Behind it were two tins of Gourmet Gato. He grabbed one of them, showed it to Butch. "Is this what you want?"

Butch came to him and rubbed against his arm.

"You're such a kiss ass." He opened the tin and placed it on the floor. He watched Butch eat, his nose buried in the tin. It was hard to believe Butch was so dainty when it came to meal time, but such a stumblebum around the house. He thought about the earring Butch had knocked out of his hand.

"If they find that earring on me, I'm in deep shit," he said. He replayed the phone conversation in his head. He imagined handing over the earring. Might as well give Laurie the shovel to dig his grave. But no, he had to get rid of it. "So, what do I do with it, Butch?"

Butch finished the meal. He shook his head to free his whiskers of leftovers and jumped onto the counter. His feet hit Will's unopened mail, and some of it slipped to the floor.

"You're such a damn klutz!"

Will picked up a flyer wooing him to buy a season's pass for Raccoon Mountain, a local ski area. He stared at the flyer, then smiled. "Of course," he said.

Butch licked his paw, then ran it over his head.

"I'll mail the damn earring to the police station. Let them wonder where it came from." He leaned over to give Butch a pat.

Butch pulled away, leapt off the counter, strutted down the hallway and into the bathroom.

LAURIE TOOK A SIP from her wine glass. "I talked to one of the EMS people who picked her up," she said. "He thinks Dee died of a broken neck. He said the medical examiner palpated a fracture between C-Two and C-Three."

"She didn't have a mark on her."

"We'll have to wait for the report to see if it was the cause of death." She placed her glass on the table. "Has Jonathan called you?"

"No."

"He does, I want to know."

"Any special reason?"

"Just keep me informed." She looked down at her plate and began twirling spaghetti with her fork.

Will drained his glass. Seeing her there made him forget temporarily why she had come over. He studied her hand manipulating the fork and followed her precise motions as she tightly spiraled a neat coil of spaghetti. He wanted to feel her touch again. "I thought we'd never get together like this," he said. "A romantic candlelight meal." He jabbed at his spaghetti. "Kind of ironic, huh?"

Laurie put her fork down. "Don't start with this." She used her napkin to dab at the corner of her mouth. "Now, you want to tell me what happened up there?"

"Have some wine." Will tried to top off Laurie's glass, but she put her palm over it.

"Just tell me what happened."

He paused and looked at the bottle and shrugged his shoulders. "More for me." He poured a glassful for himself and drank half.

"You think you could slow it down a little?"

He brought the glass down. "You think I'm getting drunk?"

"I want you as lucid as possible."

Will sat back in his chair and began his story.

Laurie looked across at him, her elbows on the table, fingers locked together.

By the time he finished, the glass was empty, and he felt lightheaded. How many glasses had he had, anyway? Maybe it was the two Laphroig's before the meal. "You didn't take notes," he said.

"Didn't have to."

Will toyed with his spaghetti, which had gotten cold. "There are too many unanswered questions."

"Like what?"

"How Lamont knew I went back to Pasaconaway that weekend. Who told him?"

"We've been through that."

"I know."

She paused. "You still think I told him?"

"I'm trying not to think that, but you're the only one who knew."

"I didn't tell him."

It sounded genuine enough. Either she was the best liar in the world or she was telling the truth. "Here's another question. Why did Lamont suddenly want to go up to Pasaconaway? He had to know Dee's body was up there."

"And you think I told him that, too?"

"I don't know!" He put his fork down and shoved his plate away. "Doesn't any of this seem odd to you?"

She thought a moment. "So, the same person who tipped off Lamont also killed Dee."

"Can you come to any other conclusion?"

"But who?"

"I don't know who. I've been trying to find out who. I can't get anybody to believe there's a 'who' out there." He didn't like the way this was going. It was the wine and Laphroig talking, he could tell, and he didn't like the helplessness he heard in his own voice. A wave of nausea passed through him.

"I want to believe you, Will, but I need evidence."

He threw his napkin down on the table. "Well, honey, you've come to the wrong place—because I sure as hell don't have any." Shit. He was drunk. He could hear it in his voice.

She crossed her knife and fork on the plate, then pushed her chair back.

"Where are you going?"

"To the ladies'."

After she left, Will sat, head in hands. Butch hopped up on the table and began licking Laurie's plate. He cuffed him off and poured himself another glass of wine. He didn't care anymore. He just didn't care.

Laurie took a long time in the bathroom. When she returned,

she looked as if she had been crying. "I think I'd better go," she said.

Will stood up from the table. "No, please don't." He shoved his chair back and it tipped over. "Oops." He bent to pick it up and his head swam, then started doing laps, and he had to hold onto the table for support. Laurie came to his side and helped him to the couch. He leaned against her, and the smell of her perfume stirred him. He tried to kiss her but she pushed him away.

"Damn it, Will."

"Sorry, sorry, sorry." He collapsed on the couch and kept one foot on the floor to try to keep from falling off the boat. Through his bleariness he was vaguely aware of her eyes. Her tears were real. She had not betrayed him.

TWENTY-ONE

WILL READ IN the paper there would be a memorial service at the school honoring Dee. Jonathan had flown in to recover the body and would attend. The article hinted he would give a speech.

Will knew he should probably stay away, but he felt compelled to be part of it. He arrived at the school an hour before the memorial service and used a side entrance to the auditorium. The lights were dimmed except for the AV booth. He climbed the circular stairs and opened the door.

Ronnie Lee Allen swiveled on his stool. "Mr. Buchanan!"

"I startled you. I'm sorry. You don't mind if I watch from up here, do you?" Will knew Ronnie Lee from biology class last year and they had gotten along well. Right now, the kid looked like he was the only Christian in the arena and they had just let in the lions.

"It's kind of cramped."

Will smiled at him. "Just pretend I'm not here." He leaned against the back wall and watched as Ronnie Lee fiddled with buttons.

Soon, students carrying baskets of flowers filed in and placed them on the stage. The auditorium began to fill. Will recognized faces from the press conference crowd.

Ronnie Lee brought up the stage lights and the fresnel aimed at the podium. The houselights remained dim. He cued up the tape player and pressed play. Palestrina's *Pope Marcellus Mass* resonated in the room.

Will spotted Laurie. He leaned forward and placed his hands on the counter and watched her move up the aisle. She chose a seat in the rear by the exit. The last time he saw her he'd passed out on the couch and woke in the morning to find her gone.

Someday he would win her back. Her eyes had told him that. She was soon followed by Jonathan Tyler and the ever present Peter, who sat in the front row.

When Perry entered, Ronnie Lee began fading the Palestrina piece. The doors closed. Father Malloy from St. Andrew's Episcopal mounted the stairs and Ronnie Lee cut off the music.

Father Malloy offered prayers of invocation and Will bowed his head. Churchy things always made his collar feel a little too tight and made him think of lost Sundays as a youth when he couldn't go fishing. He always heard the words but found it hard to concentrate on what they meant. Then his mind drifted to the Bible he had found in the duffel bag in Franco's apartment. The starred passages would lead him to the truth, he was sure, and he was determined more than ever to find their meaning.

Perry took the podium: "At moments like these we are reminded of the fragility of life. We ask ourselves why it had to happen, why such a beautiful young girl had to be taken from us so suddenly. We are angry and confused." He paused and looked out over the audience. "There are no ready answers, but we have to help each other. Our healing has to come from all of us, from the strength we share as a community. Let us all come together in praise of Dee's life."

Anita spoke after Perry. She eulogized Dee without sounding maudlin. "I only knew her a few days," she began, "but during SMOOT we became friends. She made me laugh. She kept talking to her backpack, telling it to lighten up. I shall miss her for the good times I know we would have had together. She was just plain fun to be with." It was a simple, eloquent speech, and Will felt his eyes tearing. He swallowed hard to choke them back.

The school chorus sang "Amazing Grace," always a grabber, and Will layed his hands flat against the back of the booth to help steady himself enough to get through it. What was it about that simple tune that held such power?

Then it was Jonathan's turn to speak. He wore a white three-piece suit with a solitary rose pinned to his lapel. "I want to thank you all for your kind words about my daughter. Hearing them makes me feel that she was in the right place, that good things could have happened here if it hadn't been for this tragedy." Jonathan sounded as if he had undergone a change of heart about the school, but was it enough to change his mind about the lawsuit? For a brief moment, Will felt a stirring of hope that this would all go away, that somehow the tragedy would promote forgiveness.

Jonathan took a handkerchief from his pocket and dabbed at his eyes. "Dee came to Saxton Mills a troubled person, and I know that where she is now, those troubles are finally over." He cleared his throat and held the handkerchief tight in one hand. "We are here to celebrate her life, but we cannot honor her until we bring her killer to justice." He paused. "I promise you, Dee. I will do just that."

Jonathan sat down. No, there was no change of heart. Jonathan was out for blood.

Father Malloy gave the benediction. Ronnie Lee punched in the first movement of Bach's Brandenburg Concerto #5 and brought up the house lights a notch.

That was it. A mercifully brief half hour. The service was over.

WILL HUNG AROUND in the back of the booth until the last person left the auditorium.

Ronnie Lee stopped the tape and pushed the rewind button. "I'm going now," he said.

"It's okay. I'll make sure the lights are out."

"You know where the switches are?"

"Of course."

The machine whirred and stopped. Ronnie Lee took the tape out and put it in a cassette box.

Will reached out and touched his shoulder. "You don't have to tell anyone I was up here."

The kid jumped back like he had been stung. He whirled and held onto the counter.

"Hey, whoa. What's the matter?"

"Nothing."

"Tell me what's wrong."

Ronnie Lee forced his way past Will. His footsteps clattered on the metal stairway. He ran to the front entrance, hit the crash bars, and was gone.

THE ABRUPT SILENCE in the auditorium left Will stunned. He walked down the metal staircase, found the rheostats on the back wall, and, one by one, turned off each bank of lights until he was in darkness. He felt his way along the edge of the back row. When he reached the side entrance, he paused. He sat in one of the seats and thought of Ronnie Lee. What was the talk on campus, anyway? Was everyone afraid of him?

Suddenly, the front entrance door opened.

Will sat forward.

Jonathan Tyler appeared on the landing, a wool coat draped over his shoulders. He was backlit, his figure in shadow. "I know you're in here, Will." Will didn't say anything. Jonathan walked down the steps into the darkness. "One of my people saw you come in. I've been waiting outside." The taps on his shoes clicked on the tile as he walked slowly along the front of the auditorium.

"I'm back here," Will said.

Jonathan stopped. It took a few moments for him to respond. "You've got your nerve coming here."

"Let me get the lights."

"No! Leave them off!" Tyler's voice boomed.

"We should talk face to face, Jonathan."

"Not feeling guilty, are you? Sneaking into the service like that."

"I didn't sneak in."

"You hid in the back."

"I thought it would be better to keep a low profile. I didn't want to cause problems."

"Seems to me you've done that already."

"I felt I had to be here. Dee was—"

"Stop it! Don't say her name!" There was a moment when nothing happened. Then Will heard him walking away. The heel clicks picked up speed until they stopped at the landing. "You should have been there when the bastards took her," Jonathan said. "You shouldn't have left those girls alone. None of this would have happened."

"You don't know that."

"Don't tell me what I know."

"Making me feel guilty isn't going to solve anything."

"Oh, I don't have to make you feel guilty, I'm sure."

"You're being ridiculous, Jonathan."

"You have obviously never lost a daughter." He paused. "See you in court, Will."

"You don't have to do this."

"You'll be lucky if that's all that happens to you."

Will got to his feet. "What do you mean?"

"I'm going to make you pay, Will."

What the hell did that mean? He thought of cement overshoes and Jonathan's rumored ties to the mob. "Is that a threat?"

"What do you think?"

"Apparently, what I think doesn't matter much."

"You're going down, Will."

"What are you going to do, kill me?"

Jonathan turned to leave.

Will shouted at him: "You just need someone to blame!"

Jonathan held the door and looked over his shoulder. "That's right. And I know who it is."

WILL DREAMED he was at his grandfather's fishing camp. He was cleaning a huge bass. He stuck the knife in, drew it sharply along the belly and the guts spilled. They kept rolling out and he couldn't stop them. They fell off the table and onto his shoes. When he first heard the knocking, he thought it came from the door of the camp. Then he woke.

He looked at the clock. 8:23 am. The knocking was insistent. He pulled on his pants and went to the front door of his apartment. He opened it a crack, saw Lamont, let him in.

Lamont entered and shoved him against the wall. "You have the right to remain silent…"

He saw Laurie behind him.

"What's going on?" Will asked.

"Hands on the wall," Lamont said. "Spread 'em." Will complied. Lamont frisked him, then pulled his arms back. He put the cuffs on and spun him around. "You're under arrest for the murder of Dee Tyler."

"I didn't kill her."

"And Jeanne Tyler."

"What?" Will looked at Laurie.

She wore her law face—cold, neutral.

Jeanne Tyler? Had he heard right?

"Let's go," Lamont said.

TWENTY-TWO

"IT'S SIMPLE, REALLY," Lamont said. "You didn't go to the summit of Pasaconaway that night. You waited until Dee left her tarp to visit the woods, then you dragged her off."

"To where?"

"You weren't working alone."

"I'm part of a conspiracy? Just who am I in cahoots with?"

Lamont paused. "I don't know yet."

Will shook his head. "You're on a fishing expedition, Lamont."

Lamont leaned over the table. "You were involved with the kidnapping, there's no doubt in my mind. Your story's the only one that doesn't wash. No one can corroborate it."

"So, let me get this straight. I dragged Dee off, passed her on to a buddy, and then had the time and wherewithal to get up to summit and wait for Franco to find me."

"That's right."

"Come on, Lamont. That's a little farfetched, don't you think?"

"Not when I find the missing piece."

"You mean my buddy."

Lamont leaned back from the table. He pulled out a chair, put his foot up on it, retied the laces of his shoe. "You could make things a lot easier on yourself if you just tell me who you're working with."

Will thought a moment. "You know, Lamont. I think you're right."

"You do?"

"Yeah. I think there is someone else involved. It's the same one who followed us on SMOOT, hung the wind chimes, split my garden hose—thank God, you finally believe what I've been telling you. Problem is, I don't know who it is, either.''

"Okay." He smiled at him and brushed at his pants. "Have it your way."

"Look. If I killed her, then why would I agree to lead you to the body?"

"An old ploy, really. Throw suspicion away from you."

Will stared at Lamont. "You really think I killed her?"

"I arrested you, didn't I?"

"You have no proof."

"The earring in your apartment matches the one Dee was wearing," he said, "which sounds like proof to me."

"So, that's what this is about. You found the earring."

"That's right."

"Isn't that what they call 'circumstantial'?"

"What are you, a lawyer now?"

"But why would I kill her?"

"Ah, the motive." Lamont smiled at him. "I have my own theory, but I want to hear yours first. Seems to me I remember you're good at theories." Will sighed. Lamont took off his jacket, pulled a cigar from the inside pocket, placed his jacket over the back of the chair and sat. "Look, let's stop dancing."

"I didn't kill her."

"But you know who did."

"No!"

"You're lying."

Will paused. "There's nothing more to say to you, Lamont. Do what you have to do."

Lamont lit up his cigar. "What I have to do is transport you to the Federal court in Concord. You need a lawyer."

"You plan to sneak me out of here?"

Lamont puffed away. Blue smoke filled the back room of the police station. "Nice and neat. No convoy. No press." He drew the cigar out of his mouth. "Especially no press."

Will batted the smoke with his hand. "Can I talk to Laurie?"

"You plan to tell her the truth?"

"Just let me talk to her."

Lamont pushed his chair back. "Let's get you locked up."

"You're not going to let me see her?"

"Later, maybe."

"Wait a minute," Will said.

"What is it now?"

"How's Jeanne involved with this? Why am I accused of killing her?"

Lamont shook his head. "Now, come on, Will. You know the answer to that."

"I don't."

Lamont sat down again. "Actually, this is the most interesting part of the case. You see, Jeanne was wearing those earrings the night she died—there are witnesses to confirm this, by the way. When they found the body, the earrings had somehow disappeared."

Will sat forward. "Oh, God."

"That's right, my friend. Your ass is in a ringer."

"YOU WANTED TO see me?" She stood before him in the holding cell, her hands cupped in front of her like a choir girl.

"You're not frightened, are you?"

She relaxed her hands. "Of course not."

"Good. I want you to help me get out of here."

"I can't do that."

"I'm innocent."

"You need a lawyer, Will."

"Can't afford one."

"You're being stubborn."

"I'm being railroaded." Will got up from the cot. He looked through the barred window, wheeled around and stepped toward her. "I want you to look me in the eye and tell me you think I killed Dee."

She faced him. "The law has to decide that."

He shook his head. "You think I did it."

"It doesn't matter what I think. You're in trouble, and you can't afford to be stupid. If you don't get legal counsel you'll be assigned it by the court."

"Fine."

"Is there something else you wanted? If not..."

"You're busy? You have to file something? Polish Lamont's shoes?"

"This is going nowhere, as usual."

There was a slight tremor in her voice that surprised him. After a few moments he said: "Maybe you're right: I'm asking too much."

"I don't think you did it."

"Right."

"I know the courts will—"

"Forget the courts! If I end up in jail, whoever killed Dee Tyler will go free."

"And if you're innocent, you don't have anything to worry about."

"That's pretty naive, don't you think? Especially coming from you. Maybe that's what they drilled into you at the police academy, but it doesn't wash." He moved closer to her. He wanted to touch her arm, but checked himself. "Don't you see, Laurie? Someone's set me up, and he loves to play games. The only way we're going to find him is flush him out. He knows I'm sitting in a cell, and he's probably feeling pretty smug. If I escape, he'll come after me." For a brief moment, her eyes said she believed him. She looked at the floor. He turned and peered out the window at a car roof. "I guess you can't do it."

"You were right about Lamont," she said. "He had seen the earring in your apartment."

It was a peace offering. A little belated, but it didn't matter. Right now he needed to grab onto something. He turned back to her. "I knew that bastard had been snooping around."

"He's not a bastard, Will."

"He's your friend now, is he?"

"No, he's not my friend. He desperately wants to find out who killed Dee."

"I thought he found him."

"I told you. I don't think you killed her."

"But Lamont does."

"The truth will come out. I have faith in the law."

It sounded like she meant it, but she was looking away from him when she said it.

"Okay, just tell me one more thing," he said. "And I want the truth."

She looked up at him.

"Did Lamont send you to pick up the earring at my place the night we had spaghetti?"

"Yes."

JUST BEFORE DAWN, Lamont came into Will's cell, handcuffed him and led him out the rear door to an unmarked car. Will sat in the back seat with Laurie.

"No reporters," Laurie said.

Lamont started the car. "Which means no leaks."

"Why the hush-hush?" Will asked. "I thought you'd be crowing about solving the case."

Lamont pulled the car out into the street and headed toward Interstate 93. "I could give a shit what they write about me."

"I don't think you're worried about the press at all," Will said.

Lamont gunned the engine when he hit the ramp to the highway. "That so?"

"I think you're worried about the guy who's been following me."

Lamont's silence seemed to corroborate that feeling. "I've got to hand it to you," he said. "You don't give up."

"You've got your doubts. I know you do."

"I don't believe in ghosts."

When the speedometer hit sixty-five, Lamont put it on cruise control, and leaned back in his seat. "It's not too late to change your story. It's getting close to crunch time." He found a cigar in his pocket, lit it, and cracked open the driver's side window.

Will looked at Laurie.

She turned away from him and looked out the window.

He leaned his head back and closed his eyes, surprised he wasn't nervous. All he felt was an overwhelming tiredness because he hadn't slept all night. He dozed, then was jolted awake when his head slid sideways and slammed against the door.

A beige van raced alongside Lamont's car. Will couldn't see who was in the passenger seat, just an arm out the window, a pistol aimed at the car. Was he dreaming? "Hey, Lamont!"

Before Lamont could respond, the gunman in the van fired, and Lamont slumped over the wheel. The car careened onto the shoulder. Laurie reached over the seat and grabbed the wheel, but Lamont's weight was too much. She couldn't move him away from the wheel.

Will put his cuffed hands over his head and ducked. The car smashed into the guard rail, flipped, and rolled down an embankment. He bumped against the seat, then hit the rear window before the car came to rest on its roof.

He could wiggle his toes. He was okay down there. His head hurt. He ran his hands along the side of his head. He was bleeding.

Laurie had landed in the front, on the roof of the driver's side. Lamont slumped upside down in his seat belt. The cigar had come to rest on his cheek; his flesh was burning.

Will crept toward the front, removed the cigar, checked Laurie's carotid—she was still alive—searched her belt, found the keys to the handcuffs, and freed himself. He leaned back, raised his legs over her, and drove his boots against the passenger side window. He crawled over Laurie and out through the window, reached back in, grabbed hold of Laurie's coat and pulled her out.

He checked her airway—it was clear. She moaned and began to stir.

A voice came from above him, on the highway: "You okay, mister?" Several vehicles were parked along the guard rail. No beige van.

Laurie sat up. "Will. What...?"

"Sorry," he said. "I've got to go."

Will ran past the wreckage, up the embankment. The man who had called to him met him near the guard rail. He was heavy set and had a thin mustache. He stared at Will's head. "The ambulance is coming—you should just wait here."

Will looked back. Laurie staggered up the embankment. Will pointed to an idling Chevy 4×4. "That your truck?" The man nodded. "I have to borrow it."

Before the man could protest, Will was in the driver's seat. He engaged the four-wheel drive and tromped on the accelerator. He drove across the median divider and headed north on the highway.

TWENTY-THREE

HE GOT OFF at the Lincoln exit. He kept checking the rear-view mirror. As far as he could tell, he was still one step ahead. He throttled down to the speed limit going through town past the old lumber mill that had been converted into a fancy mall, past the condos that lined the Kancamagus. The traffic was moderate and moving.

He gunned it near the entrance to Loon Mountain. He had a straight stretch to the hairpin about eight miles ahead, where the road started to climb. The pickup shook at 90 mph, but he kept the accelerator punched to the floor. He soon got behind a refrigerated truck and couldn't pass. Forty-five mph felt like a crawl. A line of traffic began to build behind him. He watched in the mirror as one car leap-frogged along the line: They were after him and he had no choice but to stay in line. The truck in front geared down when it reached an incline; since Will had his eyes glued to the rear-view mirror he almost rear-ended the truck. The road curved to the north. He passed the truck on the right and stayed on the shoulder. The truck driver must have seen him coming and hit the brakes, but Will slipped by him and back onto the road, saw the opposite lane open, and hurtled past three cars before slicing back into his own lane.

Before the hairpin he saw the sign for the Greeley Ponds Trail. He pulled off the highway into the trailhead parking lot. There was only one other vehicle, a pock-marked Toyota truck with a cap.

He shut the engine down and leaned over the steering wheel, his head on his arms. His pulse was pounding. He closed his eyes, but that wasn't such a good idea. His head began spinning.

He repositioned the mirror and looked at his head. There was a lot of blood, but most of it had caked. As far as he could tell, the laceration was closing. Without stitches he would have an impressive scar.

He got out of the truck. Once in the woods, he could wash in a stream.

As he opened the door, a car skidded into the parking lot. Laurie jumped out, her pistol raised. "Hands on the truck."

"You could have killed yourself driving like that," he said.

"Do it."

"I'm going into the woods."

She walked toward him in a crouch. "You're not going anywhere."

"Don't you get it? I didn't shoot Lamont, so somebody else did."

She kept the pistol leveled. The right side of her face was bruised. "Just put your hands on the truck," she said.

Will complied. "Lamont was onto something," he said. "He was getting too close."

"To what?"

"The truth."

"That doesn't change anything. I'm going to take you back."

"Wait. You believe me?"

"Lamont dug up something, and it probably got him killed."

"You don't know what he found?"

"No."

"But you think the guy who shot him is the same one who's after me."

She hesitated. "Maybe."

Will removed his hands from the truck.

"Put your hands back." She wagged the pistol.

He did what he was told. "My best chance is in the woods," he said.

"No."

"I've got to flush him out. If I don't, we'll never catch him."

"The safest place for you is in my custody."

"You're trying to tell me you're worried about my safety?"

"I'm telling you Lamont was."

"Oh, bullshit."

"It isn't bullshit. He told me that last night. Now, let's go."

Will took his hands off the truck. "Then I was right: He knew I didn't kill Dee. He wanted me in jail for my own protection."

"I think so."

"What else did he say?"

"Nothing."

"Did he know about us?"

"Yes."

"And that explains why he didn't trust you."

"Lamont's no dummy. He had to consider everything."

Will smiled. "I guess he didn't know you very well."

"What?"

"You would never let your heart get in the way."

In the distance, from the highway, came the whoop of a police siren.

She took a step toward him. "Don't move."

"I can't go back. It isn't over."

"You have to, Will. You're under arrest."

"You want me to beg?"

She shook her head. "I want you to stay put." She stiffened her aim, both arms straight.

He raised his hands. "Listen: Let's take a walk in the woods. I'll be your prisoner—think of it as the long way to jail."

The police siren was joined by another.

"I've got to get out of here." He kept his hands in the air. "You got two choices, Laurie. Follow me, or let me go."

Her jaw dropped. "You bastard. You're giving me choices? I'm the one holding the gun."

"Use it then!"

"Damn it, Will!" She kept her arms locked, her aim steady.

"Goodbye, Laurie." He turned away from her and ran.

He headed up the trail and across a footbridge spanning a bog. He could hear her giving chase. A shot rang by his ear. The bullet slammed into the tree in front of him, showering bark. He veered left off the trail. Another crack of the pistol. And another.

He climbed away from the bog into the dense brush. After a few hundred yards, the firing stopped. He doubled back, dropped to his knees, and listened for footfalls. He could hear her coming. He crawled off to the side, waited, and when she passed him, grabbed her from behind and wrested the pistol from her hands. "That was easy," he said. He pinned her arms. "Too easy."

Her breath came hard. "You don't have a chance," she said. She struggled to free herself. "Let me go!"

"Let's stop playing games. What you did back there—you put on a show. You could have dropped me if you wanted to." He released her.

She faced him. "All right," she said. "Now what?"

Will looked at the pistol in his hand. He brought it up slowly and aimed it at her. "How does it feel looking down the barrel of this thing?" She didn't say anything. He flipped the pistol around and handed it to her, butt-end. "I can't stand guns," he said. "Here."

She didn't move. "What are you doing?"

"You'd better take it before I hurt myself." He placed it in her palm. He let his other hand linger on hers. She jerked her hand away. "You might just as well keep it in your holster," he said. "You're not going to use it on me."

"I wouldn't put money on it."

"Why don't you go back? Let me do what I have to do."

"I'll say it again: You're my prisoner."

"Tell them you lost my trail. You covered your ass by shooting at me."

"If Lamont's right, I have a responsibility to protect you," she said.

"Well, thanks. I feel a lot safer."

"Don't patronize me."

"This is my turf, Laurie; I don't need your help."

"You expect me to believe you know what you're doing?"

"Give me some credit, will you?"

"What's the plan, then? Run through the woods?"

He looked at the sky through the trees. "We have to lose the tail first. I came in on this side of the highway because I want them to think I'm headed for Pasaconaway. With luck, they'll concentrate on this area."

"Then what?"

"Bushwhack. Cross the highway at Big Rock Campground."

"A hell of a plan."

"It'll buy time to flush out whoever's following."

She shook her head. "You honestly think the person who shot Lamont knows where we are?"

"Yes," he said. "He knows exactly where we are."

THEY WALKED due south until they reached the first of the Greeley Ponds. They stayed close to the east side of the pond, hopping across rocks to hide their trail and then turned northwest, backtracking until they were once again close to the highway. They would have to keep up a strong pace to reach Big Rock Campground by nightfall.

"Tell me the truth," Will said. "You really don't believe that story about the earring."

"I don't feel like talking about it, Will."

"I want to know what you think, that's all."

"I think it's strong physical evidence."

"Yeah, but it's too perfect. I don't know much about the law, but I doubt it would stand up in court."

She stared at him. "I guess that's something you're going to find out."

THEY MOVED WEST and recrossed the trail. The terrain flattened and they made better time. At dusk they rested near Pine Brook.

Laurie sat by the water, hugging her arms.

"You cold?"

"I'm all right," she said.

"We better keep moving."

"How much farther?"

"We're almost there." He helped her to her feet and led her closer to the highway. In another half hour, he could see the entrance to the campground across the road.

Will waited until he was sure the highway was quiet and crossed over, his arm around Laurie. He stayed to the left of the entrance and went deeper into the woods along the edge of the campground. It looked empty.

"Is this it?" she asked. "Do we have to walk anymore?"

"You can rest."

She sat near a birch tree and rubbed her arms.

"You want me to hold you? Warm you up a bit?" He touched her shoulder.

"Keep your hands off me." She drew herself into a ball. "I'm fine. I just need some sleep." He was surprised how quickly she drifted off.

The night chill had a sharp edge to it, which gave him cause to worry about hypothermia. He searched for pine boughs, or any broadleaf deadfall that might help keep her heat in. He stacked what he found over her and mounded leaves on top. It was the best he could do.

Clouds scudded across the moon. He felt his forehead. The blood had caked hard. He rested his head on his arms and fell asleep, too.

He was awakened by the whine of a small truck engine. The headlights jabbed at the darkness as the truck swung into the parking lot. He ducked down and watched a lone camper get out of the truck, turn on his flashlight, and illuminate a small dome tent.

Will watched until the flashlight went off, pondering his next move. Laurie was a liability; she would slow him down. If she was going to stay with him, she would need warmer clothing, plus they had no food and no equipment, which, of course, he would need, too.

Laurie was still asleep. He placed his hand on her forehead; her temperature felt normal. She stirred but didn't wake under his touch. He removed the loaded Smith & Wesson from her holster, and moved closer to the edge of the campground. He doubted the man in the truck was the stalker, but he couldn't be sure. It was a brash move driving into the parking lot like that. Then he remembered the wind chime, and realized that brashness might be standard practice for this killer.

TWENTY-FOUR

DAWN CAME on subtly in muted orange above the trees. He stole across the parking lot to the camper's truck, checked the truck bed and found a backpack. The truck was unlocked, but the keys weren't in the ignition. He crept toward the tent, knelt outside the door, and listened: The camper's breathing was deep and nasal.

He stuck the pistol in the pocket of his anorak and unzipped the door of the tent.

The camper didn't move.

He reached in, grabbed the bottom of the bag, pulled, and dragged the camper outside the tent.

"Jesus H... What the fuck?"

"Good morning," Will said.

The camper struggled to get out of the bag.

Will pulled the drawstring tight and held him down. "Relax. I just want to ask you a few questions."

The man wore a few days' growth of beard. His face, ringed by the sleeping bag, made him look caught in a larva state. "Let go of me," he said. He kicked his feet in the bag.

Will pulled the Smith & Wesson from his anorak and pointed it at the man's head. "Stop squirming."

The man's eyes widened. "You're the guy the cops're looking for," he said.

So the word was out. His picture must be plastered all over the news. "I'm not going to hurt you. I just want to know what you're doing here."

"What the hell do you think? I'm camping."

"Come up here often?"

"Yeah. So what?"

"Little late in the season."

"I like it that way." He shifted in the bag. "Where's the other one?"

"Who?"

"The lady cop. Your hostage."

Will pushed the pistol against his forehead. "How do you know about her?"

"Hey! Take it easy. I only know what's on the radio."

"That's what they're saying?"

"On the news."

"What else?"

"Nothing."

Will pulled the pistol away, seeing an imprint of the barrel end on the man's forehead. He pulled on the drawstring. "Out of the bag," he said. The man didn't hesitate. He stood in polypro underwear. "Now your keys."

The man scratched the stubble on his chin. "You want to steal my truck?" He showed a trace of a smile but stifled it quickly.

"Just hand them over."

"Under the mat. Driver's side."

Will gathered the sleeping bag. "Stay here," he said. He headed for the truck.

"Watch she doesn't overheat," the camper said. "Thermostat's iffy."

"I'll take my chances."

Will took the backpack out of the truck, rolled up the sleeping bag and tied it to the frame. He searched the pack and found a heavy sweater and some canned food—also a roll of duct tape. He returned the pack to the truck bed and walked back to the tent, duct tape in hand. "You must be a woodsman if you carry this stuff."

"It'll fix anything," he said. The man looked frightened.

"Don't worry, I'm not going to hurt you." In the tent, Will ran the tape around the man's thighs, his wrists, then his head and over his mouth. He said, "You're tied up pretty good, but you should be able to shuffle to the highway. Somebody will pick you up." He grabbed the man's pants, and his jacket, then gave him a pat on the shoulder. "Sorry about this. It's an emergency." Once outside, he left the tent door unzipped and returned to the truck.

It took several tries for the truck, a '70-something Ford F150, to start. Will pumped the accelerator to keep it going. The muffler vibrated and rattled against the undercarriage. He drove slowly out of the parking lot.

Laurie came out of the woods, leaves clinging to her shirt, before he reached the highway. Will pumped the gas pedal again. The timing was off and it really ran rough. He reached over and opened the passenger side door. "I want you to stay here."

She held onto the door. "You stole this, didn't you?"

"Never mind."

"I thought you didn't like guns."

Will reached inside the anorak and handed her the pistol. "I just borrowed it."

She took it from him. "Whose truck?" she asked.

"Someday I'll tell you about it."

She raised the pistol and pointed it at him. "Tell me now."

"Not this again." He tried to close the door, but she held onto it. He popped the clutch and jerked the truck forward. She clung to the door and ran alongside.

He slammed on the brakes.

She catapulted forward but held on to the passenger side rear-view mirror. Her face appeared again at the door. "You trying to kill me?"

"Let go of the door."

"No."

He gunned the engine and the truck lurched forward.

She gripped the door hard. "Damn it, let me in. I'm not going to let go!"

Will let his head rest on the steering wheel. "Shit."

She slid onto the passenger seat and slammed the door. "You're not going anywhere without me."

Will floored it. The tires spun, sending up a shower of gravel. He headed west on the Kank toward Lincoln.

LAURIE SAT WITH her arms folded, staring straight ahead. "I really can't trust you, can I?"

Will didn't answer her since he was keeping an eye on the temperature gauge: The needle was riding high. "I'm dumping the truck at the Lincoln Woods Trail," he said. "I think you should drive it into town."

"Why would I do that?"

The truck whined in fourth gear and the needle crept higher.

"You can tell them I held you hostage, then abandoned the truck."

"I don't lie as well as you do."

"You don't have to lie. That's what they think already."

"How do you know?"

"Camper told me." A car passed them in the other lane. Will brought his hand up to the side of his face and stared straight ahead.

"You think I'm a real burden," she said.

"I just don't want you to get hurt."

"That's very noble of you." She turned away from him and looked out the window, her chin resting on her hand. She said, "I want you to promise me something."

"What?"

"If nothing happens in twenty-four hours we come out."

"What do you mean 'we'? You're taking the truck into town."

"Sorry, Will. We're joined at the hip now."

"What if it takes longer?"

"Doesn't matter. We still come out."

Will thought a moment. "How about after twenty-four hours you come out?"

"No."

"You can't put a damn time limit on it!"

"I want you to promise."

"No deal."

She faced him. "Come on, Will, use your head. By now they have the search well-organized. They'll find out we're not in the Sandwich Range—they'll have choppers combing the area. We'll be lucky if we *have* another twenty-four hours."

"Is that supposed to encourage me?" He checked the rear-view. A gray van was gaining on him.

"I'm not kidding, Will!"

"All right, all right."

She studied him. "I don't think you mean it," she said.

"What do you want me to say?"

"We've been in the woods since yesterday, Will. Where's the phantom?"

"He'll show."

"When?"

"Soon."

"Twenty-four hours, Will."

Will flexed his hands on the steering wheel. "I know I'm right," he said.

THERE WERE a handful of cars in the parking lot at the Lincoln Woods Trail, one a '67 Dodge Dart that Will recognized as belonging to a ranger. He shut off the engine and surveyed the area.

"What are we waiting for?" Laurie asked.

"I'm making sure we weren't followed."

She twisted in her seat and looked out the back window of the truck. "It's all clear," she said.

Will opened the door of the truck and pulled the backpack out of the truck bed. "You coming?" He put on the pack and began hiking at a fast clip across the parking lot.

She caught up to him at the footbridge over the Pemigewasset River. "Don't walk off like that! You're still my prisoner."

He stared at her but didn't say anything.

They walked together. The Lincoln Woods Trail followed an old railroad bed that served the logging industry in the late nineteenth century. They stayed on the trail for a few hundred yards, then entered the woods and headed in a northeasterly direction.

Laurie was on his heels, parting branches with her hands. "It's so nice to bushwhack again," she said.

"We're not going far." Will kicked up the leaves as he walked, humming a tune.

"For a woodsman, you make a lot of noise."

"I want to make sure he knows we're here."

"You think it's a game, don't you? Fox and hound."

He looked back at her. "That's right," he said. "That's exactly what it is."

They stayed close to the Pemigewasset River. In a few hours, they stopped at a clearing on the bank of Cedar Brook. "This should do fine," Will said.

"For what?"

"For whatever the hound has in mind."

She stared at her feet a moment. "I must have been crazy to buy into this," she said.

"Why don't you get into the sleeping bag? You must be tired." He turned away, walked to the edge of the brook, listened to the water rushing over the rocks. He stooped down for a drink when his eye caught something. "I'll be damned!"

"What is it?" Laurie rushed over.

He showed it to her. The oak piece was spherical. "See the knot here. How it's raised?"

"So?"

"Looks like a coin with a duck's head."

"So?"

"So it's nice."

She slumped to the ground and sat, her hand on her forehead. "You're a trip, Will."

"What's the matter?"

"You're wanted for murder, you just stole a truck—and you still have time to add to your stupid collection."

"Stupid!"

"Yes, stupid!"

"But that's what found art is." He tried to explain. "You don't go looking for it. You just find it."

"Jesus."

The oak piece fitted nicely in the palm of his hand. He stuck it in the kangaroo pocket of his anorak. "Every man needs a hobby," he said.

TWENTY-FIVE

THE SUN DROPPED below the tops of the trees. The air turned cool. Will found a tin of baked beans in the pack. He used the small knife on the chain that held the truck keys to open the can. He stuck in two fingers and trenched out some beans. "Want some?" he asked, offering the can to Laurie.

"No, thank you."

He shoved the can at her. "Come on. You've got to eat."

She hesitated, then reached for it. She dipped her fingers into the can and made a face when she ate. She handed it back. "Couldn't you steal something better than beans?" Her hand was shaking.

"You cold?"

"I'm all right."

He chewed slowly, watching her. She shivered. "You are cold."

"Eat your supper."

Will put the can down, unzipped the sleeping bag, and brought it over to her. "Come on. Lie down with me." He put the bag around her shoulders and pulled her to him.

She resisted at first, but he wouldn't let go of her. Finally, she let him hold her.

He guided her slowly down to the bed of leaves. For a few moments, neither spoke. Then Will said: "I've missed holding you."

"Don't talk. Just keep me warm."

"But we have to talk." He tried to look down at her face, but she held him so tightly he couldn't move. "Your badge is digging a hole in my chest," he said.

"It's good for you."

"You want me to suffer?"

"I want you to keep me warm."

"Look at me, Laurie." She stared up at him. He kissed her.

She didn't fight it. Her lips were surprisingly warm. He ran his hand down her side.

She turned her head. "No."

He released her.

She sat up. "Let's not get carried away."

He smiled at her. "It was nice while it lasted, you have to admit."

"It shouldn't have happened. My guard was down."

"You mean I took advantage of you?"

"No. I wanted you to hold me."

"Does that mean things have changed for the better?"

She pulled the sleeping bag tighter. "Don't be smug. I let you kiss me, so what?"

He hesitated. "Laurie. I want to tell you something."

"What?"

"I know how hard this is on you out here. I want you to know I appreciate…"

"Oh, shut up, Will. Just stop talking."

"Sure, okay." Laurie looked away from him. She shivered.

"You're still cold. At least let me hold you, again." he said.

"I'm doing fine, thank you."

"No, you're not. I don't want you to go hypothermic on me." He came closer. "I promise not to try anything."

She let him hold her again. They lay together, the sleeping bag spread over them. He fought sleep, but he knew he couldn't hold out much longer. He had cat-napped most of last night, and the adrenaline spurred by the chase was wearing off. At least one good thing had come out of all of this trouble: He knew he wanted Laurie and he would fight to keep her.

"Sometimes I hate you," she said.

"Are you feeling warmer?"

"And sometimes I don't."

He tucked the bag underneath her legs. "I think you are warmer."

THE MOON ROSE high above the trees. He heard the distant hooting of an owl. Laurie slept in his arms; his arm was numb from cradling her head. He shifted his weight and tried to get comfortable. The wind picked up. When it settled, he heard scratching noises. It sounded like a small animal digging at the bark of a tree.

He slowly pulled his arm from underneath Laurie's head; she stirred but didn't wake; he tucked the sleeping bag around her. He listened and heard the scratching again. This time it was more deliberate. It came from a stand of trees near the bank of the stream.

The rushing water made it harder to pinpoint the scratching—it seemed timed to lure him; whenever he stopped, it began again.

The trees near the brook appeared as dark outlines against the sky. He took careful steps. The leaves rustled under his feet. He had to walk up a slight incline to get to the stand. Where it flattened out he felt something pull at his boot. He heard a metallic ping.

He bent down, and his hand snagged on a long wire. He followed the wire and found a looped pin on the end—nearby, a nest of five hand grenades.

He heard footsteps behind him. Someone was near the stream bank. He could barely make out the dark outline. He didn't move.

The figure walked up the bank. It stepped into the moonlight and Will saw it was Laurie. She had her pistol drawn.

"Over here." His voice was a hoarse whisper.

She approached. "Are you crazy?" she said. "I almost shot you. Next time tell me you're leaving."

"Look at this," he said. He led her to the nest of grenades. "A booby trap."

"What?"

He pointed to the grenade lodged in the center. "That's the one I tripped. See the pin missing?"

She studied the nest. "Are the others live?"

"I doubt it." He stepped back. "It's just the hound playing with us."

She bent down and touched the wire. "I don't know."

"Come on, Laurie. Who else could have done it?"

Laurie didn't answer him.

AT DAWN, Will found fresh footprints. They led away northeast of the stream bed. He followed them for a few minutes, then stopped.

"What's the matter?" Laurie asked.

"Feels like a trap."

She looked behind. "What should we do?"

"I don't know. Let me think."

She sat on the ground and picked up a maple leaf that had turned deep scarlet. "Tell me about the war," she said.

"Why?"

"I know you were in 'Nam, but I don't know what you did."

"Who cares what I did?"

"The hound, maybe?"

He looked down at his boots, placed one on top of a footprint. It was smaller than his size 11, maybe a man's size six or seven. "I try not to think about the war," he said.

"Maybe you should."

"It was a long time ago, Laurie."

"But maybe you did something to somebody."

Could that be true? He tried to think about faces he'd met, an enemy he'd made perhaps, but what came to him instead were visual stills of blood-drenched pantlegs, arms hanging by ten-dons, one kid missing half a face, but still conscious enough to ask for a smoke. It took him years of sleepless nights, but with the help of an army shrink, he'd learned to control the images. They were still there, though—always would be—and it pissed him off that they were so easily conjured. He kicked the ground. "The grenades, the shell casings—all strong physical evidence. But it adds up to nothing."

"Like the earring?"

"Exactly."

"You shouldn't dismiss the evidence so easily."

"Thanks," he said. "I'll take it under advisement." He moved away from her. "Do me a favor and don't ask me anything more about the war."

"I'm trying to help," she said "You're sure there wasn't someone you might have..."

"I didn't go to war to make enemies."

She laughed.

Will spun around. "It isn't that funny."

She started to laugh again but caught it with a hand over her mouth. "Sorry. It's just that you must be the only soldier in history who didn't go to war to make enemies."

"I was a medic."

"Maybe someone's pissed you saved them."

"Look, even if the hound is somebody I knew from 'Nam, it doesn't make any difference. Not now, anyway. We don't have to know who it is, just that he's out there."

"But all the military stuff..."

The wind stirred and swirled leaves that whispered around their feet. "I don't want to talk about it," he said.

"I've heard that line before."

He turned away again, picked up a rock and winged it.

"Are we going to follow the tracks, or what?"

He didn't look at her. She was becoming a liability, getting him thinking about things that might wreck his concentration. He would try one last time. "I think I should take it from here."

She stepped toward him. "This is some macho thing with you, isn't it?"

"No, I just want to do this alone."

"You're not even armed. You think you're Superman?" She poked him in the back. "Some big bully's pushing you around, and you've got to prove who's got the bigger one. It's like your childish refusal to get a lawyer. Your manly duty to go it alone."

He whirled around. "Cut it out!"

"No. You're going to hear this." She jabbed him in the chest. "So far you been treating me like some school marm with a parasol. I've got news for you: I'm no Lois Lane. I'm a cop and you're my prisoner. You tell me to go away one more time, and I'm taking you in. I'll shoot you if I have to."

"You finished?"

"If you heard what I said. If not, I'd be glad to repeat it."

He tried to think of words that would make her go away, some magical incantation, but it was too late for them now. She chose to stay with him, and there was nothing he could do about it.

"You need me," she said. "You can't do this alone." She checked her watch. "You've got three more hours, Will."

He hiked the pack up on his hips and cinched the belt tighter. "Well, Lois, we'd better get tracking."

She punched his arm hard. "You son of a bitch!"

THE TRACKS LED upstream along the bank. They looked as if they had just been made. "We're getting closer," Will said. He held up his hand. "Listen. Did you hear that?"

They stopped. The woods were silent.

"I didn't hear anything," she said.

A gust stirred the leaves overhead. From the distance came a muted chiming.

Will turned to her. "You must have heard that." The wind picked up again and the sound rang clearer. "If that's what I think it is..."

"What?"

"The wind chime. Now you have to believe me."

Laurie strained to listen.

They walked slowly toward the chiming. The sound grew in intensity to an incessant bonging as they approached, as if someone were striking the shell casings with a mallet.

They found the contraption over a small rise suspended from the limb of an old maple.

From a distance, Will couldn't tell what bobbed on a spring in the middle of the shell casings. It looked like a badger or muskrat with feet trussed, a weight dangling from the cord that sounded the metal with each up and down movement.

"What is it?" Laurie asked.

"I'm not sure."

They moved closer.

"My God!" Will said.

Butch the cat danced on the spring, head in a noose, pink tongue poking out the center of his mouth.

TWENTY-SIX

WILL TOOK A STEP toward the wind chime. Laurie grabbed his arm. "Don't touch it."

"I've got to cut him down."

"No. You don't know what's there. It could be wired."

The wind blew and Butch bobbed, his head twirling on the noose. The weight tied to his tail banged against the shell casings.

"We can't leave him like this," he said.

"We have to."

Will turned away. He had prepared himself to face the hound on his own terms and suffer the consequences, but he hadn't counted on anything like this. It sickened him that anyone would do this to a defenseless cat, and it felt like the hound had reached inside his shirt and torn his heart out.

Laurie came to his side and touched his arm.

"He was a good cat," he managed to say after a few moments.

"I know."

They sat there for a while, and the wind was mercifully still. When it began to pick up again, though, his anger started to build. "Let's get this guy," he said. He scoured the area for footprints, his back to Butch, trying to block out the periodic clanging. "Here," he said. "They lead south toward the highway."

Laurie pulled out her pistol. "Let's go."

"Wait a minute. Maybe we should think about this," he said.

"Come on, Will. What's there to think about?"

He motioned for her to be quiet.

She lowered her voice. "I thought you wanted to get this guy?"

"I do. But we ought to work smart." Will scanned the area.

The trees blurred in front of him. "The hound's probably watching us right now, having a big laugh."

"His trail's right here, Will. Even I can see it."

"That's what bothers me: It's too obvious."

"So what do we do?"

"Wait him out."

"So he can ambush us?" She started walking.

HE CAUGHT UP to her at the edge of a clearing.

"Right through here," Laurie said. "See where the branch is broken?" She pointed with the pistol.

Will grabbed her by the belt. "Stay put!" he said.

"I see him!"

Will did, too. It happened in a second, a flash of camouflage clothing as the hound moved beyond their vision.

Laurie yanked herself free and ran into the clearing. She stopped near the center, dropped to the ground and fired.

The report echoed in the woods.

Will ran in a crouch to her side. He lost sight of the hound as he disappeared into the brush at the far end near the tree line.

"I think I hit him," Laurie said. She got to her feet and moved swiftly ahead to the protection of a fallen oak. She waited, then began crossing over to the side where the growth was more dense.

The hound rose up out of the trees, took aim.

Will had a good view of him standing there, his head covered by a balaclava. "Laurie! Look out!"

She dove to the ground just as an arrow slammed into the tree behind her. She rose, firing, and emptied the clip.

Will ran to her position under the cover of her fire. "That's enough," he said. "He's gone."

"I had him."

"You weren't even close." He yanked the arrow from the tree. It was short, made from alloy, a crossbow arrow. He threw it to the ground. "Let's get out of here," he said.

She reloaded. "He can't be too far ahead."

"You can chase him if you want. I'm going another way."

HE HEADED WEST of the clearing, crashing through the underbrush, moving from tree to tree, then turned north. He was making a lot of noise, but he wanted to. The way the hound lured them handily into the clearing proved that Will was up against a proven stalker, someone who had planned his moves ahead. It was up to him to break that rhythm. The forest opened to a pine grove. He picked up the pace, his feet free from cloying underbrush. The terrain dropped into a boulder field. He took off his pack.

Laurie caught up to him. Her hair was tangled and burrs clung to her pants. "I can't believe it," she said. "You let him get away."

He grabbed her by the arms. "Listen to me."

"We flushed him out. Isn't that what you wanted?"

"If you think about it, he was leading us by the nose."

She tried to free herself from his grasp. "Let go!"

"I said listen to me!" He pushed her against a boulder and held her there. "It's a game, remember? As long as we chase, he dictates our movement. We've got to make him follow us."

"And have him at our backs? That's suicide."

"Maybe. But it's my call."

"Your call?"

Will paused. He released his hold. "Look, why don't we both calm down? We have to agree on a few things before we go any farther."

Laurie relaxed her shoulders. "Fine. I'm listening."

"We can't both be making decisions out here; we'll be working against ourselves."

"So, stop fighting me."

"You're going to get us killed."

"You forget one thing."

"What's that?"

"What I say goes. You're still under arrest."

Will shook his head. "The rules have changed, Laurie. The hound is real and he's out there."

"Why should I listen to you?"

"I know these woods! That's one thing we've got over the hound. You have to trust me."

"I don't have to do anything."

"You'd better if you want to stay alive. He could have killed us at any time back there. He led us into the clearing just to show his face, to lure us into chasing."

She hesitated. "You're guessing."

"This guy's been playing with me for months. I know his head. I'm sure he followed me that weekend I went back to Pasaconaway. He planted the earring and tipped off Lamont about Dee's body."

Laurie leaned her back against the boulder. "You really think he's that good?"

"I'm sure I've been under the microscope for months. He had to know I loved to pick up things, otherwise the earring wouldn't have worked. We can't go chasing him all over the place. We need a plan."

"Like what?"

"It's too flat here, and we have to watch all sides. We need to put some distance between us."

"There's nothing new here. You just want to keep running."

"I know exactly where I want to lead him. There's a place where he'd only be able to get at us from one direction. We'll wait for him, then we'll make our move." He put the pack on. "Well?"

She sighed. "We'll try it." She picked burrs off her shirt. "For a while, anyway."

THEY RAN EAST on the Wilderness Trail to a junction and turned north up the Thoreau Falls Trail. In another mile or so they reached Jumping Brook. Will checked the sky. The sun told him it was almost noon. They went off trail, followed the brook due west, hopping rocks. The brook led them slowly uphill.

"I need to rest," Laurie said.

"Soon. Keep moving."

"Where are we going?"

Will didn't answer, but pushed on. The sky was clear above

the trees. The air was cool near the rushing water where the brook widened. He walked across a large flat rock and moved back into the woods. He waited for her to catch up, and they rested in a thicket with a clear view of the brook.

He held up his hand for silence and watched the rushing water as it coursed downhill. No sign of the hound. He turned to her. "He won't come upstream, it's too exposed," he said. "Our rear end's covered from the west, down the slope of Mount Guyot. He'll have to cross the stream if he comes from the north."

"Which leaves the east."

"That's my bet."

"And we just wait him out?"

"You said you needed a rest." Laurie stretched out her legs. "Why don't you close your eyes and try to sleep," he said.

"I can't."

"Try. I'll take the first watch."

She rubbed the arms of her jacket for warmth, lay down and curled up in the leaves.

Will focused on the trees in front, his eyes shifting. He was in a stand of birch whose leaves had long since fallen. His view was clear except for a patch of spruce trees.

"I lost it back there, didn't I?" she said.

"Go to sleep. We'll talk about it later."

The sun dropped behind Guyot and the shadows grew long.

Despite her protests, Laurie slept.

Will dozed, too. When he shook himself awake, the light was falling fast.

HE HEARD A LOW rushing noise coming from the spruce grove. At first he thought it was the wind, but the sound kept coming when the wind settled. Then he understood: a gas stove. The hound was cooking dinner.

He woke Laurie. "Follow me." His boots crunched through the brush. He stopped, then took another step and waited. He saw the light from the stove.

The hound stooped over it, cast in shadow. They could hear him humming to himself above the rush of the stove.

Will motioned for Laurie to move to the hound's flank and indicated he would approach in a straight line. He moved forward in a crouch.

The hound had chosen to make camp in a small depression shielded by the trees. It was good cover. Will's approach would not be easily detected—unless it was a trap, and the hound was waiting for him.

The thought stopped him. Should he hold off for better light? It was too late to pull back; Laurie was circling. The hound huddled over the stove; Will could see part of his back through the trees. He had not moved since Will first spotted him.

Will took careful steps and reached the line of spruce. The stove rushed and intermingled with the hound's humming. But it was a different sound now, like the hound was putting words to the music.

He moved through a space in the thick growth and studied the ground ahead to make sure he wouldn't stumble on anything. The hound was just a few feet away.

Will sprang from the trees and tackled his tormentor, but he wrestled with air—there was nothing but coat and stuffing. The hound had propped up the camo jacket over a small spruce.

Laurie appeared out of the cover of trees, her pistol leveled.

Will threw the coat on the ground, followed the sound of the singing and picked up a tape recorder. He turned up the volume.

Laurie came to his side. She took the tape recorder from Will and hit Fast Forward, then Play, twice. "These are all Jonathan Tyler songs," she said as she shut it off.

The water boiling on the stove bubbled over. Will turned the stove down and sat in front of it.

"What are you doing?" Laurie whispered. "We've got to get out of here."

"Where to?"

She sat next to him. "He knows we're here."

"If we move, he'll just follow. He wants us to panic."

"So, what do we do?"

He turned to her. "I think we should make tea."

TWENTY-SEVEN

WILL POURED the tea water by the light of the stove, shut it off and they sat in darkness.

"I can't stand the thought of him out there looking at us," Laurie said.

Will blew on the tea and took a sip. "What's the big deal?"

"I don't know how you can be so casual about it."

"He's been watching us since that night you walked out on me, Laurie."

"What!"

"This is a surprise? I thought you knew."

She blew over the top of her cup. "You're just trying to scare me."

"The hound was in the house. How else would Butch have gotten out? The window latches from the inside."

"You mean he was watching us in bed."

"That's exactly what I mean."

"Good God."

Will dumped out the dregs of his tea. "If you'd listen to me, you might have found out sooner."

Laurie was silent. She shivered and wrapped both hands around her cup for warmth.

"Anyway, he won't bother us tonight."

"How do you know?"

"I keep telling you to trust me."

"We have to do something. We just can't keep running from him."

"Patience." He set his cup down and lay back, his hands behind his neck. "He's going to make a mistake."

"Listen to me, Will. You may know these woods, but you're a lousy tactician."

"Keep your voice down, will you?"

"Why? He knows we're here. What difference does it make?"

"I'll say it again." His voice cracked when he forced a whisper. "Part of his game is to set us against each other. I would prefer he didn't hear us arguing."

She moved closer to him: "I'm not arguing. I just think we should do more."

"Like what?"

"Split up. Can you track him in the morning?"

"Most likely."

"We'll start off like we're moving together. When his trail gets hot, I'll veer off but keep you in sight. You flush him out and I'll drop him."

"It won't work. He's too smart for that."

She shifted away from him. "You give him too much credit. He's got you hoodwinked."

"You know, Laurie," he said. "I think you're the one turning this into a macho thing."

She slammed her cup down. Part of the tea water spilled on her hand and she shook it. "Shit."

"You okay?"

"What I'm suggesting makes sense."

"Yeah?"

"It's a classic military tactic."

"What the hell do you know about the military?"

"A pincer movement."

"What about divide and conquer? I'm sure he wants us to separate."

"Just try it my way for once. It'll force his hand." She crept closer to him. "We can't stay out here forever."

Will didn't say anything for a moment. He closed his eyes and replayed Butch bobbing in the middle of the wind chimes. He wanted one good shot at the hound. That's all. One good shot.

"So, what do you think?"

"We'll talk about it in the morning. You take the first watch."

"Exactly what am I watching for?"

"Just stay awake, will you?"

"You said the hound wasn't going to bother us tonight."

His eyelids were heavy with fatigue. "I don't want to argue." He draped his arm over his eyes.

"Will?"

"What is it now?"

"The tape. The Jonathan Tyler songs. Isn't that proof that he's involved with this?"

"I don't know," he said, and fell asleep.

WILL DIDN'T KNOW if he heard something in his sleep or had been dreaming, but when he woke with a start the hound was standing in the dawn mist twenty yards in front of him, his lower body hidden by scrub pine. He had recovered his camo coat. The balaclava hid his face. He held the crossbow casually draped over one arm.

"Who are you?" Will said.

The hound didn't answer.

Laurie stirred next to him.

Will got to his feet. "Talk!"

The hound raised his crossbow and pulled the trigger. The arrow zipped by Will's ear.

Laurie drew her pistol and returned fire. The round hit a spruce tree above the hound's head. It left a deep white cut.

She fired again. The hound disappeared in the mist.

"You think I got him?"

"No."

"Come on!" She ran over to where the hound had been standing. Will caught up to her. "Damn it," she said. "Where is he?"

The hound came into view again. He had skirted around to his left and moved up the slope. He raised the crossbow. The arrow snapped into the brush to their right.

Laurie pumped several rounds into the mist, like shooting at a ghost. "You trail him," she said. "I'll be on your right."

"No. We have to stay together."

She ignored him and moved uphill deeper into the woods through a thicket of deadfall.

He caught up to her and grabbed her arm. "Are you trying to get us both killed?"

Suddenly, the hound let loose a high pitched wail, like the cry of wounded animal.

Will felt a chill run along the base of his neck.

Laurie turned to him, her eyes wide, but didn't say anything. She moved to Will's flank.

Will headed in the direction of the scream. He picked up the hound's trail and followed it. The terrain rose steeply as he pushed through patches of dense growth.

WILL COULD HEAR Laurie to his flank keeping pace. He kept telling himself that she was right: If she could just maneuver into a clear line of sight, it would be over. But in the back of his mind was the nagging sense he was playing the hound's game again. The hound had caught them off guard, rising from sleep, lured them into chasing without thinking. Will stepped cautiously, mindful of branches that might be booby-trapped.

Soon, the terrain flattened, then dropped into a deep ravine. The mist began to lift. He stared down at the trail left by the hound. The tracks were clear, but there was no sign of him.

The forest floor was thick with deadfall. He had to scramble over several blowdowns to stay on the hound's course. At the bottom of the ravine, he stopped and listened for Laurie's footfalls. A squirrel chattered annoyance nearby, interrupting his concentration.

He picked up the hound's footprints again and found the track moving off to his left. He started following, but his eye caught other prints heading the opposite way.

He did a quick search of the area and discovered more. They led off in various directions like spokes on a wheel.

In an instant Will understood. The hound had set the tracks earlier and led him into a web of choices. He looked up at the sides of the ravine. The best way out was the way he came in.

"Laurie," he yelled. He called her name again.

The sound of his voice set the squirrel nagging.

HE WAS ALMOST at the top of the ravine when he heard the first shot. It echoed down the back side of Guyot. Another report. Two more in rapid succession. The last helped him zero in on their location.

He discovered the hound's trail again ten yards ahead. The prints told him the hound had doubled back at the top of the ravine, that he hadn't even descended.

Less than fifty yards down the slope he found where the hound and Laurie had struggled. The ground was stirred up and lower branches were broken off trees. He dropped to one knee and searched through the leaves. No sign of blood.

He examined the area. As far as he could tell, where Laurie had fought him off was confined to a ten-foot diameter. He defined a circle, walked to the edge of it, and began working along the perimeter. He leaned over as he moved, his eyes pinned to the ground.

The discipline involved in the tracking helped quiet his rage. He could see where the hound had jumped her, where she put up a good fight. The leaves were matted, indicating he must have thrown her to the ground and held her there.

Closing in toward the center he found a spent shell casing. Then another. Laurie must have stood and fired at him. He reminded himself there were four shots. He rummaged through the leaves and found two others, but couldn't locate the third. He pocketed what he had.

He worked his way back to the perimeter again, this time searching outward. He discovered the hound's and Laurie's footprints heading in a northerly direction. Laurie was walking on her own, but her gait was uneven. Still no blood.

He began following their tracks, though it was difficult to mask his footfalls becasue the whole area, like the ravine, was tinder dry with deadfall. He moved slowly, afraid to pick up the pace. He took a step and heard something behind—then another, stopped, and listened.

A gust blew up suddenly. Branches clacked above his head. The wind settled, leaving an anxious silence.

He began walking again, his ear tuned. There was a crunch of brush behind. This time he was sure. He was being matched, step for step.

He turned.

The hound stood with crossbow raised.

Will dove to the ground. He rolled behind a small maple and heard the thung of the crossbow as it released. The arrow pounded into the tree. He waited for the hound's approach but nothing happened. He eased around the tree.

The hound had vanished again.

He found the arrow. There was a note attached:

> *Hey, Will!*
> *She's dead if you don't catch me.*

The note was scrawled in pencil. He examined the handwriting to see if he could recognize it, but the block lettering didn't offer any clues. He put it in his pocket and took stock. The hound had captured Laurie, but it also meant he wouldn't be able to move as fast. Alone, Will had the ability to adjust more quickly. It was a small advantage, but he was grateful for anything that might tip the scales his way.

He headed back to where the hound had confronted him and found where his footprints led uphill; Will traced them to another spot. The brush was flattened where Laurie must have been tied up while the hound was busy shooting at him. He soon located a double set of tracks that traversed the slope, then headed in a more northerly direction.

The hound wanted him to chase, and he had to oblige. But if he kept his head, he still might force the guy to make a mistake. He thought of Grandpa Hank and told himself to stay focused.

Soon, the hound's track turned to the west, directly up the slope of Mt. Guyot. Above, there was nothing but dense growth until he could hit the trails that skirted the ridge. It would be tough going toward the top.

Despite the difficulty of the terrain, the hound and Laurie moved fast. In a few hours, Will knew they were all getting close to the top. At times, the trees were so stunted and packed together he had to get on his hands and knees to crawl through. He ripped a hole in the sleeve of his anorak.

Dark clouds gathered above his head. They moved across the sun, sent showers, then moved away.

It was near noon when he finally broke on to Twinway, the trail that traverses Mt. Guyot. The tracks were easy to pick up. It was off season, and the rain had helped. Laurie's steel-tapped service shoes had a star on the heel prints. They were headed south toward Mt. Bond. He couldn't be that far behind.

Walking along the trail out of the underbrush felt like being released from prison. He thought of running to catch up but settled on a steady pace, concerned he might come upon them suddenly, putting Laurie in more danger.

A half mile past the access path to the Mt. Guyot shelter, he lost Laurie's prints. He went off trail to see if he could pick them up, but there was nothing there. What he did find was more of the hound's. He followed them back to the trail. He bent down and traced the boot heel with his hand. It looked like army issue.

The wind was picking up from the north, blowing away the front. The air was cold and dry.

He remembered the note: "She's dead if you don't catch me." It said nothing about catching Laurie. The hound must have carried her off trail. With luck, Will might be able to find where he left her, but it would be a long shot.

It was clear the hound wanted him to keep chasing and Will sensed why: from the beginning, all the hound wanted was to torment him and then force a confrontation. But why? Suddenly Will thought of something that stopped him in his tracks. He recalled the starred entries in the Book of Revelation, and one line especially: "Behold, the devil is about to throw some of you into prison, that you may be tested, and for ten days you will have tribulation." Yes, it was all starting to make sense, and he would soon find out who had been testing him. With Laurie out of the way, it would come down to the two of them—and he was ready.

WILL HEADED SOUTH on the Bondcliff Trail following the hound's footprints. The trail dropped down into a col and then ran up to the summit of Mt. Bond. Blue sky poked through racing clouds, and the sun drove hard against the cliff.

From the summit of Mt. Bond, Will stuck to the trail that rolled slightly and ran the ridge under the protection of trees. He was soon above tree line and the cliff that bore the trail's name opened up before him. It followed close to the ridge, marked by cairns, neatly piled rocks that show the way in open terrain. The wind howled and cut through his anorak.

He knew if he stayed close to the cairns, they would lead him around the edge of the cliff and back into the woods farther along the trail. He was exposed out here, and he sensed the hound chose the cliffs for that reason.

He moved away from the trail near a large cairn and proceeded to the southwest, down the bald face. He retraced his steps and returned to the cairn, then headed parallel to the trail until he found a depression in the rock large enough to hide in. He had no idea if the hound had been watching, but he had a good view of the trail from either direction. He was out of the wind and the sun poured down.

THE CLIFFS opened views of Mt. Lafayette and Mt. Liberty to the west. The granite top tilted downward at a sharp angle, then fell off on to craggy ledges.

Will had led one SMOOT trip up here and swore he would never do it again. It had taken him more than two hours to talk a student with vertigo off the rock. There was really no danger of falling as long as the cairns were followed, but the fear of stepping into dizzying space was constant.

He had never been off trail this far down on the rock. He knew as soon as the sun went down he would have to seek the shelter of the woods. He decided to give it another hour. He huddled inside the depression, his feet digging into the downhill slope.

Then, out of the cover of trees came the hound. He stalked in a crouch, his face still hidden by his balaclava, holding the cross-bow in one hand.

Will ducked his head, sure the hound hadn't spotted him.

The hound knelt and ran his hand along the rock, then moved in Will's direction. He reached the cairn where Will had set the false trail, faced west and paused.

He was only twenty feet away and Will could hear him humming. Something about the tune stirred inside him.

This was the first time he could watch the hound without trees in the way or an arrow aimed at his head. The way he carried himself seemed familiar, and Will was convinced he was no stranger. He knew him from somewhere—maybe long ago—but he knew him.

The hound paused, then followed the false trail toward the edge of the cliffs.

Will knew it was his chance to move now, with the hound's back to him. He stood and was about to take a step toward him, when the hound suddenly stopped.

Will ducked back into the depression of rock.

The hound surveyed the area. He had only followed the trail a few feet when he must have realized the ruse. He walked back up to the cairn and sat on a rock, holding the crossbow over his knees. Will sensed the hound knew he was near, and like a patient hunter was waiting for his prey to move. But Will wouldn't flinch; he'd outwait the guy.

Soon, the hound was humming again. Then, without warning, he broke into song:

Oh, hard is the fortune of all womankind
They're always controlled, they're always confined...

The voice! It was sweet and clear—one he hadn't heard for a long time.

"My God," he said, the words out before he could control his surprise.

He stood.

The hound rose slowly.

They faced each other across the open expanse of rock.

TWENTY-EIGHT

THE HOUND STOPPED and peeled off the balaclava, and with a quick toss of her head, let loose her long hair. The voice had prepared him, but he still couldn't believe it: Grace Diccico.

She smiled. "Hello, Will."

"Where's Laurie?"

"Never mind about her; she's unimportant." He took a step closer. "Keep your distance!"

"What have you done to her?"

"You should be worrying about yourself." He took another step. "Stay there!" She trained the crossbow on him. "Sit!" He complied. "Good dog." She squatted in front of him, the crossbow at her side.

Will studied her. She hadn't changed much in twenty-five years—only harder, more muscular. "Why, Grace?"

"Why what?"

"Why the games?"

She smiled at him. "Let's say it's just part of the plan."

"The plan?"

"An agreement I have with God."

There was a cool serenity about her that was unnerving. An agreement with God? He thought about the Bible in Franco's closet. "Where's your partner?"

She smiled. "I don't know who you're talking about."

"Franco Delacorte."

"Never heard of him."

"Those *were* your clothes in the duffel bag in his apartment, weren't they? And your Bible."

She shrugged. "Whatever you say, Mr. Smart Guy."

Yes. It had to be. The shock of seeing Grace was beginning to wear off, replaced by a strong sense of vindication. He had been right: Franco had been involved from the beginning. "Tell me more about this agreement with God."

"What do you want to know?"

"Did the agreement include killing Dee?"

She paused. "She wouldn't behave."

Will thought a moment. "And Jeanne, too. That's why the earrings. Why you planted them to make it look like I did it."

"I had to. For Jonathan's sake."

"Jonathan! You're telling me Jonathan Tyler knows about this?"

"Of course not. Jonathan would never be involved in anything like this. He's pure, like fire! He's been touched by God!"

Her outburst didn't surprise him. He had seen this intensity before—in fact, the last time he and Grace were together. They'd been in a bar. She was hysterical because Jonathan had gone off to the islands with Jeanne. At the time, he thought she was just angry over the split-up of the group and not with their love affair. He hadn't been much help consoling Grace, his own jealousy raging. He remembered getting drunk, leaving Grace with her head slumped on the table.

Grace stared at him. Her eyes were motionless as glass. "It was the women," she said. "They were confusing him. He never lost his love for me; he only forgot it for a while. But now Jonathan has only me."

The women. He understood now that Grace's mission was to get rid of all of rivals, to have Jonathan for her own—all under the guise of some bogus divine prophecy that gave her freedom to kill. He thought of Dee's cold, China-doll body lying stretched out at Pasaconaway. He spat at her feet. "Jonathan Tyler doesn't even know you're alive."

Her eyes narrowed. "You're an evil man."

He watched as she sat back against a rock. "I haven't done anything to you," he said. His eye caught a knife strapped in a scabbard to her leg. If he could keep her talking, then he might be able to distract her enough to make a lunge for it. "Tell me about the Book of Revelation."

The question brought her up short. "It's a holy book," she said. "It should not be talked about."

"Why did you star those particular passages?"

She looked up at the sky. "They are my instructions."

So it was her Bible in the duffel bag. Her clothes.

"I was there for him," she said. Her voice was distant, wistful. "I made that song famous for him." She turned her head and looked hard at Will. "And what did he do? He dumped me for Jeanne. And you know how that happened, don't you? You remember the night; I know you do. You're the one who introduced Jeanne to him; you're the one who started this whole mess. You're an evil man."

"It wasn't my fault."

"Don't try to deny it."

So, this was his crime. In her eyes he was the one who caused Jonathan to turn from her. But was it a real affair she had with Jonathan? Will doubted it. "Is that why you're torturing me?"

"I'm preparing you." She sat up, got on her knees. "Please. Won't you pray with me?"

"What!"

"Help me pray for your soul." She held her hands out in an attitude of supplication.

"Save your prayers for yourself," Will said.

"That isn't nice, Will. You wouldn't want to add blasphemy to your sins."

"Blasphemy?"

"God's will and peace hath blessed me." She raised her hands and widened her eyes. "He hath said that if I prepare you for hell, he will allow Jonathan and me to be together for eternity." Her voice rose higher. "What you have suffered on earth is nothing compared to what you'll see in the bowels of hell. Oh, the horrors, the stench of hellfire and brimstone, the screams when you can't pluck from your eye the worm that feeds on it." She jabbed a finger at him. "Evil man. I have been sent to deliver you."

Will watched her. The words flowed easily off her tongue, full of bitterness and corruption. "I think I understand," he said. "When I'm out of the way, you'll kill Jonathan."

She didn't say anything.

"Then yourself. Is that it?"

She lifted her hands toward the sky. "Then we'll all be free."

Will saw his chance and lunged. He tackled her, brought her down, and grabbed for the knife strapped to her leg.

He forced his full weight on top of her. He could feel her wiry strength as she fought him. He had to release pressure on her other leg to grab the hilt. He yanked the knife out of the sheath.

She squirmed, freed her foot, and kicked.

The blow caught his shoulder and forced him back, but he had the knife. He brought it above his head and thrust downward.

Grace deflected the strike with her forearm.

He sat on her and tried to pin her down. He ground the heel of his hand under her nose as she grabbed his throat and squeezed. Her grip was strong and he felt his arms going numb. He tried to stab once more, but she brought her knee up and caught him in the groin. He rolled off, sucking for breath.

She stood above him. "Get up!"

He fought to get to his knees. He still had the knife.

"Come on. Kill me. I'm waiting."

If he could just get back far enough, he could throw the knife. He stepped away from her in a crouch. He felt the slant of the granite becoming severe under his feet and tried to move uphill around her position.

She stalked him, one arm forward, the other cocked next to her ear, coiled to strike. "Where are you going, Will? I'm here." Her legs seemed to move separate from her body on pivots, her ankles hinged, feet sure on the granite as she moved forward, her trunk turned sideways. She closed in on him.

He took the knife by the blade and raised it above his head.

In an instant, she had made up the space between them. Her foot kicked high and struck his arm. The knife shot out of his hand. It rose in the air, fell on the ledge, and slid downward. It came to rest at the edge of the cliff.

She laughed. "Now look what you've done," she said. "You

made me lose my knife.'' She bent her knee, and her leg shot forward.

Her heel caught him flush on his face. He heard the crack as his nose caved in. He fell backwards and rolled, the pitch increasing his speed as he scrabbled for purchase. He finally came to a stop toward the edge of the cliff. His fingers felt on fire from trying to grab rock. He heard her voice above him: ''While you're down there, get my knife!''

He tried to focus on her, but she was a blur of camoflage. He attempted to stand but his legs collapsed. His rage blinded him. ''Get it yourself!'' He tasted blood in his mouth.

She was down on him in a few swift movements.

He crouched and tried to shield himself from what he expected was coming. He heard her laugh.

''You are pathetic, you know that?'' she said.

''Why don't you just kill me?''

''When I'm ready. Now, get my knife.''

He spat blood. ''When I'm ready.''

''Oh, you are an evil man, Will Buchanan. You're beginning to anger me. But I guess I can't expect much when chivalry is dead.'' She moved toward the edge of the cliff and bent to retrieve the knife.

Will stumbled to his feet, rushed her. She seemed far away, and his legs couldn't bring her closer. He imagined their struggle—then sailing through the air in an odd embrace.

She turned.

He was expected. The blows came as he tried to cover himself. But he would not die. He would not give her that satisfaction.

WHEN HE REGAINED consciousness the sun was dropping over Mt. Liberty. The wind had died.

Grace sat with knees drawn up, watching. The knife was in the sheath on her leg. The crossbow lay beside her. ''Welcome back,'' she said.

He struggled to clear his vision. ''You didn't finish the job?''

''I wasn't trying to kill you.''

He touched his face, his nose. "You're going to pay for this, Grace."

"My conscience is free."

"How can you say that after all those deaths?"

"God's will."

"You honestly think Jonathan will have anything to do with you once he finds out?"

She shook her head. "You seem preoccupied with Jonathan and me."

"I find it interesting."

"I'm taking him to another place. Far away. One radiant and pure."

"And I'll be there to haunt you."

"You? You couldn't even save your cat!" She turned away from his gaze and picked up the crossbow. "Get up, Will."

The mention of Butch stirred his guts. He fought to stay in control. "I don't think you want to kill me, Grace."

"I said to get up."

Will pushed himself to his feet.

She smiled. "Let's just have one more game, shall we?"

"You want to torture me some more?"

"It'll be fun. Rock Hide 'n' Seek. It's something new I just invented." She looked pleased with herself. "I turn my back. I give you five minutes. Then I look for you. You have to stay on rock, though. That's the rule."

"You just can't kill me at close range, can you?"

"Let's go. While there's still light." She loaded the crossbow and turned her back. She began walking up the slab. "One one thousand, two one thousand..."

She was giving him a chance to get away, but what kind of chance was it? His groin was on fire. She had hurt him just enough so that he could move, but not move far. His legs protested, burning from welts and bruises, but there was nothing broken down there. His busted nose gave him trouble breathing.

He searched for a good spot to hide, but there was none. A rock outcropping near the edge seemed the only place. He headed for it, then changed his mind. Too obvious. She would know right away.

He could see her back still turned to him. There was no place to go. A rigged game.

The sun had gone down over Liberty's ridge, the twilight heavy. If he could just buy time, make darkness come.

But it was too late. Grace wheeled. "Here I come, ready or not." She stared down at him.

He was in the open, close to the edge of the cliff. He didn't move.

She scrambled toward him. "What are you doing?" she yelled. "You're not playing the game right." She stopped twenty yards in front of him.

"This isn't a game, Grace. I have no place to hide."

"What do you mean? There are plenty of places."

He gestured with his arms. "Where?"

Grace looked around. She pointed to the rock outcropping Will had avoided.

"Where else?"

"What do you mean, where else? I'm supposed to find places for you?"

Stall. Stall. "Give me five more minutes. Let me look around."

"No."

"This is a turkey shoot." His mind raced, seeking options. He had to get her focus off the game. An image of the Bible in the duffel bag came to him. He raised his hands, not in surrender, but in prayer. "And in the end, the Lord God will save me. He will minister unto my soul. He will ensure me justice in the afterlife. He is preparing a table before me in the presence of mine enemies. My cup runneth over."

"Stop it. Blasphemer!"

"When the arrow is loosed, He will strike. Right now, He is damning your soul to everlasting hell."

She smiled. "Dying is easy, Will. It's God's poetry." She raised the crossbow.

The arrow struck him in the stomach, pushing him backward.

He tried to regain his footing, but his toe caught the edge and he tumbled into space. For a moment he felt suspended, like he was gliding in a calm wind, feeling nothing. Then he was falling harder, with the wind singing in his ears. A curious peace settled over him. He was ready to fall forever beyond the sun, but something abruptly stopped his journey.

He looked up: The sky was dark above his head; the stars danced. Was he still alive? He became aware of his hands; they were clinging to something. So he wasn't dead. He looked down at a yawning blackness. Slowly, he understood: A small ledge, sprouting tough-minded spruce growth had broken his fall.

He could feel the arrow boring through his middle. He closed his eyes, waiting for death.

TWENTY-NINE

THE DARKNESS behind his eyelids was deeper than the night. He was thankful there was no pain, but he was afraid to look at the wound. He lay there thinking it was only a matter of time before it would all be over.

When he opened his eyes the sky was rose-colored, the dawn light a milky gray. He was still on the ledge. He looked down. Mist rose from the crevasse below. He felt dizzy and held on. He had been dangling there all night. He tried to steady himself. He hugged the rock face and stood.

The protruding arrow scraped the rock when he moved. He had not looked at the wound for fear of what he would see. He finally found the courage to run his hand down the shaft of the arrow. It was lodged firmly in his stomach. He pulled his hand away and look at it. No blood. He wiped his hand on the anorak where the arrow had entered and checked it again. His hand was clean. Something wasn't right, but still he couldn't bring himself to look at the wound. He grasped the shaft, this time pressing it against his stomach.

Then he understood. A small cry of wonder escaped his lips. The found art! The arrow had pierced the palm-sized piece of oak in the pocket of his anorak.

The joy was short-lived. He wasn't dead, but his reprieve was only good as long as his wits could keep him alive.

He held on and studied the cliff. The face was ragged, marked by a series of ledges. If he had fallen a little more to his right he would have plunged another hundred feet to a ledge below. He looked up and estimated the distance to the top to be about twenty feet. Did Grace know he was there?

She probably saw him lying on the ledge after the fall with the arrow sticking out of his middle. But it was almost dark. She would wait until morning to make sure he was dead. He had to climb out before she came back to check.

He tested his legs. They were stiff from the beating, but they moved. The pitch of the cliff looked to be a 5.8 or 5.9—not the toughest climb, but a mid-range challenge for sure. As a younger man, Will had led climbs higher in grade, but this would truly be a free climb. If he slipped, there would be no rope to catch his fall, and he had to rely on boots, not rock shoes.

He tried to pry the arrow from the piece of oak, but it was stuck. He stabilized himself, slipped off his anorak, and tied it around his middle. The arrow rested on the small of his back.

He began the climb. He told himself to keep looking at his feet, to concentrate. He had difficulty feeling the rock through his boots, but he climbed in a zone of intensity, choosing each move in a deliberate manner. As he moved up the cliff, he felt the sun warming his back. He was going to make it.

It went well for the first few moves, his boots holding on the dew-soaked granite. But when he brought up his leg to a flake that had served as a previous handhold, it suddenly gave way. He could feel his other foot slipping as he transferred his weight. He scraped at the ledge with his boot, but the flimsy toehold gave way.

He dangled from his arms, momentarily. He knew he couldn't hold this position for long, and his stretched tendons began to burn. He was almost there, damn it! He was almost there.

He pushed higher with his right leg and the edge of his boot caught a knob. He put his weight on the leg and rested a second. The knob held, but soon he began to lose strength in his leg—it began to shake, what climbers call a sewing machine leg. At best, he knew he had one move left in him. His breath came in short gasps, and he fought panic. His left hand began to slip. He gathered his strength and pushed hard against the knob with his leg, and at the same time shot his left hand upwards, hoping to snag a blind handhold. His fingers found a small crack. He dug them in and hung on. He brought his left leg up and found a small shelf. He pressed his boot in and immediately relieved the tension on his left leg. He hung there for a while, getting his breathing back to normal.

The cliff edge was just above his head. He fought the urge to grab for it. He was too close to make a mistake. He steadied himself. Slowly, he moved his right leg higher and shifted his weight. He released pressure from his left foot and drove it higher. His left hand could reach the edge, now. He had a nice handhold. He pulled himself up and over.

HE SCANNED the broad expanse of granite. Grace was nowhere to be seen. He headed for the rock outcropping and hid behind it.

Perhaps she wouldn't return. He would be free, then. He would know what to tell the police. They would pick her up and lock her away for good. But if she did come back, if she found him no longer on the ledge, her pursuit would be relentless.

Will untied the anorak around his waist, put it on. The arrow still stuck through the piece of oak and protruded in front. He again worked to dislodge it, but it wouldn't budge. He gave up and watched the slab for movement. As he waited, a plan began to form. The arrow was key. He had surprise on his side.

He didn't have to wait long. Even though he had prepared himself, Grace's entrance onto the slab sent a chill through him. He watched her dart toward the edge of the cliff and warred with himself to stay put or follow through on his plan. He would be the ghost of Will Buchanan, replete with an arrow through his middle. It was a long shot, but he felt he understood her thinking, knew her fears.

He waited until she reached the place he had stood last night before plummeting over the edge. He slipped away from the outcropping of rock.

Grace knelt and looked down into the abyss, her back to him.

Will walked softly and made it to the spot where she had fired the crossbow, and placed his feet where she had stood. He raised his arms in the same attitude of prayer he had used the previous night. "Grace!" he intoned.

She spun. When she saw him, her mouth dropped open. She let the crossbow fall, and it clattered on the rock.

"Your arrow can fly but it cannot kill," Will said. "You have killed too many!"

"No!"

"As long as you live I will follow. The Lord God has spoken! He has said the word." Will took a step toward her. Then another.

Grace grabbed the crossbow. "You're an evil demon!"

Will kept walking, his arms held high.

She reached for an arrow in a quiver on her belt. Her hands shook as she tried to pull one out.

Will moved faster. He stopped a few feet in front of her and pointed his finger. He gathered the full strength of his voice. "You are the evil one! You are condemned to crawl on your belly in the bowels of the earth."

Grace started to raise the crossbow, then stumbled. Her foot hit the edge, and she struggled for balance. The crossbow sailed from her hand and flew over the edge, looking like a bird shot from the sky.

He closed the distance.

She reached out for him, but it was too late. One foot gave way. Their eyes met for a brief instant as she struggled for balance. She smiled at him, as if to say even now he couldn't win. Then her eyes grew wide in horror, and she fell, clawing at the air. She screamed, the same high-pitched wail he had heard when she had stalked him, and it grew louder as she fell, echoing off the cliff walls until she hit the ledge a hundred feet below. Then there was silence.

WILL DROPPED TO his knees and stared down at Grace on the ledge for a long time, expecting her to rise up to meet him for one last standoff. He swore he saw her soul separate from the body, watched it ascend, then plunge as her screams echoed again in the chasm. He shook his head to clear his vision, rubbed sweat from his eyes. He looked down again, not trusting she was dead, but her body didn't move.

It was over. He had done it. He became aware of how close his boots were to the edge. He backed off, turned, and began walking up the rock ledge to the trail. The relief he felt was momentary, though, for his thoughts soon focused on Laurie. There was a chance she was still alive and he had to find her. He stumbled across the rock face, trying to locate the cairn-marked trail that would lead him back to Guyot.

Following the trail helped clear his head. He tried to think how long Laurie'd been missing, tried to separate time in the blur of his memory. He made it to where the trail entered the woods and kept a steady pace as it dropped down into the col. He stumbled in a bend in the trail and fell. It was only when he turned around that he realized he'd been tripped.

FRANCO DELACORTE held a pistol on him. "You've really made a mess of things, don't you think?"

Will stared at Franco, then at the pistol: Laurie's stainless steel Smith & Wesson 659. "You were watching. You saw everything."

"And I'm afraid there's more work for you." Franco clucked. "You shouldn't have done that to Grace."

"I didn't do anything; she fell."

"After you scared the shit out of her. Pretty clever, I must admit."

Will's mind was spinning. "So, all along you were working together."

Franco laughed. "That's right, my friend."

"From the start," Will said. "I mean—you were the one who put the coat on Butch."

"He was a feisty sonnavabitch, that one."

"He was a good cat. Tell me, Franco, did you have a fun time stringing him up like that? Did it make you feel like a big man?"

Franco shrugged. "Wasn't my doing. Grace seemed to enjoy it, though."

"What did you do? Watch?"

"Never mind. Get up."

"Where are we going?"

"To pick up climbing gear." Franco grabbed Will by the hood of his anorak and forced him to his feet. "Grace has something I want," he said. "You're going to get it for me."

Franco walked behind him, poking him with the pistol, until they reached the bottom of the col. "Through there," he said. He gestured to the east, off the trail.

There was nothing but a thick growth of juniper bushes. "Where?"

"To the left."

Will parted branches and a space opened up. He moved in farther from the trail and saw Laurie.

She was tied up, her mouth taped.

He turned to Franco. "Let her go," he said.

"She'll be all right. She's resourceful."

Will went over to Laurie. She shook her head as he approached. There was fear in her eyes.

Franco yanked him by the sleeve. "Get the rope," he said. "And that pack."

Will looked around the clearing. For the first time, he was aware of the cache of food, the climbing gear. "A moveable feast," he said.

"Yeah. And I'm sick of moving it. You are a slippery bastard."

He picked up the climbing rope. "This is from your closet, isn't it?"

"My closet?"

"In your apartment. When you were away. It was Grace who came back to get it, right? You must have forgotten it. And it was her duffel bag under the bed. The one with the Bible in it."

Franco looked puzzled for a moment, then his face brightened. "Buchanan, I'm surprised at you; you sneaked around my apartment. You really can't be trusted."

Will opened the pack. Inside, a rack of climbing gear—nuts, chocks, slings, friends—even jumars, mechanical fixed-line ascenders. "Planning an assault on Everest?"

Franco chuckled. "Not really. More like a descent."

"You want me to go down on that ledge?"

"That's right. It's really a bother, I know, but you have only yourself to blame."

"It's my fault?"

"Of course. I had my money on Grace. I thought you were a goner."

"What is it, Franco? What's Grace got that you want so bad?"

"Dog tags."

"You want me to retrieve dog tags?"

"That's right. It's all fitting and proper, don't you think? A good dog like you must have a proper set of tags."

"You're a funny man, Franco."

"Let's go."

"Wait a minute. You mean if Grace had done me in, you would have killed her for the tags?"

"It had come to that. After Grace killed Dee, she just wasn't the same. This was supposed to be a simple kidnapping." His hand flexed on the pistol grip. He aimed the pistol at Will's eyes. "It was an accident."

"I don't believe it for a minute."

"Believe what you want."

"Face it, Franco. Grace suckered you. She told you it was going to be a kidnapping to get your help. She was going to kill Dee from the start. What a chump!"

Franco raised the pistol and struck him.

THIRTY

THE CLIMBING ROPE WAS tied in a butterfly coil. Will flung it on his back and attached both loose ends around his middle. He took one last look at Laurie. The lines of fatigue on her face were deeply etched.

"Don't forget the pack," Franco said.

Will hefted it. "You could help out, you know."

"I've carried that thing enough. Get moving." He shoved Will's shoulder with the pistol.

"You don't have to keep doing that."

"No. I guess I don't." He jabbed him again.

Back on the trail, the sun was riding high, beating down on them. Warm air blew gusts in their faces from the south. Indian Summer had indeed arrived, and Will fantasized about throwing Franco over the side so he could stretch out on a rock slab and sleep in the sun. His bones ached and he carried his tiredness like an extra load on his back. Maybe if he got Franco talking, he might get distracted and leave him an opening to pounce. "How did she get you to do it, Franco?" Will asked. "She just call you up and say, 'Hey, let's kidnap Jonathan Tyler's daughter'?"

He laughed. "It was a little more involved than that."

"Tell me about it."

"Just keep walking."

They started uphill out of the cold. Will stopped.

"What are you doing?" Franco asked.

He pointed to his boot. "My lace is undone." He dropped the pack and knelt to tie it.

"I'm watching you, Will." Delacorte said, holding the pistol on him. "Don't try any funny business."

"You're not going to shoot me, Franco."

"I'm not, huh?"

"Not yet, anyway. You need me to fetch those tags."

"Just tie the damn boot."

"The thing I don't understand is how you got the job teaching at Saxton Mills. Was that part of the plan?"

"It's none of your business."

"Come on, Franco. Tell me. What have you got to lose?" He finished knotting the lace and looked at him.

The familiar smirk appeared. "Let's just say our original plan didn't hinge on my employment, but getting the job meant I could have more fun. It was my idea to approach Perry. I came cheap. I made myself irresistible." He winked. "You know how I can do that, right?"

Will nodded. "Your social skills are the source of great envy."

The smirk turned into a broad smile. "Ah, Will. I'm going to miss our little encounters. They've been wonderful fun."

"Your file. Are you really a Ph.D?"

"What do you think?"

"I think you're less than truthful."

"In that case, you wouldn't believe me if I told you."

"It's all fabricated, isn't it?"

He sighed. "Oh, I do so many things, it's hard to keep track. I'm a professional itinerant. I like to keep moving." He held the pistol to Will's head. "So, let's go."

"How many languages do you know, anyway?"

"Enough to get by."

"You going to tell me what's on the tags?"

"No."

"Ah, come on."

"Anticipation is all, Will."

In another half hour they reached Bondcliff.

Will dropped the pack, and untied the rope around his middle. "Okay. Now what?"

"You figure it out."

"There's no place to tie in, Franco."

"Plenty of pitons in the pack."

"Pitons! You want me to desecrate this rock? I'm disappointed in you."

Franco laughed. "Sorry, I'm no purist." He caught his breath, then laughed some more.

"What's so damn funny?"

"Your nose, Will. You really ought to get it fixed. It tends to light up when you get excited."

His nose must have been something to see because it felt like it belonged on a much larger man's face. It was swollen and sore. When he looked down, it actually blocked part of his vision, like he was looking over the hood of a car.

Will dumped out the contents of the pack. The gear scattered on the rock and made a racket. He picked through it, and found a piton and a hammer. He turned to Franco, hammer in hand.

"Don't even try," Franco said.

"What?"

"I know what you're thinking—you're just dying to throw it at me."

"You have no idea what I'm thinking." Will walked toward the edge of the cliff, found a fissure in the rock and began banging in the piton—a V-shaped metal wedge, like a spike, with a circle cut out of one end to attach a sling or a carabiner—a metal ellipse with a gate on one side that pushes inward to hook onto something or slip a rope through.

The rock was warm to the touch. The metal clanged as he pounded. Will hadn't used pitons for years, and they were certainly out of fashion in the climbing community—too much environmental impact, something that Franco could care less about. "Truth is," Will said, "I want to stick around to watch you fail. You're screwed." He whacked the piton one last time. "You'll never make it."

"I guess we have a difference of opinion."

"Without Grace, you're lost."

"You should be thankful for my voice of reason. Oh, the things she wanted to do to you."

"I should thank you?"

"You don't know the half of it."

"Which one of you shot Lamont?" Franco hesitated. "Come on. I'm curious."

He smiled. "You know what happens to cats that get curious."

Will pointed the hammer at him. "I'll say it again: Killing Butch was rotten. Far too heavy-handed for you, Franco."

"I told you I had nothing to do with that. Grace was just doing her thing."

"Yeah. And I'm the tooth fairy."

"I argued against it, I tell you. I liked the old boy."

"Well, we know who was boss then, don't we?"

Franco smiled. "You're not going to make me mad, Will. So you can just stop trying."

Will paused. "She shot Lamont, didn't she?"

"Of course. She's much better at that sort of thing."

"And you drove the car?"

"I'm a much better driver."

"Figures."

"What's that supposed to mean?"

"Means you don't have a stomach for blood."

Franco's hand flexed on the pistol. "That's a theory you probably shouldn't test. I'm too close now, Will. I can smell it."

Will got to his feet. "Stinks, doesn't it?" He let the hammer drop.

"Get ready," Franco said. "I'll start setting up the rope."

"You mean you're going to help?"

"Just hurry up, will you!"

The climbing harness still had the price tag on it. All the equipment looked fresh out of the box. "How did you know you'd need this stuff, anyway?"

"We were prepared for anything; Grace was quite meticulous."

"And look where it got her."

"She wasn't always lost. Shame really. I know you don't believe me, but killing Dee wasn't part of our original plan. That's the truth. I only came on board for the ransom money."

"But Grace had other ideas. She wasn't interested in the ransom to begin with."

"I don't know how you can be so sure."

"The Bible tells me so."

"The Bible?"

"See Chapter Two, verse Twenty-three of the Book of Revelation. She suckered you, Franco."

Franco exhaled loudly. "Yes, you've said that already."

"What a loser."

Franco smiled. "I haven't lost yet."

Will studied him. "You going to tell me what's on the tags?"

Franco uncoiled the rope. "Plan B," he said. He handed Will a rope end. "It's time."

Will located a figure-8 rappel device in the pile. The device is named after its shape, but the figure is irregular with a smaller circle of metal, used for attaching to harnesses, sitting on top of a larger circle which guides the rope through on the rappel. Using a locking carabiner, one with a threaded gate, he attached the smaller circle of the figure-8 to the climbing harness. "She would have killed you," Will said. "You know that. You knew too much."

"You're probably right."

"Just like Lamont."

"That man loved to dig."

"He knew about you, then?" Will asked, surprised.

"Let's just say he was getting close."

"Grace probably gave herself away with all the meddling."

"I tried to get her to stop calling the police station, but she was having too much fun setting you up."

Will took a step toward him. "Kind of ironic, isn't it?"

"What?"

"Her games are going to drag you down, instead. I'm sure Lamont had you in his sights. The FBI knows about you."

Franco sucked at the corner of his mouth. "It doesn't matter. I'll be out of here, soon."

"I doubt that."

"Sure I will. It's going to take a while for them to sort this all out. By that time I'll be long gone."

"Did you have to shoot Lamont?"

Franco chuckled. "Grace thought he was the devil." He paused. "Actually I think she was more concerned with keeping you alive. Lamont was taking her toy away and she wasn't finished playing yet. You made a great pawn, Will." He walked over to the pile of climbing gear, grabbed carabiners and slings. "I'd love to talk more, but we've got to get busy."

"Am I'm supposed to climb back up here? That face is at least a five-ten."

"The top part's the hardest. We're actually standing on a roof that extends over a cut in the granite. From the side, it's a big scoop, like an apostrophe. You'll have to dangle a bit on your rappel. Coming back up, I think a fixed rope ascension is appropriate. Just pack the etriers, the daisy chains, the ascenders, and you should be fine."

Will shook his head. "For a bungler in the woods you talk a good game."

"There's a lot you don't know about me, my friend."

Will had seen what Franco had described off to his left on his way up the face that morning. The rappel wouldn't be half as scary as the free climb, but Grace had hit the ledge farther down and to the left of where he had fallen, and coming back up on a fixed line would take some time.

Will drove two more pitons into the rock to make a three-point anchor. He attached a locking carabiner to each piton and ran a sling through them. He adjusted the sling so the loop ends met and were self-equalizing, then joined them with two more carabiners.

Franco handed him the climbing rope. Will inserted the end through the two carabiners attached to the sling—the arrangement acting as a runner for the rope—and tied off to his harness with a double figure-8 knot on a bite. He double-checked the carabiners to make sure the gates were offset, a safety measure to ensure that the rope would not slip out.

He released the figure-8 rappel device from his harness, made a loop in the rope, and pushed it under and through the larger circle of the figure-8, then tugged it over and under the smaller circle. He clipped back into his harness and put pressure on the rope to test for tension and drag.

Franco coiled the loose end of the rope and tossed it over the edge. "No screw ups," he said. "Just get those tags and get back up here."

WILL STEPPED OFF the edge and let out rope. It slithered through the figure-8 ring, and he dropped farther down. His hand on the loose end of the rope, he pushed it against his hip, and felt the rope tug against the ring. He made his way over the lip of the roof, then dangled in space as he fed out rope, and braked himself periodically to control his descent past the scoop in the rock face. Soon, his feet met rock again, and he rested.

He looked down at Grace on the ledge. She didn't seem much closer. He pushed away from the rock, released pressure on his brake hand at the same time, and dropped another ten feet. Up and off to his right, he saw the ledge he had landed on the night before, the tough spruce growth that had broken his fall.

Directly above, Franco was watching. "Keep going," he yelled.

Will focused on the mechanics of the rappel: releasing his brake hand, stepping out, letting the rope slide through the ring. When he figured he was at least three quarters of the way down, he stopped and checked his position.

He could see Grace clearly. She had fallen on her back, one leg skewed across the other at an extreme angle. Her eyes were wide open.

When he reached the ledge, he swung to the right to avoid stepping on her. He touched down with little difficulty.

The ledge was about five feet wide—not much room to maneuver. He closed Grace's eyes, slid his hand down to her neck, reached in under her shirt, found the tags, gave a yank on the chain, and snapped it.

The tags looked like they were made of gold. There were numbers stamped on them. He shoved them into the pocket of his anorak.

Franco's voice boomed from above: "Did you find them?"

Will took his pack off.

"What's taking so long?" Franco yelled.

Will ignored him. He stayed on the ledge with Grace. It was now Franco's move.

THIRTY-ONE

WITH HER EYES CLOSED, Grace looked at peace. Will studied her leg. She had a compound fracture; the white shattered bone end of her tibia had burst through the skin. He tried to line the leg up to the other one but it wouldn't straighten out; the tendons had contracted. He found her knife still strapped to the broken leg, removed the sheath, strapped it on his leg, pulled the knife from the sheath and hefted it. It was the survival type, one a Navy Seal might wear.

He glanced toward the sun, closed his eyes, and let the sun's warmth seep in. He imagined throwing the knife, hearing the thud as it hit Franco's chest. Fatigue settled over him, and he slept.

At first, he thought the rumble overhead came from a dream, but it didn't go away. He got to his feet. Then he saw it, a helicopter heading north toward Guyot. The dull thumping grew more distant. It stayed its northerly course, then shifted toward the east and disappeared.

It meant others were out looking. If he could just hold off, buy time.

From above, Franco's voice hurtled down: "Hey, Will."

He looked up.

Because of distance and perspective, Franco's head was no bigger than a tennis ball. Then another tiny head appeared, and he could barely make out that Franco had Laurie by the hair. He forced her head over the edge of the cliff. "I wonder if she can fly?"

"Let go of her!" He could barely hear what Franco was saying, but it didn't matter. He knew he would have to go back up on the line.

Franco pushed Laurie forward until her arms dangled over the cliff. She hung limply and didn't struggle or scream.

Will admired her strength. She wouldn't give Franco the satisfaction. "All right," he yelled. "I'm coming."

Franco gave Laurie a tug and she disappeared over the top.

Will knelt down. "Say goodnight, Gracie," he said, and rolled her off the ledge.

AN ASCENDER EMPLOYS a cam that allows it to slip freely on the rope in one direction but grip tight when pulled the opposite way. Will clamped it onto the rope and tested it.

He attached a daisy chain, a sling with sewn-in loops, to the ascender, and clipped the other end into his harness.

He prepared another ascender in the same manner. The idea was to push the devices up the rope, the top first, then the other, as he climbed.

To provide a place to stand as he moved up the rope, he also clipped in etriers to each ascender, ladder-like slings he could step into.

He put on the pack and started to climb.

He slipped the top ascender up the rope, and placed his right foot into a loop on the etrier and stood. He then pushed the bottom ascender upwards, which, in turn, raised the etrier attached to it. He lifted his left foot and stuck it through a loop higher than where he was currently standing and shifted his weight. He nudged the top ascender farther up the rope and began the process again.

After ten feet of climbing, he stopped. Since he was still tied into the rope, the upwards movement meant he was dragging the end of the rope with him, creating a large loop. He pulled up the excess rope and re-tied himself into the harness closer to where he was actually standing. In that way, if the mechanical devices failed, he wouldn't plummet the length of the rope. He reminded himself to do this periodically.

The afternoon sun beat against the cliff wall, but it was losing its intensity. The air was noticeably cooler as he climbed past the scoop in the rock. It took him a little more than a half hour to reach the top. He grabbed for a handhold on the rock and hauled himself over.

FRANCO HELD THE PISTOL on him. "Okay, where are they?"

"What's that, Franco?"

"Come on. Hand them over." He pointed the pistol at Laurie and fired. The shot ricocheted off the rock in back of her.

"Hey, take it easy!" Will reached into his pocket. "Here they are. See?" He held the tags out for him.

"Just put them down and back off."

Will looked at the tags in his hand, then threw them. They caught the air and landed a few yards up the rock slope.

"You just had to do that, didn't you?" Franco said.

"It made me feel good."

Franco scrambled for the tags.

Will lifted his pant leg and slipped Grace's knife out of the sheath. He waited for his chance.

In the distance, the helicopter veered and headed back toward the cliffs. The blades throbbed and beat the air.

Franco turned, tags in hand, and searched the sky.

In one swift motion, Will let the knife fly.

It caught Franco in the shoulder. He stumbled and fell to the rock. The pistol dropped from his hand.

Will rushed him.

Franco saw him coming and fumbled for the weapon. He picked it up and fired.

The shot hit at Will's feet, splintering rock.

Laurie screamed at him: "Over here!"

He ran back to her.

She grabbed his arms and pulled him behind the rock where she was hiding. "Are you crazy?" she said.

"I think I hurt him." He looked at her. Her face was puffed and swollen. "You okay?"

"Am *I* okay? Have you looked in a mirror lately?"

He peered over the rock to check on Franco. As far as he could tell, the knife was still lodged in his shoulder. All his woodsman's practice throwing axes and knives had paid off, but still he was disappointed. He had aimed for Franco's heart.

Franco fired again. This time the shot sailed high.

Laurie tugged on his sleeve. "Stay down! You don't need to do anything—we've got help."

The helicopter rose out of the chasm and hovered over them. Franco shot at the helicopter and took off up the slope.

Will pulled himself free from Laurie's grasp and went after him.

"Damn it, Will!"

The prop wash from the helicopter kicked up pebbles and sand. Will squinted to keep from being blinded.

Franco was slow. He had trouble keeping his feet.

Will thought about closing in on him, but he still had the pistol. Better to keep him in sight. Let him run himself out.

Franco followed the cairn-marked trail. He reached the edge of the woods where the trail dropped down into the col. He turned and fired. He pulled the trigger again, but nothing happened. He let the pistol fall. It skidded down the rock face and came to rest below the trail.

Will could see it, but he left it there. He wanted Franco, and with a knife stuck in his shoulder and no pistol, it would be easy to catch up to him. He looked behind at the hovering helicopter. A ladder dropped. By the time he turned back, Franco had disappeared.

Will found blood on the rock at the top, where the trail entered the woods. He followed Franco's tracks that led down the trail into the col.

There was blood-soaked ground near the bottom of the col where Franco had fallen. The scratch lines in the dirt indicated he had dragged himself to the side of the trail. He had struggled to his feet again, using the scrub growth along the edge of trail to pull himself up.

Then Will heard him. He was just a few yards ahead off trail, beyond sight in the brush, thrashing his way toward the cache. Will took a few steps toward the sound and hesitated. He had to be careful; this was like tracking a wounded animal. He chose an indirect route.

When he reached the clearing, Franco was waiting for him with what looked like an AK-47 in his hands. Franco laughed.

His body began to shake and he winced at the pain. His face twisted into a smile. "Gotcha."

Will watched him teeter, then catch himself. He took a step toward him.

Franco set off a few bursts of the AK-47. The shots raked the brush at his feet. "Don't even try," he said.

Will didn't move.

"You shouldn't have bothered following. You're no match for me." Franco slapped the rifle. "I told you, Grace was prepared for anything."

"How's the shoulder?"

"I must admit, that was a hell of a shot." He struggled for balance again.

"You can't hang on much longer."

Franco raised the weapon. "I'm going to enjoy this." He sprayed bullets into the ground.

Will dove for cover, rolling through the brush that lined the edge of the clearing.

Franco fired wildly in short bursts. "Stand still, you son of a bitch!"

The rounds crashed above Will's head. He crawled on his belly over a small rise and dropped down behind it, hugged the ground as a hail of bullets slapped the earth in front of him. He could hear Franco stumbling toward him.

Franco shredded the top of a juniper bush to Will's right.

Will stayed put. There was a lull in the firing, and he guessed Franco was catching his breath. He feinted left, then ran until the brush tripped him up.

Franco sprayed the air in a wide swath of erratic fire.

If he could keep from getting hit, he knew Franco couldn't chase for long. He heard the distant pulsing of the helicopter again; the search was still on. He doubted the commotion of the AK-47 would be enough to give away their position, but if he tried to flag the chopper down he would make himself an easy target for Franco. The helicopter veered to the west, near the cliff edge, then headed back in their direction.

Franco's weapon was suddenly quiet again.

Will took a chance. He stood in a crouch. He could see Franco clutching his shoulder, studying the movement of the helicopter. Will took off.

Franco fired but the shots were off line.

Will ran for several yards, then dropped to the ground. He saw a thick patch of brush to his left and crawled to it, pulling himself forward on his elbows.

The chopper came closer; flying low to the ground it whipped the trees above his head. The sound beat against him in concussive waves.

Will guessed Franco was hiding, that he wouldn't signal their position by firing at the chopper. As soon as it roared over his head, Will rose out of the brush and started running again. He didn't look back.

There was no response from Franco's weapon. Will dodged through spaces in the thick brush until he dropped down near a small stand of spruce. He waited and listened.

The helicopter, now a dot in the sky, was circling back to the west.

Then he heard Franco: "They've all gone home, Will." He coughed and spat.

Will tried to gauge the distance of his voice. He could hear the brush crackling under Franco's feet as he came toward him.

"I know where you are," Franco said.

Will doubted it. Franco hadn't fired at him for what seemed a long time. He would stay in his position.

Franco coughed again and staggered toward him. He was getting closer, close enough for Will to hear the touch of the scrub growth against his pant leg. His breathing was labored. He coughed and spat again.

Will began to second guess his decision to stay put. His deep mistrust of Franco kept playing on his nerves. Maybe Franco knew exactly where he was and the lack of fire was just another head game. It didn't take long for the answer.

The automatic weapon came to life.

Splinters showered over him. He ducked and covered his head with his arms. He crawled on his belly out of the stand of spruce.

On the other side, toward the east, the terrain opened up into a boulder field with thick blueberry patches. He had somehow maneuvered himself into the open.

He glanced at the sky and picked up the helicopter flying a zig zag course back in his direction. He ripped his shirt off and began waving it just as Franco showed himself.

Franco set off a few rounds at Will's feet. "They can't see you, Will," he said.

Will let his hand fall, his fingers still looped in the shirt. "You don't have to kill me."

"But I want to."

"They'll find you; they know where you are."

Franco winced. He had lost a lot of blood.

Will watched him closely. He couldn't just let him fire away. The chopper moved in a straight line now, dipping close to the ground. They must have spotted him waving.

Franco raised the AK-47 to waist height. "It's been fun, Will."

Will wanted to charge, but his feet wouldn't move. He stood, lulled by the sound of the helicopter bearing down on them. He had been wounded once in the arm. It felt like hot ice. He imagined lasers cutting into him.

The shot came from Will's right.

Franco's head snapped back and he fell heavily to the ground. Will turned.

Laurie held the Smith & Wesson straight out in both hands. Slowly, she brought the weapon down. She let it fall to the ground and walked toward him.

THIRTY-TWO

WILL PULLED HIMSELF from sleep and stared at the clock: almost 9:30—but was it morning or night? It had been the better part of a week now since he'd come out of the woods. After two days in the hospital he had spent most of it in his apartment, sleeping.

He rolled out of bed and lifted up the blanket he had tacked over the window. The light hit his eyes, and he let the blanket drop. He considered it a good sign he was up at all.

He sat on the bed and held his face in both hands. He remembered that Laurie's deputy, Ray Carson, had been to check on him saying that Laurie was back in the office and that he'd patrol, keep reporters at bay. But how long ago was that? Maybe it was just a dream. Maybe it was all just a dream.

He thought about going back to sleep but soon became aware of his sides aching. His kidneys were bloated. He threw on his robe, stumbled to the bathroom, and released a torrent into the bowl. He lifted his head and stared at the strips of peeled paint on the ceiling as he relieved himself.

When he finished, he tried to escape without looking at the mirror over the sink, but it was a wide oval and difficult to ignore. He switched on the light and pondered the image that stared back at him. His nose looked like it belonged in a clown's makeup kit. His face was still swollen, his eyes raccooned in deep purple.

He stepped back, not believing the image belonged to him, when his eye caught the reflection of Butch's empty cat bed on the floor. He left quickly, slamming the door behind him.

He leaned his back against the door and closed his eyes. An image flashed of Butch bobbing in the wind chime. He headed down the hallway, drawn by the morning light pouring into the living room.

In the kitchen he made coffee. As he waited for it to drip, he leaned his elbows on the counter and stared through the slats in the blinds. Light seemed to be pulling him into the world, but he wasn't sure he wanted to come back.

Just then the doorbell rang. He thought it might be Ray or Laurie, but when he opened the door he found Anita.

"Mr. Buchanan? Is it okay to come in?" Behind Anita stood Michiko. She looked up at him with dark eyes. Patty and Elsa brought up the rear. The only person missing from the SMOOT group was Dee.

"Sure. You're welcome any time."

"Not according to that cop who keeps chasing us," Anita said.

So, he hadn't dreamt it. Laurie was back at work. Will led them into the living room. When he sat down, he realized they were staring at him like he was on exhibit. "I apologize for my appearance."

"Oh, no. Don't even think about it," Anita said. She turned to the girls: "We understand, don't we?"

The girls nodded and Michiko giggled.

"What exactly do you understand?"

"Oh, we've read everything about it," Anita said. She sighed and looked at him with big moon eyes.

Will had seen the look before, but it was usually reserved for rock stars like Jonathan Tyler. He squirmed in the chair. "It was nice of you to come over."

"Oh, we won't stay long," Anita said. "We just wanted to tell you how much we miss you at school."

"And we hope you'll come back soon," Michiko chimed in.

Will looked at their faces. They were full of light.

Elsa pulled something from inside her coat. "And we wanted to give you this." It was a kitten. It mewed as she handed it to him.

Will took it from her. It was so tiny, he could hold it curled in one hand. He brought it close to his chest.

Anita's face turned serious. "We thought about getting you a big Angora like Butch, but we fell in love with this one. It's kind of a cross, but mostly a yellow tabby."

Will didn't know what to say.

"Well, we'd better be going," Anita said. "I hope we didn't bother you."

"No. Not at all." He felt the kitten purring against him. "Listen. Does it have a name?"

Anita smiled. "Oh, about fifty or so."

The girls laughed.

"We couldn't decide so we're leaving it up to you," Elsa said. "We hope you like it."

Will stroked the kitten's head. "Thank you," he said.

After the girls left, he put on a sweatshirt and jeans. He threw on a coat and stepped outside. The sun was bright on his face. He set the kitten down and watched it bat at leaves that flew through the air.

"Mr. Buchanan?" Will turned, saw Berkeley Hutter. "It's a nice kitten, isn't it?"

"What are you doing here? Shouldn't you be in class?"

"I'm just missing a study period. I wanted to come with the girls, but they wouldn't let me. They said the kitten was a gift from the SMOOT group and that I didn't belong. I rode my bike over anyway."

The kitten found an acorn and tried to handle it with both paws, but it kept popping out.

Will walked up to Berkeley and placed a hand on his shoulder. "It's okay. I appreciate you wanting to be here."

"It's not fair, Mr. Buchanan. I wanted to help pay for the kitten, but they wouldn't let me."

Will smiled. "Maybe you could get it a new collar."

Berkeley brightened. "Yeah. That's a good idea."

Will snapped his fingers and called to the kitten. Amazing. It actually came to him. He scooped it up. It seemed to like being held. He turned to Berkeley. "You should get back to school before you get into trouble."

"I know. I guess you'll be back soon, too."

"Probably next week sometime."

Berkeley smiled. "That'll be great." He stroked the kitten's head. He looked up at Will. "See you next week, then."

"Thanks for coming over, Berkeley." He was almost out of the yard when Will called to him. "How's Mr. Malboeuf?"

Berkeley looked back at him. "He's okay. You were right. You just have to keep your distance."

WILL WATCHED AS Berkeley disappeared around the corner of the apartment. He stuck the kitten inside his coat and began walking toward the police station.

The sun slid behind cumulus clouds ushering in cold air. It wouldn't be long before the first real snow. Will snugged the kitten closer. He liked the feel of it purring against him.

The walk to town was just under a mile, but after a few yards he wondered if it was a good idea. His body ached, each step an effort, but the bite in the air made him feel alive. He pushed on down Pleasant Street, past bungalows built during the heyday of the logging industry.

As his legs warmed up, he began to feel human again. It was as if he had spent the last week in a cave and was finally set free. He reveled in the sounds of the traffic blowing by, in the simple act of an elderly man raking leaves in his yard.

When he took a left down Islington he was aware of someone following. He thought nothing of it at first until he realized whoever was behind him was trying to match his footsteps. He stopped and bent to tie his shoe. Out of the corner of his eye, he saw a man wearing dark glasses, his hands thrust into the pockets of a wool overcoat. He was looking away at traffic.

Will adjusted the kitten in his coat and began walking again. He picked up the pace, but the man stayed on his heels. When he reached the corner of Center Street, he crossed, went past the front window of LaPierre's Market, and ducked into the alley between the market and Sander's Hardware. He braced himself against the wall, and waited.

The man had slowed down, but he was still coming. Then he stopped.

Will could hear him breathing. He said, "What do you want?"

The man stuck his head around the corner of the building.

Will studied his face. "Christ, it's you."

"Mr. Tyler wants to see you."

"So what?"

Peter walked toward him, adjusting his gloves. "You coming with me?"

Will smirked. "Suck eggs."

Peter grabbed him by the jacket.

Will straight-armed him. "Get your hands off me!" The kitten squirmed inside his jacket.

Jonathan's voice came from the front of the alley: "That's enough, Peter." Peter held on. "I said, let him go."

Peter slowly relaxed his grip.

Will shoved him away.

Jonathan stepped closer. "Bring the limo around, Peter."

"Mr. Tyler. I don't think..."

"Do it!"

As the big dog watched, he began to feel human again. It was as if he had waited his last breath in a daze and was finally set free. He revelled in the sounds of the night, down by, and the scuttle-act of an elderly man raking leaves in his yard.

Will saw the now-silent down in front of him. He was aware of him no following. He thought nothing of it at first until he realized who ever was behind him: there was Trung. As though the familiar dog stepped and came to the impasse. Out on the corner of his eye, he saw a man running once; close, his hands clutched into his pockets in a tired overcoat. He was looking away at traffic.

Will nudged the kitten in his coat and began walking again. He picked up the pace, but the animal stayed on his back. When he reached the corner of Chase Street, he crossed a were and the man shadowed Lawrence's Market, and ducked into the alley between the market and Sondler's hardware. He backed himself against the wall, and waited.

The man had slowed once, but became still dropping. Then he stopped.

Will could hear him breathing, the safer, "What do you want?"

The man stood, his limo beneath the canopy of the building. Will smiled. It said, "Christ, it's you?"

THIRTY-THREE

"WHAT DO YOU WANT, Jonathan?"

"I want to know about Grace. What she told you."

"Grace was sick. What she said made no sense."

"I've been reading the papers."

"Probably not a good idea." The kitten felt tense inside his coat. The little claws kept digging in.

"It's true, isn't it? She carried this thing for me since the group split."

"Like a cancer."

"She loved me that much?"

"Like I said, Grace was sick."

"But you can understand it, can't you? You know what it means to love like that."

Will pulled the kitten out of his coat. He ran his hand down the length of its back to calm it down. "It was a rotten thing you did back then."

"I seem to recall you were the one who left the group."

"And why did I leave, Jonathan?"

"Jeanne went with me because she chose to."

"After you lured her with dreams of making it big."

"I didn't kidnap her, for God's sake." Jonathan's voice cracked.

"Poor choice of words," Will said.

The limo appeared in the front of the alley. Will could see Peter watching them through the driver's-side window. "Look. Why don't you just get in the car and drive away."

"I can't understand it. Why now? Why did Grace wait so long to do this?"

"I've thought about that myself. I think it's the re-release of those old songs that did it. That was about six months ago, right?''

"You think that's it?''

"It had 'Waggoner's Lad' on it. Maybe Grace didn't like it. Come to think of it, neither did I.''

"You still get your royalties.''

"You've got a big heart, Jonathan.''

Jonathan didn't respond. He reached inside his coat. "I have something for you.''

"I don't want anything from you.''

"It's Jeanne's journal. I want you to read the entry from your last visit.''

"What the hell are you doing with it? I'm sure what she wrote wasn't for your eyes.'' Will forced his way past him. Jonathan grabbed his arm. "Let go of me!'' Will said.

"She still loved you. Don't you want to hear about it?''

"No.'' Jonathan's hand felt small on his arm. "It's taken a long time, Jonathan. Too long, but I'm ready to move on. I suggest you do the same.''

"I don't think I can.''

"Then you might end up like Grace.''

Will pulled away from him and walked out of the alley. Jonathan followed. Peter got out of the car and stepped in front of Will. "It's okay, Peter.'' Jonathan said. "We're finished.''

Will stared at Peter, "You should do something about your lackey, Jonathan. His manners are atrocious.''

Peter's eye twitched. He looked ready to strike.

"Let's get out of here,'' Jonathan said.

Peter walked back to the limo, opened the door for Jonathan.

Will watched as the limo pulled away and slowly disappeared. He put the kitten inside his coat again, with her head sticking out, which he stroked gently. Soon she began to purr. It seemed a miracle he could calm her down.

LAURIE WAS SORTING through folders at her desk when Will walked into the police station. She let the folders drop and walked over to him. "You're feeling better, I guess.''

"Out and about." He pulled the kitten out from under his jacket. "See my present?"

Laurie looked at it. "That's nice." She returned to her work, opened a folder, and spread the papers out on the desk.

Will rubbed the kitten's neck. "I don't get it. Women usually go goo goo over kittens."

She looked up from the desk. "I'm sorry. I guess I'm a little preoccupied. Let me see the little dumpling."

Will handed her the kitten. "I knew you were capable of goo goo."

Laurie frowned. "Maybe you should go back to bed."

"Feel perfectly fine."

"I don't know. If you're saying things like 'goo goo' maybe your head's still on crooked." Laurie rubbed the kitten's neck. "Does it have a name?"

"Not yet. The girls from the SMOOT group gave it to me."

"How thoughtful."

"It doesn't look anything like Butch."

"Probably a good thing." She lifted it up. "It's a girl."

"We could call it Bitch."

"Very funny." She handed it back to him.

"Actually, it'll be nice having a female around the house," he said.

"Too bad she doesn't cook and sew."

"I was thinking more in the line of sensitivity training."

Laurie smiled. "You could call her EST."

"Too severe. Maybe Gloria. You know, after Gloria Steinem."

"You want to stand on your doorstep and yell 'Gloria'?"

Will put the kitten on the desk. He put both hands on her waist and pulled Laurie to him. "No. I want you to stand on my doorstep and yell 'Gloria.'" He kissed her.

"Will! Cut it out!" She pushed him away and retreated behind the desk. She straightened her uniform and brushed hair away from her face. She pointed to the kitten. "Get that thing off my desk."

"Thing?" He picked up the kitten and sat on the edge of the desk. "Gloria, did you hear what she called you?"

Laurie shook her head. "You're really not going to call it Gloria, are you?"

"Why not?"

"Because it's a stupid name for a cat." She sat back in her chair.

"That's what you said about Butch." Will got up from the desk. He held the kitten an arms' length. "Okay, Gloria. I guess we know when we're not wanted."

"Don't go yet, Will."

"I thought you wanted us to leave."

"A few things happened you should know about."

"Yes?"

"Lamont came out of his coma."

"He's alive?"

"I talked with him this morning. He has a partial paralysis, but he'll make it."

"I'll have to send him some cigars."

"They won't let him smoke."

"I'll smuggle them in."

"He also wanted you to know he thought it was Grace who kept giving him the phone tips. That's why he demanded you go up to Pasaconaway."

"And also how he knew I was away that weekend retracing the SMOOT route."

"That, too."

"I guessed as much." Will stroked the kitten's neck.

"You wouldn't believe Grace's story. It's all here," she said, tapping a folder. "FBI reports."

"I'm sure it's a hell of a read."

"Did you know she was in Vietnam?"

"At this point nothing surprises me."

"She was a pilot and so good at it she was a trainer."

"Amazing Grace."

"She flew a lot of recon missions through army intelligence. That's where she met Franco. He was a top decoder."

"Of course. That explains a lot." Will paused. "Did she join up right after the group split?"

"No. She dropped out of sight for a while. We know she spent some time in a fundamentalist commune before she enlisted."

"And that was the start."

"The start of what?"

"Grace going down the tubes."

Laurie hesitated, then picked up the folder. "You know, there's a lot of information here, but none of it tells me why she did it."

"I know. At least I think I do."

Laurie sat back in her chair. "I'm listening."

Will told her about Grace and the connection with the Book of Revelation, how she thought God would grant her heavenly peace with Jonathan if she got rid of all the females vying for his attention, how she would earn this only by putting her enemies, Will Buchanan in particular, through a series of trials before killing them, leaving only Grace and Jonathan—murder/suicide would complete the plan. When he finished his explanation he said, "I'm still a little confused about the dog tags, though."

"Maybe I can help you there," Laurie said. "After the war, Grace flew drugs out of Columbia. She made a lot of money."

Will snapped his fingers. "And probably stashed it in a Zurich Bank."

"You've got it."

It was all coming clear now. "And the account numbers were on the tags."

"Engraved in fourteen-karat gold."

"God, no wonder Franco wanted them."

"It's all in here," Laurie said. "I can't let you take this stuff, but you're free to read what you want."

"I want you to tell me the story."

"I don't have time."

"You can stretch it out—for years if you want." She looked at him, but didn't say anything. She turned back to her desk and sat in the chair. He followed her. "I've been thinking of telling

Perry I'm not going to run a dorm next year. I'm going to get my own place."

"That'll be nice," she said.

He took her hands, and pulled her gently from the chair. "I know what you're going to tell me. You're not sure about things, that you're going to need time. That's fine." He tried to kiss her, but she turned her head. "Look," he said. "The only thing I'm after is a commitment to have dinner tonight. Can that be arranged?" She broke away from him. "Come on, Laurie. I thought things were better between us."

She hesitated. "There's some unfinished business."

"It can wait, whatever it is."

She shook her head. "I guess you're right. We'll take care of it after you've fully recovered."

He placed the cat on the desk. "Okay. Let's have it."

"You sure? I hate to do this after what you've been through— it's nothing personal."

"For Christ's sake, will you just tell me?"

"You remember the truck you stole?"

"Yeah. So?"

She searched the desk and found an official looking form. She handed it to him.

He looked at it. "A warrant?"

"It was the duct tape that did it. Mr. J. Wilcox Handy thinks you went a little overboard when you tied him up. It took him two days to get the tape out of his hair."

Will looked up from the document. He forced a smile. "This is a joke, right?"

"No joke."

"The guy's pressing charges? Doesn't he realize there were special circumstances?"

"Just a piece of tape over his mouth would have been enough. You wrapped him up like a Christmas present."

Will ran a hand through his hair. "This guy—what's his name again?"

"J. Wilcox Handy."

He smiled at her. "Come on, you've got to be making this up."

"I'm not."

"Nobody has a name like J. Wilcox Handy."

She took the document out of his hand. "I'm serious, Will."

He watched her as she found a manila folder on the desk and placed the warrant inside. He said, "Can J. Wilcox Handy be reasoned with?"

She opened a side desk drawer and filed the warrant. "What do you mean?"

"Can't we plea bargain or something?"

"I'm not your lawyer."

"Christ. I don't believe this." He slumped in a chair by her desk.

"I don't think Mr. Handy's being malicious about it, Will."

"No?"

"He's just making a point."

"I guess I'm missing it."

"That's not surprising."

He leaned forward in the chair and let his elbows rest on his knees. He stared at the floor.

Laurie came to his side. She touched the hair on the back of his neck.

The gesture surprised him. It had been a long time since he had felt any tenderness from her at all. He didn't dare move his head. He talked to the floor: "So, what happens now?"

She twisted a lock of his hair. "I don't think Mr. Handy wants to cause trouble. A few nights in jail might convince him to drop the charges."

"You think so?"

"I think it'll help." She removed her hand from his neck and let it fall to her side.

He looked up at her. "Well, I guess I better start doing time."

"It won't be so bad."

"The mattress is lumpy."

"You'll survive."

"On bread and water?"

"Maybe a little wine."

"What?"

She placed her hands on her hips. "You were talking about dinner, weren't you?"

"I thought I was going to jail."

"You are."

He cocked his head. "We're dining in a jail cell?"

"Sure. I think I can scare up a candle somewhere."

"How romantic."

"You prefer bread and water?"

"No. Hey, forget what I said."

She picked up the phone and dialed the Burger & Brew. "I think shrimp would be nice. I hear they have shrimp in Saxton Mills."